THE GRAY AND GUILTY SEA

THE GRAY AND GUILTY SEA

SCOTT WILLIAM CARTER

WRITING AS JACK NOLTE

FLYING RAVEN

PRESS

FOR J.D.M.

WITHOUT YOU,
THIS BOOK WOULDN'T
HAVE BEEN WRITTEN.

Chapter 1

THE WOMAN WASHED UP on the beach at sunset—
a girl, really, eighteen or nineteen by the looks of her,
dressed in black lace panties and a white tank-top. No doubt she
was dead. Gage had seen enough dead bodies to know.

A fierce wind blew back his hair. His bare hand, gripping his
cane, was numb from the cold. The approaching storm stretched
along the horizon like an old metal coil, the hint of orange like
rust in the dark, tightly-wound clouds. Above the clouds, the sky
was flat and sterile like dull silver; beneath the clouds, only the
white-capped swells broke up the gray monotony of the ocean.
It would be dark in twenty minutes. Gage, groggy from an early
bourbon, had almost skipped his evening walk. How different
his life would have been if he had.

The girl had the look of an exhausted swimmer, body half out
of the surf, half on the sand, head resting on one outstretched arm.
But one ankle was tangled in sea kelp, sand and mud streaked her
milky skin like paint splatters on white porcelain, and both eyes
were wide and unblinking. Even from twenty paces, he could see
her eyes—two slashes of white in all that gray.

The beach was deserted. Far to his right, two miles away,
Gage could make out the twinkling lights of the Golden Eagle

Casino. To his left were the beginnings of the many cliffs that gave the city of Barnacle Bluffs its name. Gage hesitated, watching the girl, hoping for some sign of movement even when he knew there would be none, then ambled toward her.

His right knee throbbed. It was always worse in the winter, when the damp air seeped into all those cracks in his surgically repaired knee. It never got *that* cold on the Oregon coast, which was one of the reasons he'd moved there after Janet died, but it got cold enough. It didn't take much for Gage to feel cold. Not anymore.

When he reached the girl, his heart was pounding, and he knew it had nothing to do with physical exertion. He'd thought he was past all this.

It was only up close that he saw the lacerations on her wrists and ankles, the bruise-marks on her thighs, the sunken eye sockets that made her face look like a skull. Her dark blond hair tangled around her face and neck like seaweed. Her mouth was open in a silent scream. She was maybe five-two, ninety pounds at most. He doubted she'd been dead more than twenty-four hours. She didn't smell like death yet. She just smelled like salt water.

"Where did you come from?" he said.

There was no answer.

It was raining by the time the police arrived. Gage didn't own a cell phone, or any phone for that matter, but there was a pay phone at the gas station across the street, just on the other side of Highway 101. Gage could have made the call from Mattie's house, up the hill behind the station, but that was another ten minutes of painful walking and he'd wanted to be back at the beach by the time the police arrived. He didn't know why. It wasn't like he wanted to be involved. It was more that he felt obligated by finding her.

That had been his second mistake.

There was still enough light to see, though barely. Two police cars arrived, sirens blaring, the threads of rain visible in the beams lancing over the beach. The parking lot was up ten feet on the bluff, behind the metal barricade. Seconds later two officers charged down the grassy dune. Both ran with their right hands over their holsters. One of the officers was much heavier than the other.

Gage's leather jacket had no hood, and the rain quickly soaked his hair. Cold water dribbled down his forehead. The thin cop, a kid with a Brad Pitt face, continued to the body while the larger one charged up to Gage. He had a doughy face, a thick brown mustache, and no hair but a fine brown ring around his scalp. The brass badge on his navy blue coat shimmered in the rain.

"What time did you find her?" he asked.

"What time did I call it in?" Gage said.

"Are you trying to be a smart alec?"

"No, I just don't wear a watch."

More sirens, more headlights appearing up on the bluff. The young cop dropped to his knees and felt for a pulse on her wrist. He looked at them.

"She's dead," he said.

"Well of course," Gage said. "Isn't that what I told you on the phone?"

The heavier one blinked a few times at this, then looked back at Gage. There were more cops barreling down the dune, and two paramedics carrying a stretcher. The heavy cop in front of Gage flipped open a little black notebook. Water speckled the white paper.

"Your name, sir?" he said.

Gage shivered; the water dribbling down his back was ice cold. There was commotion all around them now—the paramedics trying to revive her, the cops conferring. Up on the bluff, a few looky-loos had come of the houses lining the beach and peered down at the spectacle from their decks. The heavy cop slipped the little pen from the side of the notebook. When he noticed Gage hadn't answered, he glanced up with a questioning look.

"Problem?" he said.

"Oh, no," Gage said. It was a lie. He hadn't planned on giving his name, and now he saw how stupid it had been to wait around. An anonymous call would have been fine. But what could he do now? "Gage. Garrison Gage. I live just on the other side of the highway."

"And you've never seen this girl before in your life?"

"No."

"Why do you think she was here?"

"How the *hell* should I know?"

The cop grimaced. "What's your phone number?"

"I don't have a phone."

"You don't have a *phone?*"

"No."

The cop sighed. "What about an address, Gary? Do you have one of those?"

"Don't call me Gary."

"Okay. What should I call you?"

"Don't call me anything."

The cop narrowed his already narrow eyes. Gage felt his frustration rise, creeping into him like the coldness in his knee. He'd forgotten what most cops were like. One of the other cops was taking digital pictures of the girl, the flash strobing the body. The paramedics were readying their stretcher for her.

"Are you *trying* to be a problem?" the cop said.

"No. I'm not trying to be anything at all."

Then he gave the cop his address. He answered the rest of their questions. And when they said he could, he went home.

Chapter 2

A LITTLE AFTER NINE the next morning, someone knocked on his door. Gage was nearly finished with the crossword in the latest *Oregonian*. The first knocks were tentative, three gentle raps that he could barely hear over the whistling wind. But when Gage ignored these, the next knocks were more forceful.

He put down his pen. Looking beyond his dining room table, piled with enough books and magazines that someone might have mistaken it for a library rummage sale, he saw the wide expanse of the ocean through his bay window, above the rooftops of the houses on the slope below. The clouds had cleared overnight, the sky a bright cobalt blue. It might as well have been summer. But it was a deceiving sky, because he knew from when he'd stepped out to get the paper how cold it had been, how brittle and strong the breeze.

When he'd moved to the coast, he'd disabled the doorbell and put up both *No Solicitation* and *Beware of Dog* signs. That had mostly done the trick. But there were always a few people who knocked anyway. Illiterate fools.

He limped to the foyer, the peeling linoleum like ice against his bare feet. The smell of burnt toast hung in the air; he could never get that damn toaster working right. He tied his bathrobe and flung open the door.

"What is it, then?" he said.

He expected a vacuum salesman or a kid hocking magazine subscriptions, a frivolous interruption. Instead a sober-faced man in a gray trench coat stood on his concrete stoop; he wore a narrow blue tie, a white shirt. He had thinning gray hair and bushy black eyebrows, his face long and gaunt. He made Gage think of a slightly heavier version of Mister Rogers. Still, there was no denying he was a cop. Gage had seen thousands of cops over the years and they all had the same look about them—a wary earnestness.

The arbor vitae at the back of Gage's property swayed in the breeze. The cool air penetrated his thin cotton robe, making him shiver.

"More questions?" Gage said.

The man smiled kindly. He had yellow teeth, and one of his incisors was capped with gold. "Garrison Gage?" he said.

"That's right."

"I'm Percy Quinn. Chief of Police in Barnacle Bluffs."

It was a small town, and deaths like the girl on the beach were rare, but he was still surprised that the Chief himself was paying a visit. "Well, thank heavens," he said. "You're a few months late, but the kids playing the loud music live just down at the end of the drive."

Quinn chuckled. He had that look about him of a patient grandfather. "Can I have a few minutes of your time?"

"Why?"

The man's smile stayed the same, but his eyes changed; it was like watching water freeze. "Humor me," he said.

Gage shrugged and stepped back so Quinn could enter. Standing close, Gage caught the whiff of cigarette smoke, and he could just make out the outline of the revolver holster beneath Quinn's coat.

Without a word, Gage limped to his table and settled into his chair. He took a drink from his coffee, which had grown cold; it was black, except for just a splash of Irish cream, just the way he liked it. A log in the stove crackled. Quinn stood behind one of the other chairs, hands gripping the walnut frame. He glanced at the coffee cup as if waiting for Gage to offer. Gage didn't.

"I don't want to take much of your time—" Quinn began.

"Well, that's good," Gage said.

The man looked a bit pained. It really was like insulting Mister Rogers. "I'm hoping we can be friends."

"Hope can be a dangerous thing."

"Man, you're not going to make this easy for me, are you?"

"Make what easy?"

Quinn pulled out the chair. He turned it around backwards and straddled it. "You see the news this morning?"

"I don't have a television," Gage said.

"No television. No phone. You're quite the character."

"Thank you. I mean that sincerely."

"Look," Quinn said, "this is really just a courtesy call, that's all. I want you to know that we didn't give your name to the media. We just told them a homeless man stumbled upon the girl."

"Well, that's an upgrade for me," Gage said.

"I thought you'd appreciate it. You see, I . . . I know who you are, Gage. I know all that business you were involved with before. All that work you did with the FBI. I . . . know what happened back in New York. I am sorry about your wife. About what they did to you. Everything."

Gage said nothing. He looked at his crossword. Ironically, the theme was the ocean. The clue was *broken boat*. Eleven letters, and it ended with a "d."

"Shipwrecked," Gage said.

"Huh?"

Gage wrote it in.

"Oh, right," Quinn said. "My wife's into those too. Though she's more into that other thing—what's it called? The thing with numbers."

"Sudoku," Gage said.

"Right. Look, here's the deal. You kind of slipped into

Barnacle Bluffs under the radar. That's fine. I can see why you're here. Lots of folks come here for the same reason. To get away. To forget. Whatever."

"I just like the view," Gage said.

"But here's the thing," Quinn went on, "we're a small town. We might seem big because of all the tourists, especially in the summer, but when you get down to it this place is just a village. This thing with the girl, it's already all over the news. A Portland crew showed up here this morning. It'll be front page in tomorrow's *Oregonian*. That's more than enough attention. We don't need your name getting mixed up in this. It'll turn this place into a circus."

"Who doesn't like the circus?" Gage said.

"Can't you be serious? Even stupid reporters can type your name into Google. Then they'll be swarming this place, getting the wrong idea, wondering how you're all mixed up in the girl's death when we both know you got nothing to do with it. I'm just asking you to lie low, that's all. I don't mind you living here—"

"That's very generous of you."

"—but if you could just, well, stay retired, I'd appreciate it. And we'll keep you out of it."

Finally, Gage looked up. "Do you know who she is?"

"What?"

"The girl. Who is she?"

Quinn's brow furrowed, his enormous eyebrows like mirrored checkmarks. "Why?"

"Just curious."

"Well, we don't know yet. No ID on her, obviously. And nothing came up in the databases on her fingerprints. They're doing an autopsy on her now, so maybe we can find out more."

"They know the cause of death?" Gage said. "Was it drowning, or did she die beforehand?"

Quinn hesitated. "I'm getting a bit uncomfortable with these questions, Mister."

"I'm a bit uncomfortable when a girl washes up on a beach below my house—especially one like that with marks on her wrists and ankles."

Quinn offered up a tight-lipped smile. "If I didn't know better, I'd think you were opening up an investigation."

"Well, it's good that you know better."

"Gage, I wish you wouldn't make this hard. We got this thing covered, all right? Right now she's a Jane Doe. Maybe she was a runaway. Maybe she was abducted. Maybe she's even a local, but nobody's come forward. It'll come out in time, trust me. We have a deal?"

Gage looked at his crossword. He'd stopped trusting cops a long time ago. He'd stopped trusting pretty much everyone—not that he ever really did. There was a faint flicker of curiosity in the back of his mind, but he wasn't going to let it turn into anything. Not now. Not after so much time. How long had it been? Five years? He wouldn't even know where to begin.

"I don't see any reason to get involved," he said. "I'm not a private investigator any more. I'm just a guy who does crosswords. That's my whole purpose in life—doing crosswords. I've probably done thousands of them. I'll probably do thousands more."

Quinn laughed. Gage, not smiling, looked at him.

"I wasn't joking," he said.

Chapter 3

THAT NIGHT, GAGE DREAMED he was lost at sea. It was a wild and churning sea, a bubbling gray broth with no land in sight. It was not cold at all, but hot—scalding, as if he'd been dumped into a boiling cauldron. Clouds as wild as the sea streaked the sky like the hurried brushstrokes of a mad painter. Thunder rumbled, and hot rain pelted his face. He struggled to keep his head above the surface, thrashing about, taking in great mouthfuls of warm, salty water. Something was wrong with his arms—they weren't working the way they should.

When he got them up in front of his face, he saw that he had no hands. There were only stumps.

Then something floated into view—a buoy of some kind, two adjoining logs jutting out of the waves. Kelp tangled around the logs, fastening them together. He paddled toward them and wrapped his stump-arms around them. The logs were cold, but strangely soft. It was only then that he realized what it was.

It was the girl from the beach.

She was upside down, her bare, lacerated legs sticking out of the water—and that's what he was holding.

Gage finally woke, heart pounding, face drenched in sweat, the sheets tangled around his legs like the sea kelp tangled around that girl.

"Christ," he said to the darkness.

A couple days passed. It rained one of the days, a brief shower, but otherwise remained cool and bright. Except for checking on Mattie once, his ailing housekeeper who lived in a cottage down the hill that Gage owned, he spent the time reading or doing crosswords at his kitchen table. In the *Oregonian*, news about the girl's death went from garish, front page headlines, to equally garish headlines on page 8, to not even warranting a mention at all.

It was the way of things. Gage had seen it lots of times. People lost interest quickly. They lost interest even faster when there was no story to keep them hooked. She was just a dead girl on the beach. She could have been anybody, and if she wasn't anybody, then she was a nobody. It was hard to care about a nobody. It was like trying to hang a picture on an invisible wall.

Still, the more Gage tried to forget her, the more she crept into his thoughts. He was still thinking about her when he went for a walk Thursday night, exactly one week since he'd found the body.

He trudged north along Highway 101, the night air crisp, the moon full and resplendent. Cars and trucks roared past, headlights piercing the darkness; the big semis and their moving walls of wind forced him to stop and clutch his fedora with one hand and lean on his cane with the other.

Most of the lodging was farther north, near the outlet stores. Both sides of the highway were lined with little shops that specialized in various things—Christmas knick-knacks, homemade quilts, high-end chocolate, low-end jewelry. To his right in the hills above the shops were houses like his own, tucked among the Douglas firs, the hemlocks, and the occasional oak trees. Across the highway and below the shops were two blocks of other houses and then, below them, the beach.

While he walked, he kept going over in his mind what he knew about the girl. Only the local *Barnacle Bluffs Bugle* kept the story front and center. He was actually impressed. Up until six months earlier, the paper had carried nothing but snippets about the latest happenings at the senior center or badly written human interest stories that always seemed to feature someone who'd fought in World War II. But lately, there'd been real investigative journalism—embezzlement at the casino, backstabbing between local politicians, a major drug traffic exposé that actually scooped the cops.

It was impressive because it was all the product of a single person, Carmen Hornbridge, who'd become the sole proprietor/ editor/writer six months earlier when the original octogenarian owners had finally decided they'd rather play shuffleboard on cruise ships than squabble with local advertisers. It was even more impressive when he looked at her photo; he didn't expect a blond bombshell to write and publish such hard-hitting journalism.

But people often surprised Gage. It was one of the things that kept life tolerable.

From reading the articles, Gage learned that they still hadn't identified the girl. For a few days, the police withheld information while they did an autopsy and then searches based on dental records and fingerprints, but when nothing had turned up, they'd become more forthcoming.

Her life had been reduced to a series of details. Shoulder-length blond hair. Brown eyes. Most likely nineteen or twenty years of age. Five feet four inches tall and weighing a hundred and nineteen pounds. Fair complexion. Double piercing in both ears, plus a stud on her tongue and her bellybutton. A ring of dolphin tattoos around her left ankle. Dressed in Intimissimi black lace panties and a white Hanes tank-top. They'd posted a sketch of her rather than the actual photo; he guessed they probably didn't want the abundant senior population choking on their lime jello.

At first, they'd withheld the cause of death, but eventually they'd released that information too. The autopsy determined she'd died by drowning. Suicide could not be ruled out, but the bruising and cuts indicated some sort of struggle. The sea had washed away any chance of fingerprints, but there were signs of recent, violent sexual activity. According to blood tests, she'd also been a heavy user of methamphetamines.

None of it, according to Ms. Hornbridge, had led anywhere. The police had gotten lots of tips, but they'd all been dead ends. The theories ram the gamut:

She was a runway from a severe cult out of Utah.

She'd worked for a secret highbrow Oregon call girl company.

She was the girlfriend of an Italian mafia hit man who'd traded her for a younger model.

She'd been abducted by aliens, who performed sexual experiments on her, and then discarded her in the ocean.

Nonsense, all of it. The truth, Gage knew, was usually more mundane.

About a quarter mile from his house, one block east of the ocean, was a bar called Tsunami's. It was hard to see from the highway. It had a neon Budweiser sign in the window and posters of local events plastered on the door. The windows were all black, but he could hear the pulsing music from across the street. The gravel parking lot was packed with dusty cars and motorcycles. People milled about in the parking lot smoking cigarettes.

He'd been inside exactly three times, all of them on his birthday, each time at his friend Alex's insistence. All three times, it had been so loud that he couldn't even hear himself speak, much less Alex.

He didn't know what made him do it, but he decided to cross the street and go inside—hobbling fast during a break in traffic. Opening the heavy door, it was exactly what he expected: hot, crowded, and raging with dozens of obnoxious, alcohol-fueled gabfests, everybody shouting to be heard over a jukebox belting out songs at a volume that would have melted butter.

No wide-eyed tourists here. This place was for the locals, and it contained everyone from the Native American blackjack dealer fresh off her shift to the pudgy bikers in shiny new leather trying to forget that they worked as accountants during the day.

The joint stank of sweat, peanuts, and beer, and every table was packed. One of the funny things about Tsunami's was that despite the name, there wasn't the usual sea-themed kitsch so common to the coastal restaurants. There were scuffed wagon wheel tables, funky lava lamp lighting, and posters of Clark Cable, Marilyn Monroe, and Gandhi. He pushed his way to the bar, ordered a bourbon on the rocks from a mop-haired bartender, and lucked out when a black guy in a grease-stained mechanic's uniform slugged down the rest of his beer and staggered away, leaving a wooden stool open.

Gage settled on the stool, placing his hat on a countertop that was layered with hundreds of scuffed bumper sticks. He was shoulder to shoulder with the guys on either side. When the bartender brought his drink, the guy to his right stared at Gage.

"Hey, I know you," he said.

The voice was familiar. Gage looked at him. Sure enough, of all the strange coincidences that could have happened, he'd walked into a real whopper. It was a doughy fellow with a thick brown mustache—the very cop who'd taken his information on the beach. The guy was dressed in a ghastly orange sweater that may have once been used as carpet in some seventies lounge.

"No, you don't," Gage said.

The guy squinted, eyes disappearing in his round face. He pointed a pasty finger. "Yeah," he said, "you're the guy who found the girl. The smart alec. Gage, right?"

"I'd appreciate it if you point your finger somewhere else. I haven't eaten any dinner."

"Still the smart alec, huh?"

"Some habits die hard."

"Christ." The guy shook his head, then looked at the bartender. "Can you believe this guy, Mac? Thinks he's better than the rest of us."

"My name's not Mac," the bartender said, and left for the other end of the counter with two frothy mugs.

The cop looked at Gage again, and he dropped his voice—not much, but enough to make it seem like he was whispering when he was still practically shouting to be heard over the din. "They sent around a memo. Said you used to be a big time private dick in New York."

"Must have been somebody else," Gage said.

"I looked you up. That was some big time shit you were involved with back then. Had your name all in lights, huh? Serial killers. Russian mafia. Must have given you a pretty big head. But now look at you. You're wife gets knocked off and now you're nothing but a fucking cripple."

Gage looked at him, conscious that a bubble of silence had spread from the two of them. At least a dozen people were watching. "Watch your mouth," he said.

"Oh, what are you going to do, hit a cop?"

"You're not a cop. Not right now, anyway. And probably not ever."

"Fuck you, pal."

Gage smiled. "If I was a homosexual, which I'm not, I'm pretty sure I could do better than you. Even if I *am* a cripple."

It turned out to be more than a little pasty cop with a Napoleon complex could take. With a guttural roar, he launched himself at Gage. But his drunkenness, combined with his general ungainliness, meant this amounted to little more than a wobbly stumble in Gage's direction. In his orange sweater, he made Gage think of a big orange traffic cone.

Without leaving his stool, Gage delivered a swift forearm to the cop's neck. The guy dropped like a sack of beans on the peanut-strewn floor. He coughed and hacked, and finally glared at Gage, red-faced. He tried to speak but couldn't manage it between the coughs.

The room fell silent. The jukebox was between songs. Gage left a five on the table, thanked the bartender, and hobbled for the door. His knee had stiffened, so his limp was more pronounced. All eyes followed him. The thumping of his cane on the hardwood floor was the loudest sound in the room.

Gage pushed through the crowd into the open air. The cop, struggling to his feet, cursed at him. He heard somebody yelling for the cop to settle down, then the door swung shut.

The air had thickened, golden halos ringing the street lamps. His heart was doing the wild mambo, so loud in his ears he couldn't even hear the cars whizzing up behind him. He walked as fast as his worthless body would take him, and when he reached the gas station, he was breathing heavy. The sweat in his eyes blurred the numbers on the payphone as he dialed.

When the person on the other end said hello, the sound of a sizzling frying pan in the background, Gage said, "It's me. Can you do me a favor? I'm investigating a case."

Chapter 4

THE NEXT MORNING, Quinn kept Gage waiting for half an hour before finally buzzing his secretary to send him back. By then, Gage had downed three cups of coffee that tasted like bean-flavored water, read more than he'd ever wanted about golfing from the wrinkled magazines on the end table in the waiting area, and been given the suspicious eye by at least two dozen cops.

When he entered the office, bright sunlight glared through the cracked-open blinds. Through watery eyes, he saw the vague shape of a person behind mounds of manila folders and white binders.

"How can I help you this fine morning, sir?" Quinn said.

It was spoken with forced politeness. When Gage's eyes adjusted, he saw Quinn's gentlemanly face looking up at him over the tops of thin reading glasses. In his plain white shirt and a plain blue tie, his right pocket full of pens, pencils, and other items, Quinn had the air the studious professor.

A computer with two monitors sat a smaller adjacent desk; the screensaver was a bright-eyed yellow lab, the picture bouncing around the screen.

"I've been thinking about that girl on the beach," Gage said.

"I was afraid of that. Shut the door and take a seat."

Gage took one of the two black plastic seats across from the desk, the kind designed for maximum discomfort. He rested his cane against the side of the chair, holding one hand on it so it wouldn't slip. Even after all these years, he was never quite sure what to do with the damn cane.

Quinn removed his glasses and placed them on a stack of papers, then leaned back in his swivel chair. He rubbed his eyes. "I thought we agreed you were going to keep a low profile."

"I'm still going to keep a low profile."

"But you plan on investigating her death?"

Gage shrugged. "I guess so."

"You *guess* so? You don't sound very determined there, my friend."

"My determination will depend on how much help you need."

"I thought I made it pretty clear we don't need any help."

"Yes, you did. I kind of like to make my own decisions, though, you see."

"I looked it up, Gage. You don't even have a license in the state of Oregon, and your New York license expired three years ago."

"Oh well. I sometimes forget to return library books too."

They looked at each other, the silence stretching between them like a receding fishing line. The question was, which one of them was the fish? The lights on Quinn's phone flashed yellow. There was boisterous laughter in the waiting area. Outside, he heard the droning of motorboats on Big Dipper Lake.

Finally, Quinn sighed. "Gage, we're going to get along much better if you just butt out of all this."

"Yeah," Gage said, nodding, "us not getting along would sadden me. We seemed to be starting a beautiful friendship."

"Okay, so who's your client? Somebody's paying your way, right?" There was a new edge in Quinn's voice.

"I'm doing it pro bono."

"For who?"

"Let's say the girl."

"But Gage, you don't even know her!"

"Yeah. Nobody does. That's what bothers me."

Quinn shook his head. "I don't need this. We really have it covered."

"Think of me as a gift. Like a free sample that showed up in the mail."

"I think of you as a fucking pain in the ass, that's what."

"Well, I can be both. That's usually how it works."

"You really don't care what you poking around is going to do to our own investigation, do you? When Nancy Grace and Anderson Cooper and all the other media whack jobs show up in our little town, it's gonna be a nightmare. I didn't think you wanted all that attention."

"I don't," Gage said. "That's why I'm going to try to keep a low profile."

"Not in this town, pardner. There's more gossip here than beachfront." He sighed, and this time his sigh was deep and lasting and filled with years of built-up petty anguish—the long sigh of the overwhelmed small town police chief. "Okay, not much I can do to stop you if you're determined to be an idiot. But why, exactly, are you here? I take it you didn't come just to announce your intentions?"

"I was thinking you might put me on your payroll."

Quinn stared, dumbfounded. "You're joking."

"Yeah, I'm joking. Actually, all I wanted was copies of the autopsy photos."

"No way."

Gage had expected this reaction. He'd hoped for voluntary cooperation, of course; it would have made his life easier. But once Gage had gotten his teeth into something, he wasn't going to let go easily. In fact, he *never* let it go. It was really the only reason he always won in the end. Pure stubbornness could take you far in life. It didn't make you many friends, but it would take you far.

"All right," he said, making as if to stand up, "I guess we're done. I'm going to head on over to the *Bugle's* office."

Quinn put out his hand. "Hold on a minute. What's this about the *Bugle?*"

"Oh, you know, I figure Miss Hornbridge might have some info to help me. She seems pretty sharp."

"Hmm."

"Of course," Gage said, "I'll probably have to do a little quid pro quo. I doubt she'll just tell me anything for free."

"Uh huh," Quinn said. "And what, pray tell, are you going to share with her?"

Gage shrugged. "Oh, stuff. You know, gossip. Probably not anything fit to print, but I'm sure she'll be interested."

"Like what?"

Gage let the silence lengthen, the tension rising. Silence could be like stretching a rubber band. Let it go far enough and the band would get very taught. That tautness could be quite useful. Of course, the trick was not to let it stretch so far that it snapped.

"Oh, you know," he said, "some stuff I heard about a particular cop's wife. Kind of embarrassing stuff, actually. I heard she did some stripping when she was down in Austin—long time ago, when she was in college. She was doped up on painkillers back then most of the time. Got busted for illegal possession. There were rumors she was doing more than stripping. Probably not true. But you know, who knows? She changed her name, then changed it again when she met a nice young cop just out of the academy. But a good reporter starts sniffing around, who knows what she'll find. Like you said, there's more gossip in this town than beachfront. Hate for that stuff to get out. Makes it hard for a prominent person in a small town, especially somebody who's been thinking about running for mayor."

Quinn's face turned into a clay mould, firming up, hardening. "That's interesting speculation," he said.

Gage shrugged.

"I guess you've still got some friends with connections," Quinn said.

"A few."

Quinn drummed his fingers on the stack of papers. "So this is the way it's going to be, huh?"

"Doesn't have to be."

"Oh, it seems it does."

His eyes smoldered, revealing a man of intense passions hiding behind his Mister Rogers facade. He wasn't somebody Gage would want to be alone with in a dark alley. He also slightly regretted having to play the cards the way he did. But what could he do? He wasn't going to play footsie with this guy, hoping to get on his good side.

Finally, Quinn smiled. It was obviously a forced smile, but it still broke the tension. "You're a son of a bitch, Gage."

"Tell me something I don't know."

"All right, you'll get your photos. One thing, though. Keep me in the loop if you find out anything, okay? It sure would be nice to save the taxpayers some money if you manage to ferret out something useful."

"I can probably do that."

"And please, please don't go to the *Bugle*. For any reason." He picked up the phone, muttering to himself. "I'm too old for this crap . . . Yeah, Alice? Gage is going to need copies of all the autopsy photos. Can you call over to the morgue? Yes. Yes, that's right."

Gage rose, mouthing the words *thank you*, and limped his way to the door. But Quinn wasn't quite finished.

"One last thing, Gage."

Gage turned. Quinn covered the mouthpiece of the phone. The intensity in the eyes was gone, and Gage was relieved to see that. Instead, there was a glint of amusement.

"I heard you had a little scuffle with one of my men at Tsunami's last night," Quinn said.

Gage shook his head. "You must have heard wrong."

"Hmm. Maybe so. But I just want you to know, Henderson's a prick. I've had problems with him for years, so it probably did him some good being put on his ass."

* * * * *

The first place Gage went, after getting copies of the autopsy photos from the clerk at the county morgue, was *The Barnacle Bluffs Bugle*. He didn't do this to spite Quinn. He'd been planning on doing it all along.

The *Bugle's* modest headquarters was a one-room walk-up above a saltwater taffy shop, in the old downtown area on the east side of Highway 101. A third of the stores were vacant, a third were long term tenants, and the other third rotated every year through the usual suspects—antique shops, art galleries, t-shirt stores, and usually a combination of all three.

The sky was a bold and cloudless blue, the kind of sky that showed up prominently on all the postcards. He parked his '71 Volkswagen van—he'd picked it up at auction shortly after moving to Barnacle Bluffs, and it was more rust-colored now than the original mustard—across the street. When he got out of the van, the wind sliced right through his leather jacket, and he pressed his fedora to his head.

After crossing the street, he smelled popcorn and peppermint wafting out of the candy shop. When he took the green-carpeted stairs, the bottom of the stairwell open to the outside world, those smells were replaced by a faint whiff of mold.

At the top there were two doors, one for an accountant, the other for the *Bugle*. That accountant's had an "Out to Lunch" sticky note stuck to it even though it was not yet eleven. He went into the *Bugle's* office without knocking, and there was Carmen Hornbridge in a room that looked like a tornado had ravaged it. She smiled at him. It was a smile that would have knocked a scrimmage line of football players on their asses.

"Hi," she said. "Want to place an ad?"

The room, no more than fifteen by fifteen feet, was a hodgepodge of desks, filing cabinets, Apple computers, and so much paper that it made Quinn's office seem sterile in comparison. With the curtains open, the full glare of the sun spilled into the room. Framed newspapers adorned most of the walls except for the one behind Carmen herself, which was covered by a giant corkboard; the corkboard itself was buried behind three or four layers of newspaper clippings, sticky notes, and business cards.

Carmen Hornbridge was seated at the messiest of the three desks, bracketed by two wide monitors. Her nimble fingers were poised over the keyboard.

Her powder blue blazer hung over the back of the swivel chair. The curly blond hair that had been let loose in her editorial page photo was now tied back in a pony tail. She was dainty, probably not more than a hundred pounds, with smooth skin, liquid green eyes, and childlike features. Her eyes gave her away, though. He'd guessed early twenties by her photo, but there was something about the intensity of her gaze and the subtle crow's feet that made him revise her age upwards a bit. Thirty maybe? She'd certainly aged well.

The lingering aromas of chicken, onions, and noodles hung in the air. He spotted the white boxes from Ching Pau's behind one of the computers.

"Chinese food for breakfast?" Gage said.

She shrugged. "Maybe I'm having dinner at ten in the morning. What can I help you with?"

He squeezed around cardboard boxes and settled into one of the two office chairs across from her desk. These chairs, unlike the ones in Quinn's office, had plenty of cushioning. He had to smile at that. You could tell who wanted you to stick around and get comfortable, at least in general principle.

Closer to her now, he heard the faint mumble of voices, punctuated by static, and saw that she had a police scanner under a pile of magazines.

"You run this whole place by yourself?" Gage said.

She looked at him, blinking, as if her internal computer was assessing what level of attention Gage required, then finally turned away from her keyboard, folding her hands in her lap. She offered up a wan smile.

"Do I look like I can't handle it?" she said.

"I'm sure you can handle it fine. I was just curious."

"Uh huh. Well, right now I do. There were two ad managers

and a part-time secretary that came with this place, but I wanted to do things myself for a while so I knew the business inside and out." Those intense eyes narrowed. "Why, you looking for a job?"

He chuckled. "No."

"I didn't think so. You don't seem like the newspaper type."

"Oh? What type do I seem?"

She pursed her lips. He noticed there was a faint scar in the shallow valley between her lower lip and her chin, a mark that looked like it would blow off as easily as chalk. He also noticed that she radiated some kind of animal magnetism, a confidence that was damn appealing—appealing, that was, if he'd been on the lookout for that sort of thing.

"Retired cop?" she said.

"Now *that's* funny," Gage said.

"All right, I give up. Who are you?"

"My name's Garrison Gage."

When he paused, she said, "Should that name mean something to me?"

"I was waiting to see if it did. But it will as soon as I leave and you look me up on your computer."

"Don't tell me. You're a retired adult film star, and you got that limp in the line of duty."

He feigned offense. "What limp?"

"You're ex-CIA, and you got shot in the cold war while running guns in Nicaragua."

"No, but I watched the Iran Contra scandal on C-SPAN."

"All right," she said, "I give up. Who are you? You better have once been in Cirque du Soleil, or I'm going to be pretty disappointed."

Gage wasn't sure whether she was flirting with him, or if she bantered like that with everybody, but he liked her. Pretty, sharp, with a bit of an edge. It surprised him. She wasn't at all like Janet. In fact, from what he could tell so far, he'd say Carmen was Janet's exact opposite. He almost felt bad having to bring such a grim reality into the conversation.

"I'm here about the girl on the beach," he said. "The one they found on Friday night."

Her demeanor changed immediately; smile vanishing, the humor going out of the eyes. "Oh?" she said.

"I'm the one who found her."

"Really?" She reached for a pen and a yellow legal pad.

"That's not why I'm here. I mean, it is and it isn't. I don't have any new information to give you other than that—not yet, anyway."

Her eyebrows arched. They were thin and perfectly shaped. That was at least one thing she had in common with Janet; they both plucked their eyebrows with the precision of a surgeon. "Not yet?" she said. "What do you mean, not yet?"

"I'm investigating her death."

"So you *are* a cop?"

"No, no."

"Private investigator?"

"Closer." When he saw the questions forming, he held up a hand. "You'll learn everything you need to know about me after spending a few minutes with Google, believe me."

"Really?" she said. "Now you've really got me intrigued. So what do you want?"

He liked that. Cutting to the chase—a woman after his own heart. "I'm here to make you a deal."

"Uh huh. How so?"

"Whether I told you who I was or not, you'd eventually learn about me once I started snooping around. No way to avoid it in this town. So here's the deal: You refrain from printing anything you know about me, and I'll make sure you get the first scoop when I find out who the girl is."

"You're pretty confident in yourself, huh?"

"Oh, I don't know."

"You said *when,* not *if.*"

He shrugged. "Yeah, I guess I did. Probably because that's the way it usually works."

"Usually? What percentage of cases do you usually solve?"

"Oh, I don't know. All of them, I guess."

Her eyes narrowed. "All of them?"

"Yeah."

"As in, you've never failed?"

"Oh, I've failed all right. I've failed plenty."

Her expression clouded. "Then I don't understand—"

"Every investigation is a series of failures, Miss Hornbridge. You try on different theories, you head down a lot of dead ends. It's just a question of how much failure a person is willing to take. That's really the only thing that makes me different than most folks. I learned early on that I'm one of those people that's willing to fail *a lot*."

She smiled wryly. "Like Edison and the light bulb, huh?"

"Something like that."

"Somehow I think there's more than that that makes you different."

"Well, sure. I was also born in a manger. So do we have a deal, Miss Hornbridge?"

"Call me Carmen."

"Okay, Carmen then."

Outside, he heard an approaching siren. Through the window, he saw cars and trucks on Highway 101 pulling to the shoulder, and then saw an ambulance, lights flashing, roar past. Carmen glanced at her police scanner. He heard a mumble of voices, but couldn't make out what they were saying.

"Chase a lot of ambulances?" Gage said.

She grimaced as if she'd swallowed something bitter. "Comes with the job, I'm afraid. How about you?"

He nodded at his cane. "I never chase something I can't catch."

"Sounds like a wise policy," she said, and then added: "For a lot of things."

She held his gaze for a beat longer than necessary, the double meaning hanging in the air, and he couldn't tell if she was opening a door or closing one. It didn't matter. "You didn't answer my question. Do we have a deal?"

"I never make deals until I know the terms."

"What's that supposed to mean?"

"It means, I'll know the terms after I've punched up your name on the Internet."

"Ah. I guess I should have expected that."

"Tell you what," she said, "you leave your contact information, and if for some reason I think the story of *you* in Barnacle Bluffs is bigger than a dead girl on the beach in Barnacle Bluffs, then I'll at least give you a heads up before I run the story."

"Well, that's very kind of you."

She laughed. "I don't want to get off on the wrong foot here, Garrison. But you have to understand my position—"

But she never got to explain to Gage what her position was. The door to the office flew open and a teenage girl dressed in black stumbled into the room—face pink, breathing hard.

"Mister Gage?" she said.

It took a second for Gage to recognize her, because he usually only saw her for a few seconds when she answered the door, and she'd never bothered to speak to him before this moment. Mattie's granddaughter. Zoe. When he visited, she usually just shrugged and retreated to her room, leaving the front door open for him. He remembered the apology Mattie frequently made about her: "Don't mind, Zoe. She's not really that rude. She tells me she acts that way cause she's a nihilist. I don't know what that is exactly, but I figure it's like having the cramps all the time."

The girl's black *Mastodon* t-shirt pictured a flaming skull. Over the summer, she'd cut her hair spiky short and dyed it black, and she now sported piercings in her nose, eyebrows, and so many in her ears that she might as well have been a traveling jewelry store.

"Not the toilet again?" he said—and then immediately made the connection to what had passed by the office moments ago. His heart raced. "The ambulance? "

Zoe nodded, hands on her knees as she gasped for breath. "Saw your van out front on the way to the hospital. She's coughing up blood."

Chapter 5

THEY TOOK GAGE'S VAN instead of Mattie's Jeep Cherokee. When they were outside the *Bugle's* office, and he saw that Zoe's hands were shaking, he insisted.

When they got to the hospital, they already had Mattie set up in a room, and a doctor who was probably older than Barnacle Bluffs itself was shuffling out her door. In the quiet tones of an undertaker, he told them that she was doing okay, all things considered. Badly dehydrated. The coughing up blood was due to a side effect of one of the pain medications she was on—it caused a certain rawness in the throat. It didn't mean her condition had deteriorated any more rapidly than it already had, but her situation was still grave.

He looked at Gage, and not at Zoe, when he said he didn't see her lasting more than a month, maybe less, especially since she was refusing further treatment. The cancer had long since spread beyond her brain. They really should think about hospice.

There was a nurse taking her temperature when they entered the room. Mattie's eyes were closed, but they cracked open when Gage closed the door. She looked like a much older woman than she really was, which was mid-fifties, aging twenty years in the last ten months. Her once rosy face had turned pale and gaunt.

Her long hair, before mostly blonde, was now gray and waxen fanned out around her head. When she worked at his house, she always had it tied up in a pony tail, but he hadn't seen her put it up that way in months. They had her hooked up to an IV to get fluids back in her system.

"Just took some of the worst god damn medicine I've ever had in my entire life," she said. "Tasted like mud mixed with vinegar."

"It'll help your throat," the nurse said, and slipped out of the room.

They drifted to her bedside. Gage attempted a smile; his face felt as hard and brittle as sun-baked clay. A heavy weight had burrowed into his stomach the moment he'd stepped through the pneumatic doors into the ER. It took enormous effort just to stay upright, putting all his weight on his cane. He'd spent too many hours in hospitals, either fighting off death himself or watching other people do the same.

Horizontal bars of light from the blinds striped her tan bedspread. The thick windows muted the outside world, but he heard the dull drone of a motorboat out on Big Dipper; the hospital was on the east side, nestled in a grove of Sitka spruces.

"Well, don't go on looking at me like I'm in a casket already," she said. "I'm still breathing as far as I can tell."

"Aw, Grandma," Zoe said, her eyes misting.

"What, I can't make jokes?"

"Sure," Gage said, "but they should at least be funny. That one stunk like a corpse."

She laughed, but it rang a little hollow; her eyes remained serious. She looked at Zoe. "Honey, can you go get me a cup of coffee?"

"I don't know if they'll like that," Zoe said.

"Well, they're not the ones drinking it. Cream, no sugar."

Zoe shrugged and left. Mattie waited until the door had closed again before looking at Gage.

"Find out much about the girl on the beach?" she said.

"What?" Gage said. "What makes you think—"

"Don't play coy. I'm a dying woman and I won't stand for it."

"Mattie, you're not going to die."

"Now you're just plain fibbing. Come on, out with it. No matter what you said last time, I knew you'd get involved eventually. What did you find out? Or you going to make me get up out of this bed?"

He put up his hands in a mock gesture of defeat. "All right, all right. I'm going to ask around a little, that's all. Haven't found out anything yet."

She smiled. It looked like it took so much effort, just smiling, that he almost wished she wouldn't. "That's all right," she said. "You will. You'll get to the bottom of it . . . The great Garrison Gage, back at work."

"Stop."

"What do I owe you for the toilet, by the way? I never did pay you." Up close, her lips looked slightly blue, webbed with thin black lines.

"Don't worry about it."

"No, no. I gotta pay something. I still got Ory's military pension, you know. I ain't totally broke."

"Really, it's nothing," he said. "I had a hose that fit up at the house."

"You're such a bad liar. Don't you think buying the place and letting us live there was already enough?"

Gage shrugged. "It was a good investment."

"Like hell. It's a craphole."

"Hey, now. You're talking about my rental property there."

"It can't be a rental property when we don't pay no rent."

"I'm keeping a tab. You'll pay it back when you get better."

She snorted, but didn't dignify his remark with the truth they both knew. He liked her sass and attitude. When Mattie had shown up to clean his house, she'd seen the picture of his deceased wife next to his bed and asked him how long ago she'd died. He'd asked how she knew, and she'd snorted and said there wasn't one woman thing in the house except the picture, and if they'd gotten divorced he certainly wouldn't have been sleeping next to her face.

He'd told her that all he wanted was somebody to tidy up a little—he'd have done it himself, except for his messed up knee—and she'd fired back that she'd clean however she damn well pleased and maybe if he got out and walked around some instead of doing crosswords all day he wouldn't be such a cripple.

That had been the *first* day.

She closed her eyes, and was so still for a moment that he thought this is it, she's going right here. But then she lifted a thin arm and patted the baby blue bedspread.

"Sit down, Garrison."

He obeyed, careful to give her plenty of room. She took a few deep breaths, then cracked open her eyes.

"You going to hit me with your cane?"

"What?"

"Look at your hands."

He did. He had the cane in his lap, and he was gripping it so hard that both knuckles had turned white.

"Sorry," he said.

"Don't go apologizing. I don't like hospitals either. I need to ask you something before Zoe comes back."

"Okay."

She smiled, and for the first time since he'd known her, she looked scared. "She's a good kid, you know. Don't be fooled by the way she dresses. She may act out some, but she's good inside."

"I know."

"She's had to grow up fast. Way too fast. I feel bad about that. She didn't need to deal with my problems after everything she's been through."

Gage patted her hand. "She's lucky to have you, Mattie."

"Yeah, maybe. But I worry about what's going to happen to her when I'm gone."

"Mattie—"

"Let's cut through the bullshit, okay? I know the clock's ticking. It really started ticking when I said no to surgery and more chemo. I also know that girl, she's practically an adult as it is. But she's not. She's only sixteen. She's only hinted at it, but I'm pretty sure she wants me to sign some papers emancipating her so that she won't end up in foster care when I'm gone. And I don't blame her. Who knows what could happen to her then."

Gage didn't know what to say.

"But see," Mattie went on, her voice growing hoarse, "I don't think she's ready. Oh, she could take care of herself all right. She's more mature than most folks twice her age. One thing I did that wasn't stupid is I kept paying on my life insurance, so at least there's a little money—not much, but a little—to help her for a few years, maybe get her going at college. But she's not *ready*. You know what I'm saying? It's not the taking care of herself part. It's the being alone part."

"Mattie—"

"No, hear me out now. Zoe, she's been alone so much as it is. Her whole life, she's hardly had anybody." She swallowed hard, and he saw the muscles of her throat contracting and constricting like the gears of an old motor. "So here's what I want to ask you, Garrison. Here's what I want to ask. I need somebody to look out for her until she turns eighteen. Will you do that for me? I know I'm asking a lot."

Gage should have seen it coming, but he hadn't. The idea of watching over a child, even one almost an adult, scared the hell out of him. "You want me to let her go on staying at the house? Because that's fine. I wasn't going to kick her out. I could check on her now and then—"

"No, no," she said, shaking her head. "I know this is hard, but I'm asking if she could live with you?"

"Live with me?"

Mattie nodded, her eyes bright and glimmering. It was strange, because it took tears to give her face new vitality. "Yes," she said softly. "I want to sign over custody of her to you."

It was one of the few times in Gage's life when he was struck speechless. The last time had been a decade earlier, when Janet had told him in no uncertain terms that they were either going down to the courthouse and getting married before the month was out, or he'd have to pack his bags and find some other girl to shack up with. But this hit him harder. He'd never wanted children. It wasn't because he didn't like them—he was indifferent, really, not having strong feelings about them either way. They were usually just something he had to maneuver around on his way to something else. But he'd definitely never wanted any of his own. It had been easy, because Janet hadn't wanted them either.

"You got that deer in the headlights look," Mattie said.

"Sorry," Gage said.

"It's not a prison sentence. It'd only be for a couple years."

"I know. It's just . . . wow. There isn't—isn't anybody else?"

She took his hand and gave it a gentle squeeze. "I wouldn't ask if there was anybody else—at least anybody I could trust."

"What does Zoe think about this?"

"To be honest, I haven't told her."

"Oh."

"I gotta be straight with you, Garrison. She'll probably throw one hell of a fit. But I'll make it my dying wish. She wouldn't dare spite me if I put it that way."

Garrison shook his head. "Are you sure, Mattie? I mean, kids, you know . . ."

"Oh, I know. Ain't something you ever saw yourself doing. But here's the thing. There's nobody I know I'd trust more than you, Garrison. Nobody. There's something about you. You're just decent right down to the core. Ain't nothing in the world could corrupt you, I think. I wonder sometimes if you know how rare that is."

"No," Gage said, "no, you've misread me. I'm selfish, Mattie. I'm about as selfish a person as there is."

"I think that's just an act."

"No. No, it's the real me."

She sighed. "I'm not going to argue with you. But I'm not changing my mind either. I realized on the way down here, I got to do this now before I miss my chance. You wouldn't turn me down, would you, Garrison? It's my last dying wish. It'd make me happy."

Garrison stared at her, bemused at her chutzpah. "I thought you were going to use that line on Zoe?"

"Oh, I will. But it's the kind of line I plan to get plenty of mileage out of."

He laughed. He couldn't help it. "I don't know, Mattie. I just don't know if it's a good idea or not."

"Well, think quickly, okay? Maybe if you thought a little about that girl on the beach, and imagined it being Zoe, it would help."

He took her hand and squeezed it back. He didn't want to tell her, but he'd already done exactly that.

When Zoe came back, they visited with Mattie another hour, then Gage asked if Zoe wanted him to drive her home—since the hospital wanted to keep Mattie overnight. Zoe told him she had a friend who worked as an orderly and she'd catch a ride with him later. She'd said it with a fair amount of bite, as if she knew what Gage and Mattie had discussed. Gage imagined many years of such biting remarks from Zoe and left the hospital more depressed than when he'd entered it.

Back in his van, he glimpsed the lake through the openings in the firs and the spruces, as smooth and blue as painted concrete. The cool breeze whistled through the gaps in his windows. Even a half mile away from the ocean, there was less salt in the wind; the air was fresher.

He pulled out the manila folder under his seat, the one containing the autopsy photos. Flipping through them, he saw there were about a dozen in all, computer printouts on glossy white paper. Somehow seeing her in the stark fluorescent lighting of the morgue was even more gruesome than seeing her on the beach that first time. She was so pale and white, and her surroundings so monochrome and sterile, that the bruises and cuts on her body leapt off the page. Who would do such a thing? It was the question that always flitted through Gage's mind when he witnessed such cruelty, but he never let himself dwell on it. He'd learned early on that it was madness to do so. He'd seen too much evil in the world to try to make sense of it.

Evil was like Mattie's cancer—a foreign invasion into an otherwise healthy body. Why was it there? There was no why. It just was, and the only thing to do was to destroy it before it destroyed you. At least, that's all Gage could do. He'd leave it to the social workers and the psychiatrists and the politicians to look for evil's cause. Maybe some good would come from that sort of thing, but he doubted it.

Because he was dealing with a Jane Doe, Gage knew there were lots of potential places to begin. It was like having a map without a destination. You could start walking in any direction and hope that where you were supposed to go would occur to you along the way.

He lingered on the photo of her ankle, the one that showed her ring of dolphin tattoos. It was the sort of tattoo a girl who loved the ocean might get. It was also the kind of tattoo a girl might get when she'd moved to the coast. There were also all the piercings. He knew there was no guarantee that she'd gotten any of it done in Barnacle Bluffs, but it was a place to begin.

There was only one tattoo and piercing shop in Barnacle Bluffs, *TP Piercings and Body Art,* in the strip mall across from the casino. It looked out of place squeezed between a Starbucks and an office supply store. The windows were so covered with colorful designs—fairies, elves, unicorns, and every other fantastical creature imaginable—that he couldn't see inside. At the far end of the strip mall, windsocks fluttered in the wind. Across the road, beyond the blocky orange buildings of the casino, the ocean filled the horizon.

The glass door chimed when he walked inside. The shop was clean, bright, and organized, and he started to think that maybe it wasn't so out of place in the strip mall. With the polished granite counter and green marble floor, it looked like what he would have expected inside the office supply store. The front section of the store was cordoned off by portable dividers, the kind so common in corporate America; matted pictures of designs similar to the ones in the windows hung on the gray felt. Thick white binders packed the metal bookshelves next to the door.

A kid who might have been fourteen wandered around one of the dividers. He was dressed in black jeans and a sleeveless black T-shirt that showed off the tattoos that covered his arms from wrist to shoulder.

"Hey, man," he said. "Here for a tat?"

"I was wondering if I might ask you a few questions."

The kid frowned. "Aw, man, I'm not buying nothing today, so if you're a salesman—"

"It's nothing like that." Gage held up the manila folder. "I have a picture of a tattoo, and I was wondering if you might tell me if you did it."

The kid hesitated. "You somebody's dad?"

"Excuse me?"

"It's happened before," the kid said. "Girl comes in and gets a tat, then Dad shows up wanting to punch the guy who did it. But if they've got ID, how are we supposed to know it's fake?"

"No," Gage said, "it's not like that at all." He hesitated, wondering what to tell him, then decided that the truth was probably best. Gage had found over the years that unless there was a good reason to lie, then the truth was always preferable. He never knew when it would lead to unexpected discoveries. "You know that girl they found on the beach?"

The kid looked taken aback. "Um, yeah."

"She had a ring of dolphin tattooed around her left ankle."

"Really? So you a cop?"

"Think of me as a concerned citizen."

"Huh. Like a good Samaritan or something?"

"Sure. I don't know about the good part, though." He extended his hand. "Name's Garrison."

The kid shook it. "Tim Paige," he said.

"The owner?"

"That's right."

"You do a good business?"

"Oh, yeah. We get a lot of folks wander over from the casino.

We really try to make it nice and welcoming for all the women over with their girlfriends. Peggy, my sister, she's real good at that sort of thing. You know, putting them at ease and stuff."

"Let me show you something." Gage opened the folder and pulled out the one showing the tattoo. The kid looked at it only a moment before shaking his head.

"Nah, not mine."

"You're that sure?"

He nodded, and motioned for Gage to follow him. "Come around back here where the light's better. I'm the only one who does tats, so it's me or nobody."

They rounded behind the office dividers, where there were two reclining, dentist-type chairs, three drawing easels, and loads of inks and needle equipment and under banks of fluorescent lighting. Gage detected a hint of the tangy, sweet odor of marijuana. So much for the whole Office Depot facade. Tim took the photo from Gage and clipped it to one of the drawing easels, then flicked on the attached light. He leaned in for a closer look, then wrinkled his nose.

"Oh, yeah," he said, "this ain't mine. I never forget a tattoo. Faces, not so much. This one, it was probably done by somebody not in business long."

"What makes you think that?"

"Because it stinks."

"Oh."

He laughed. "I shouldn't be so hard on it, but I'm kinda a tat snob. You know, like a wine snob? This one's got no flair, no style. It's small, but that's no excuse. Doubt it was even taken from flash—just probably made up on the spot. Look at how blocky it is. They didn't even use the right size needle. It was probably done by somebody real new, cause if they kept up like this, I doubt they'd be in business long. It wouldn't just be a dad wanting to punch 'em."

"She didn't do it herself, did she?"

"Oh no. Highly doubt that. It's done with professional equipment, I can tell you that much. Just badly."

"Do you think it's very old?"

The kid looked at the picture a little longer. "It's hard to say without seeing it in the flesh, but I don't think so. It doesn't have much fade or stretching. She was also pretty young, so how old could it be?"

Gage placed the photo back in the folder, then pulled out a close-up of the girl's face. Her eyes were closed at least, but it was still gruesome enough that the kid swallowed hard.

"Sure you've never seen her?" Gage said.

"I don't think so."

"You don't *think* so?"

"I told you, I'm not as good with faces. I mean, I could have seen her in a club or something. It's hard to say. But I don't think so."

Gage watched the kid closely. No dilating eyes. No hesitation in the voice. "Do you do many ocean-themed tattoos? You know, dolphins, sharks, mermaids, that sort of thing?"

He nodded. "Some. Not as many as you might think."

"Mostly kids?"

"Depends on how you define kids. Almost everybody who gets a tat is under thirty, at least around here." He pointed at the picture of the girl. "That kid, though, I'd say she hadn't lived on the coast long."

"What makes you say that?"

"It's funny," Tim said. "You'd think it would be the locals who'd get sea-related tats, but it's almost never that way. I think it's cause the kids who grow up around here don't always want to be reminded of it so much. I don't blame them, cause I grew up around here. You get past the beach, it's pretty much nowhere-ville. It's the tourists and the people who just moved here that usually get dolphins and sharks and mermaids and stuff."

Gage slipped the photo of the girl back in the folder. "Are there any other tattoo artists in Barnacle Bluffs?"

"Nope. There's others up and down the coast, though. I'd try Sandy Cove, if I were you."

"Why is that?"

He shrugged. "They've got two tat shops up there and both do a pretty good business, Zander's and Ink and Exile. Most tattoo artists apprentice for a couple years—I did myself in LA—before going it alone. I know those two have a fair amount of turnover with apprentices. None of the longtime pros around here would have done such a crappy job, and I know most of 'em. Small world, you know."

"Yeah," Gage said.

"And if they remember her, ask if you can see their release forms. Not all the tat shops do that, but most of the good ones do."

"Good idea. Well, thanks for your help. Okay if I swing back if I have other questions?"

"Oh, sure," Tim said. "Always glad to do my part. Real sad, her washing up on beach like that. You think she was killed?"

"Probably."

The kid shook his head, and started for the front of the store. "You know, I just can't imagine a person who would do a thing like that. I like *everybody*, you know. I mean, even if I disagree with them, I really like people, doesn't matter the background. Mormons, skinheads, yuppies with their kids, I get along with everybody. I just don't know why anybody would want to hurt . . . "

His voice drifted off when they rounded the corner. At some point while they were in the back, a homeless man had wandered into the store—or what Gage *guessed* was a homeless man based on his appearance. He looked like he'd gone to a Jerry Garcia look-a-like convention ten years back and spent the last decade sleeping outdoors. His face was lost within a wooly cloud of gray hair and beard and behind tinted glasses so large they could have once been portholes in a submarine. He wore a blue rain slicker, gray sweatpants with patches in the knees, and heavy black boots covered with duct tape—all coated with years of grime and grease and who knew what else.

He teetered on his feet like a man on a boat in rough seas. Outside, visible through the window, was a rusty red bike attached to a homemade wooden trailer, both loaded up with bulging shopping bags and cardboard boxes.

"Ya got any cans?" he said. He was missing a few front teeth, and the teeth he did have were as yellow as old wax. Even across the room, his breath reeked of alcohol—it hit them like a swarm of flies.

"Dude," Tim said, "I thought I told you never to bring your sorry ass in here any more! Get the hell out!"

Gage cringed. He guessed that "liking everybody" only extended so far.

Chapter 6

I T WAS GOING ON one o'clock when Gage left the tattoo shop. Thin vapors streaked the sky like scratches on blue enamel. A plastic Safeway bag bounded over cars and concrete barriers, a pair of cawing seagulls in hot pursuit. He caught the scent of grilling beef from the fifties nostalgia joint on the corner of the parking lot and his stomach grumbled.

Realizing he hadn't eaten anything since the bagel that morning, he grabbed a burger, then used the phone book at a pay phone to make a list of all the tattoo shops up and down the coast. He was already exhausted—so much had happened during the day already—but there was no point in stopping now. A cold trail would only grow colder with time.

After a quick call to make sure Mattie was still fine (she complained about the food, but did so with plenty of gusto), he got in his van and headed south on Highway 101. He planned to start with the two shops in Sandy Cove, and continue snaking down the coast, hitting the other half a dozen shops through Waldport, Yachats, and Florence. If that didn't work, tomorrow he'd head north up towards Tillamook, Seaside, and Astoria.

Usually, Gage enjoyed the drive. The coastal highway in Oregon was one of the best in the world; he remembered a long ago road trip when Dad piled them all in the station wagon and they drove from Montana to Oregon to see the ocean. The impressive vistas along the coast had made a lasting impression on him. It was no different now. The two-line highway slipped back and forth from the high bluffs over the water and the dappled shade of firs and pines. The ocean, wrinkled with white seams, stretched out like a newly made bed.

But instead of enjoying the view, he drove in a silent funk. He'd decided to take the case, and once he'd decided he always saw it through, but he felt far more uncertain than in years past. Where was his usual confidence and verve? Too much time holed up in that cave had made him uncomfortable outside it. He felt like an old sailboat left tied to a dock, ignored for years, covered with grime and scum from disuse, and now was out in the open water without anyone even unfurling the sails. He didn't feel ready. He didn't know if he could handle the open seas.

The first stop, at Zander's on the outskirts of Sandy Cove, left him even more dispirited. None of the three tattoo artists recognized the tattoos or the girl. They wouldn't even let him look at their release forms. The second one, Ink and Exile, down at the seaport where the smell of fish was heavy in the air, yielded no better results, though they were more friendly.

It was only when he was getting back into his van that he finally got some information. A rail-thin woman in black clothes and blond dreadlocks—one of the tattoo artists he'd talked to inside—charged out of the store, waving her tattooed hands at him. He rolled down the passenger window.

"Glad I caught ya," she said.

"You remember her?" Gage said.

She shook her head, her dreadlocks bouncing around like Medusa's snakes. "But I know somebody who might. If you head east on Highway 20, in about ten miles you'll come to a little town called Kooby. Not much there, but there is a pawn shop. Don't remember the name, but the guy who owns it is this fat Indian. He did tattoos a couple years. Not very good at it, and I don't think he does it no more because there's no neon sign in the window last time I passed, but you should try him."

"Thanks," Gage said, "I'll do that."

It was more like twenty miles to Kooby than ten, but the pawn shop was still there, at the top of the forested range that separated the coast from the Willamette Valley. The blocky mud-colored building was squeezed between a single-pump gas station and a string of manufactured homes that looked like hastily stacked playing cards. The words PAWN SHOP were written in black paint on the upper floor windows of the three-story building, windows cracked and streaked with mud. When he parked in front of the building, he saw that below the flat roofline were the words KOOBY HOTEL, barely visible in a slightly darker brown, where the now departed letters had protected the paint from years of sun exposure. His was the only vehicle there.

A fat, dark-skinned man slouched in a rocker next to the glass door, chewing a blade of grass. His hair, slicked straight back, was as dark as crow feathers, and his skin was gnarled and reddish brown like the stump of a sequoia. The rocking chair barely held his girth, his dirty overalls straining against the sides. His red plaid shirt was unbuttoned all the way down to the navel, revealing a wrinkled but hairless chest.

Gage parked right in front and got out of the van. The air, appreciably cooler than on the coast, nipped at his cheeks. In the shadows of the building, frost glazed the gravel. "You the owner?" he said.

The man went on chewing his straw for so long that Gage almost spoke again.

"Who's asking?" he piped up finally. His voice sounded like water gurgling through a pipe.

Gage shut the door and limped over to him, careful where he planted his cane on the gravel. He held the manila folder under his arm. "Name's Garrison," he said. "I'm looking for information about a girl."

The man stared fixatedly at Gage's cane instead of his face. His eyes were grayish black, like the charcoal remains of a long dead fire. "We don't got no hookers here," he said.

"No," Gage said, "it's not like that. It's about the girl who died on the beach."

The straw stopped moving and the man gazed at him as if seeing him for the first time.

"What girl?" he said.

"The one who washed up on the beach in Barnacle Bluffs last week. It's been all over the newspapers."

"I don't got time to read newspapers."

"I can see that. She had a tattoo on her ankle. Somebody said maybe you did it."

He squinted at Gage suspiciously. "Who said that?"

"Just somebody."

"Who?"

"What does it matter? Can I show you a picture to see if you know her?"

The man was silent. An RV pulling a fishing boat rumbled past on the highway, kicking up a cloud of dust.

"I don't know," the man said.

"It would sure be a help."

The man shrugged. "I guess it don't hurt none to look. I haven't done no tattoos in over a year, though. Don't know what the person who sent you here was thinkin."

Gage opened the folder and pulled out the picture of the girl. "I appreciate your time," he said, then added: "Mister . . . ?"

"Call me Otis," the man said.

Gage handed him the glossy print. Otis looked at it for only a moment, squinting at it through the corner of one eye, then handed it back.

"Yeah, I remember her," he said.

The answer came so quickly that Gage assumed he'd said *didn't*. He nodded, slipping the photo back into the folder, then stopped when he realized what Otis had actually said.

"You do?" he said.

"Yeah. Don't remember her name or nothin'. It was a year back maybe. Yeah, it was February, right after President's Day, cause I remember thinking how the traffic was not nearly as good as the week before. She was a bit heavier than in that photo. Think she wanted some butterflies on her leg."

"How about dolphins around her ankle?"

The man nodded. "Yeah, like I said. Dolphins."

Gage took out the photo of the girl's tattoos and held it so Otis could see it.

"Yep, that's my work," he said, nodding. "Pretty nice, huh? Shame I had to give it up cause of my 'thritis."

"You don't happen to know her name?"

Otis shook his head. "Nah. She didn't talk all that much."

"Do you keep release forms?"

He looked confused. "Release what?"

"Some tattoo shops have people sign a release form consenting to the tattoo before they do it."

"Oh." He scratched his chin. "No, nothing like that."

"Was she with anybody?"

"No. That's why I remembered her. I remembered thinking she was kinda young to be by herself."

"What kind of car was she driving?"

"She wasn't. She was hitchin'. When she left, I saw her out front. I went into the back of the store, and when I went out there later, she was gone."

"And you don't remember anything else?"

He shook his head. "Sorry."

"All right," Gage said, "I appreciate your time. I might call on you again if I have other questions."

"You can't call on me cause I ain't got no phone."

"Well, I don't have one either, " Gage said. "It's just a colloquial expression."

"A what?"

"Never mind."

Otis went back to chewing his straw, looking thoughtful, as if this was a turn of phrase that would take the rest of the afternoon to ponder. Gage ambled to his van. He was putting the key in the ignition when Otis waved at him. Gage assumed he was waving goodbye and waved back, but Otis shook his head and pointed at the van.

Gage rolled down the window. "Yeah?"

"I do remember somethin'," Otis said.

"What's that?"

"I asked her why she like dolphins. She said they were smart. And I said, oh yeah, as smart as humans? And she said smarter. Dolphins don't hurt nothin' on purpose. Then she said they was the first thing she wanted to paint when she got to the coast. And I said, oh yeah, you a painter then? And she nodded. Then I said, well, you know they got no dolphins in Oregon. It's too cold. And she was real disappointed about that so I says, you want me to draw you some orcas instead? But she still wanted the dolphins."

"You just remembered all that just now?"

Otis shrugged. "Wasn't like I been waiting around here my whole life just to get asked about it, you know? I got a busy life. Stuff like that just kind of blurs together."

"I suppose so," Gage said.

The sun was dipping beneath the ocean by the time he got back to Barnacle Bluffs. The swath of fiery orange along the horizon was like a crack in a potter's kiln. It was too late today to make use of what he'd learned, but that was all right. Gage's spirits were considerably buoyed, and he actually found himself tapping the wheel and humming—at least, until he realized what he was doing and felt mildly annoyed at himself. There was still a nameless girl in the county morgue, after all.

But there was something about having a lead, any lead, that was immensely satisfying. What had he learned? She'd come from the east about a year earlier. She'd been heavier. She'd been by herself and she'd hitchhiked. It wasn't much, but it did flesh out the picture of her a little, and that was a step in the right direction. He hadn't felt satisfied about *anything* in a long time.

It was like welcoming back an old relative, one he'd sworn would never grace his doorstep again, and yet now he couldn't remember why he'd wanted them out of his house in the first place.

Still, in addition to the satisfaction there was another feeling—a yawning loneliness that made the idea of returning to his empty house depressing. Instead, he made a pit stop just south of town.

Half the shops in The Horseshoe Mall—consisting of a dozen little ma and pa stores in a dilapidated, U-shaped building—were already closed. Few, Gage knew, even kept regular hours. When Gage entered Books and Oddities, the stacks were dark, the only fluorescent light the one over the front counter where Alex was closing up his till. The shop smelled of musty books and dust, barely five hundred square feet of retail space and every square inch packed with merchandise.

Most of the pine shelving was filled with books—a mix of dog-eared paperbacks and hardbacks in Mylar covers—but there were also the usual tourist trinkets to be found in all the coastal stores: Oregon magnets, ocean scene postcards, shiny agates, and even a few Barnacle Bluffs t-shirts.

"I'm looking for some Nancy Drew," Gage said. "Got any?"

Without fully turning away from the open cash register, Alex glanced at him over the tops of his reading glasses, silver-rimmed ones attached to a red cord. His thick gray mustache completely dwarfed his upper lip. "I suppose you've got some moldy Reader's Digest Condensed Books you'd like to offer in trade?" he said.

"Oh, much better. I've got a set of Encyclopedia Britannicas from 1968."

His friend grunted. Short as a stump, bald except for a ring of silver hair, and dressed in wrinkled tan slacks and a plaid button-up shirt loaded with a half dozen ballpoint pens, Alex Cortez had the frumpy, tired appearance more appropriate to the bookseller he'd become than the FBI agent he once was. Already on the heavy side, his paunch had gotten considerably bigger in the three years he'd lived in Barnacle Bluffs.

His dark complexion, the deep bags under his eyes, and his heavy jowls gave him an austere look.

"Been a while," he said.

"Yeah," Gage said. "Sorry about that."

"Uh huh. Don't see hide nor hair of you for three weeks. Then I get a call asking for whatever dirt I can dig up about our police chief."

"Which I really appreciate," Gage said.

"I bet. So what have you found out so far about the girl?"

Gage filled his friend in on what little he'd discovered. While Alex listened, he finished closing out the till, then took a bottle of rubbing alcohol and a white rag and cleaned a stack of paperbacks resting on the glass counter.

Watching the way he meticulously cleaned the sticker residue off a paperback picturing a particularly bosomy female on the front, Gage had to smile. After all, this was a guy who'd been in gunfights with teenage crack heads, testified against Russian mobsters, and pulled all-night stakeouts in subzero weather. Still, it didn't surprise Gage at all when Alex opened the store. He'd said for years that he'd open a bookstore when he retired. No, the only thing that surprised Gage was that Alex had opened the store in Oregon rather than his native Arizona. Alex had claimed that they'd moved to Barnacle Bluffs because Eve adored the town, but Gage suspected Alex was trying to keep a close eye on him.

When Gage finished relating his encounter in Kooby, Alex said, "Well, it's a start, I guess."

"How about the FBI?" Gage said. "They got any ideas?"

"Wow, you're expecting some serious results, my friend. It's been less than two days. You know, I *am* mostly retired, Garrison. It's not like I have the FBI on my Twitter account or something."

"You have a Twitter account?"

Alex loaded his stack of books onto a cart and pushed it around the counter, the wheels squeaking. "Nah," he said. "I don't even know what a Twitter account is. Be right back. Got to shelve these before closing up."

"You want the lights on in the stacks?"

Alex chuckled. "Nah. I'd be able to shelve these even if it was pitch black. Know the store that well." He disappeared around a corner. "So," he said, his voice floating over the stacks, "is your knee up for a lot of ambling about?"

"Why, am I going to have to do a lot of ambling?"

"Well, if you're investigating the girl's death, you are."

"I'm not investigating anything. Not officially anyway."

There was the sound of a book sliding onto a woodened shelf, and then Alex answered. "Right."

"Seriously. I'm not."

"You take lying to yourself to profound lengths, my friend. I don't suppose you've ever gotten around to seeing a therapist like I told you, have you?"

"Why would I need one?" Gage said. "I thought that's why you moved to Barnacle Bluffs—to lead my therapy sessions."

"Hardly," Alex said. "I moved to Barnacle Bluffs because Eve wanted to live here, and I figured screwing up three marriages was more than enough."

"You've done all right," Gage said. "At least none of them died."

It was a blunt thing to say, and it surprised Gage. Where had that come from? There were the sounds of books sliding into place and the squeaking of the cart's wheels. It was a few minutes before Alex finished the shelving, and when he wheeled around the corner, he looked at Gage with concern.

Gage felt the old familiar anger creep up on him. It was always there, lurking around the corner, his old friend.

"Don't do that," he said.

"What?" Alex said.

"The pity thing. I've told you before, I don't need it."

"I've also told *you* to stop blaming yourself."

"If I don't, who will?"

"Jesus," Alex said, "it's been five years."

"To you, maybe. To me it might as well have been yesterday."

Alex shook his head. "Yeah, that's the problem."

Gage, saying nothing, watched his friend push the cart around the front counter. The tightness in the chest, the heat on his face, the clenched fists—these were the signs, and Gage knew that if he *did* say something, it was liable to get out of hand in a hurry. What did anybody else know about his pain? Five, ten, twenty years, what did it matter? When an Iranian circus strongman takes a baseball bat to your knee, busting it up so bad most of the doctors tell you you'll be lucky if you walk again, and then drowns the love of your life in your own bathtub while you're lying on the floor in agonizing pain, unable to stop him, it does a pretty good job at stymieing your progress through the five fucking stages of grief. Even blasting the asshole's brains out with his Beretta hadn't been cathartic; if anything, it took away the one thing other than himself where he could focus his blame.

Alex took some glass cleaner from below and squirted the countertop next to the cash register, then used some paper towels to wipe the area clean. It left the scent of ammonia in the air.

"Look," he said, "I just want to say one last thing."

"Maybe you've said too much already," Gage said.

"Hear me out before you blow a gasket, all right? You may not think you're investigating this girl, but I think you already are and just haven't figured it out yet. And I think Janet would want you to."

Gage shook his head. "Janet hated what I did for a living."

"No, she hated that you might get killed while doing it. That's not the same thing. And I still think she'd want you to do this."

"Bullshit."

"Did she ever ask you to quit?"

"What?"

"In all the years you were together, did Janet once ever ask you to quit?"

Gage thought about it. Janet had been an elegant creature, a woman of refined tastes who'd spent her life shuffling around museums, but she'd hated his chosen line of work with a passion. If he came home late, if he came home bloodied or bruised, it was enough to send her into a rage. She'd broken a few vases—a couple quite rare—while aiming for his head. There was no doubt she would have preferred he was an investment banker, a college professor, or some other career that didn't involve ducking bullets and fists. But ask him to quit?

"No," he admitted.

"Yeah, I thought so," Alex said. "You know why?"

"I'm sure you're going to tell me."

"Because she knew you loved it, that's why. She knew it was what you were. She couldn't ask you to stop being what you were. The last five years, you haven't been yourself. You stop fooling yourself and be honest about what you're doing with this dead girl, you'll be yourself again."

"Thank you for those peals of metaphysical wisdom, Deepak Chopra."

Alex shook his head. "Laugh all you want. Both of us know it's true."

"You know, I really did just stop by to say hello."

"No, I think you stopped by because you wanted someone to give you permission to do this."

"Uh huh. And what about you, Special Agent Alex Cortez? Aren't you avoiding doing what you are?"

Alex looked around his cramped little shop. Through his thick lenses, his eyes glinted with amusement. "Nope," he said. "I spent thirty years doing what I *wasn't* supposed to be doing. This is actually me. I just do some consulting for the FBI on the side to help make ends meet. Health insurance is a bitch."

Gage would have come back with a witty rejoinder, but then the bells over the front door rang. Turning, he saw a white-haired old lady with severe curvature of the spine struggling to carry a box full of what looked like old Regency romance paperbacks into the store. Gage took the box from her and, to her effusive thanks, lifted it onto the counter. The box stank of mildew and cigarette smoke. Smiling, Gage looked at his friend, but Alex was holding up a finger in warning.

"Not a word," he said.

While he'd been inside the store, the sky had melted to black. On the drive to his place, fog blanketed the highway, moisture beading the windshield. His brain felt foggy too. Seeing Alex had lifted his spirits, but now that he was on his own the brooding melancholy returned. Inertia had carried him through the day, but now that energy was spent and he was like a rock rolling to a standstill. Why was he doing this again? She was just some girl. Nobody had come looking for her. If he stopped this ridiculous foray back into his old ways, who would care?

There was something lurking in the gray world of his past, a terrible turmoil awaiting around the next corner or the next bend. He knew that if he continued on this road, he risked plunging himself back into all that madness. After Janet was killed, there were whole weeks that passed that he had no memory of—he'd been in a walking coma, living in a world of fog and shadows. He didn't want to go there again. He didn't know if he *could* go there again, if anything could trigger that kind of strange delusion, but he didn't want to find out.

She was just a dead girl on a beach. It was an awful thing, but it wasn't his responsibility. He was a stubborn man once he'd set himself on a path, but he could talk himself out of it. Maybe, for once, he should.

This was what he was thinking when he parked his van and walked across the gravel to his front door. The air was cold and wet. The porch light was dark, but there was enough light from street lamp on the corner that he saw them right away—pieces of gravel arranged on the smooth gray concrete in front of his door.

His pulse quickened. Up close, he finally saw that the little stones had been arranged into letters, and the letters into words:

THER AR OTHR GRLS

Chapter 7

THE FIRS AND TAN OAKS murmured in the breeze. Crisp leaves skittered down his roof and floated to the ground. The night, an impenetrable murk, closed in from all sides. The thick air felt like a wet sponge, dipped in ice water, pressing against his cheeks. Gage felt a chill run down his spine, but he knew it had nothing to do with the cold.

There are other girls.

He glanced around him, searching for a person in the shadows enveloping his property—in the wall of arbor vitae, in the ivy strangling the trunks of the oaks, in the low-lying branches of the firs. For a moment, a spindly shape next to the metal garden shed looked like a crouching person, giving him a jolt, but then he remembered that it was the maple sapling still in its pot, the one he'd bought from the nursery a few weeks earlier. Bought and forgot, like so many other things.

He stepped over the gravel, unlocked his door—he was relieved it was still locked—and stepped into a dark house. The house was still except for the hum of the refrigerator, the huge uncurtained bay window gaping an ominous black.

"Hello?" he said.

Gripping his cane like a club, he turned on the living room

lights first, then did the same in the bedrooms. Nothing had been disturbed. He was going to turn on the light in his bathroom, but when he reached for the switch a terrible nausea overwhelmed him; his eyes blurred, and he felt sharp stabbing pain in his temple.

Not in there.

Never know what he'd find.

Something awful. Someone he loved, dead.

When he stumbled back to the front door, the feeling passed. His back was already greased with sweat; underneath his jacket, his shirt stuck to his skin. He retrieved his flashlight from the closet by the front door, turned on the porch light, and stepped outside.

The porch light cast its amber net over the porch, but the rest of the yard was steeped in shadows. Taking his time, feeling unsteady with his cane, Gage searched the area around the letters first, looking for footprints. He found none other than his own. He shined the flashlight on the gravel, looking for footprints or tire tracks other than those from his van, but he couldn't find any.

He started down the driveway, and there, a dozen feet from his front door, he found a footprint. It wasn't in the gravel, but in the mud sloping in on the drive—a right footprint, pointed downhill, deep like from a boot. The strangest thing was that there were no waffle-iron tread marks; the print was oddly flat and smooth. He held his own right foot over the print; whoever it was had feet quite a bit smaller and narrower than his own.

Could have been someone else, but he doubted it. Not in the winter, with the frequent rains. He walked down the rest of the drive, probing with his flashlight, but he didn't find any other tracks. Even if there had been something, Gage himself may have erased the evidence when he drove up in his van.

Back in his well-lighted house, he fixed himself a bourbon on the rocks and drank it slowly at the kitchen table. His own haggard face gaped at him from the reflection in the bay window. His hand shook when he brought the glass to his lips. What the hell had happened to his nerves? He'd never been rattled this way before, not by anything. Who was this person staring back at him, this old guy with the gaunt face and the thinning hair? Some old cripple, that's who. It wasn't the man he remembered being.

He has other girls.

Finally, the bourbon began to take hold, his cheeks warming, his hands steadying. He racked his brain for who might have left the message there. Already, there was a long line of people who knew he was investigating the girl's death—Alex, Mattie, Zoe, Chief Quinn, Carmen Hornbridge, all the people at the tattoo shops. There were the people in Tsunami's who might have overheard him when he got into that argument with the cop. All the cops probably knew who he was by now. Heck, the gossip had probably spread so fast that half of Barnacle Bluffs knew.

But somebody knew something more.

Not only did they know something, they felt compelled to tell him—without telling him all that much.

But why? Why not just send him a letter with no return address, with all the details he needed to know? Why all the fun and games with rocks? There was a lot loaded into that one sentence. He imagined rows of young women all washed up on the beach, arms and legs tangled. He imagined them all gazing up at the sky with unblinking eyes.

He didn't remember falling asleep, but he woke to someone knocking. It jolted him upright, his heart racing. He was in the leather recliner, the living room filled with pale watery light. Rain tapped on the roof and streaked the windows. Yesterday's *Oregonian* lay on his lap.

It took him a moment to get his bearings—blinking away the bleariness in his eyes, rubbing his sore neck. Whoever was at the door knocked again. What was with all the knocking? He groped for his cane, remembered he'd left it in the bedroom when he'd finally given up on sleep the previous night, then threw off the afghan. His holstered Beretta was on the floor and he covered it with the newspaper. Then he hobbled to the front door. He was dressed in a thin white t-shirt and a pair of boxers, but he could at least peek out and see who it was.

He was glad he'd swept the rocks off the patio the previous night. It wasn't the sort of information he was ready to share with anybody.

When he cracked open the door, cool air jetted inside. Carmen Hornbridge stood on his patio under a black umbrella. A shiny black Camry was parked next to his van. She wore a gray trench coat over a burgundy turtleneck, black pants, and shiny black boots. Her blonde hair, down this time, billowed in the breeze. In the early morning light, her eyes were a bold emerald green. She flashed him one of her million dollar smiles.

"You look like crap," she said.

"Why, it's nice to see you too, Miss Hornbridge."

"Can I come in?"

He was going to say something about getting more properly dressed, but it was too late. She was already standing in his foyer, water dribbling from her raincoat onto his vinyl. She folded her umbrella and turned to him, and that's when she finally saw what he was wearing. Her eyes widened.

"Oh," she said.

"I wasn't really expecting visitors," he explained.

"I can tell." Her gaze lingered, then she peered into his house. She noticed his setup on the recliner—the mussed-up green afghan, the newspaper open on the floor, the bag of chips and the half-empty glass of water. She looked at him, eyebrows arching. "Rough night?"

He was glad he'd at least covered the Beretta. "I guess one of these days I should get a phone."

"Oh, why bother entering the twentieth century when it's already gone? Maybe if you wait long enough phones will go out of style."

"Right. If you can hold on a minute, I'll put on some clothes."

"Probably a good idea."

Her eyes twinkled with an inner merriment. He couldn't tell

if she liked what she saw or if it was just the comical nature of the situation she found amusing. He caught the scent of her perfume. Jasmine? Feeling off-balance, and his head still sluggish, he left her there in the foyer. When he was in his bedroom, she heard her opening kitchen cupboards.

"Garrison?" said. "Where's your coffee beans?"

"You don't have to do that," he called out to her.

"It's no trouble. Ah, I found them. Go ahead and take your time—shower if you want. I'll make a pot for us."

Gage didn't know her well enough to leave her unattended in his house while he was in the shower, and probably wouldn't have even if he did know her better, considering that she was a reporter, but he did take a minute to splash cold water on his face, shave with the electric razor, and straighten his hair. By the time he returned dressed in tan slacks and a silver-blue button-up shirt, it had been less than ten minutes. Her trench coat had been flung over the back of the kitchen chair. The coffee maker was percolating and Carmen was getting down two mugs from his cabinet. The Irish cream and sugar were already on the counter.

She surveyed his new attire and nodded in approval. "You clean up nice."

"Thanks. Mind telling me what you want?"

"Aww. That's pretty blunt. What if I said I was just stopping by to say hello?"

"Sure."

"I'm part of the official Barnacle Bluffs Hospitality Brigade. We like to check up on all our citizens from time to time to see how they like life here on the great Oregon coast."

"Uh huh. So that's what you do for fun on Saturdays?

"Fun?" she said. "What's that?"

She poured the coffee. He took his with a splash of Irish cream; she took hers with more cream and sugar than coffee. The aroma alone was enough to sharpen his senses and add a little clarity to his thinking. They sipped from their mugs and sized each up across the counter.

"I looked you up on the Web thingy," she said.

"Web thingy?"

"That's a technical term in journalism." She put her mug on the counter and cupped it with her hands, looking into the coffee. Strands of steam threaded past her face. "You have a pretty interesting past, Garrison."

"That's one word for it."

"Why did you move out here?"

"Why does it matter?"

She looked at him. "Was it to disappear?"

"Is there something I can help you with, Miss Hornbridge, or did you just stop by for the free coffee?"

"Touchy, touchy. You knew I'd ask, right? I *am* a journalist. And you've got a past that's pretty damn intriguing to a journalist. I'd love it if you'd tell me a little more about what led you to moving to Barnacle Bluffs."

"I think it should be pretty obvious from what you read."

"That's the official version. I want your story."

He said nothing, letting the silence fill the moment.

"Well," she said, shrugging, "I guess that's fair. Maybe you'll trust me enough in time. I actually stopped by about our mutual interest. I heard you were a busy boy yesterday."

"Oh yeah?" Gage said. "Who'd you hear that from?"

She smiled. "I'll tell you that when you tell me what you learned yesterday."

"Miss Hornbridge—"

"Come on, call me Carmen. It won't kill you."

He sighed. "Carmen, I told you I'd keep you in the loop. And I will. But I'm not going to tell you every time I get some sort of lead. Most of them won't go anywhere, so it would just be wasting your time."

"Oh, so you have a lead then? What sort of lead?"

She grinned like a mischievous pixie. He had to admire her persistence. But the last thing he needed was for her to print something that would make his job that much tougher. He'd been down that road. The press could be a powerful weapon when used properly, but it was often like taking a shotgun to a problem that required a pistol. He had the feeling he was knee-deep in sleeping vipers, and one wrong move would wake them. There might come a time to wake them up, but it wasn't now.

"All right, I'll tell you this much," he said, "I think I might know why she came to the coast. That's it, though. I don't even have a name yet."

"Why she came to the coast?" Carmen said. "How'd you get that?"

"I'll tell you that if you promise not to run any stories on it."

She laughed. "You know I can't do that. It's hard enough these days to sell newspapers *without* sitting on something juicy."

"Well, then you'll have to wait on the details." He rounded the counter to the coffee pot.

"Aw, come on, Gary—"

"The only person ever to call me Gary was my grandmother. I never liked it."

"Well then, I certainly won't do it again. But you've got to give me something here. Do you know how deep in the red my little paper is? Newsstand sales have picked up after the girl's death, but I haven't had much to report lately."

"So what, you're trying pity on me?"

"No, I'm pleading with you to support a free and independent press."

"Oh, I support it all right. I just don't work for it."

He had his back to her as he refilled his coffee. He could feel her staring at him. It was strange, having an attractive woman in his kitchen. It had been a long time. He was afraid that if he turned and looked at Carmen, she'd see this on his face, and he didn't want her to see that. He opened the fridge and took out a carton of eggs.

"I think I'm going to make some breakfast," he said. "Interested?"

"Tim Paige called me," she said.

"What?"

"The owner of TP Piercings and Body Art. He told me you were asking questions about her tattoo. I know him pretty well.

He's run some ads in the *Bugle*."

He heard something in her voice. He looked at her and saw that it was in her eyes too. "You know him better than that," he said

"Huh?"

"You two date or something?"

"No! It's nothing like that."

"Hmm. I'd say the lady doth protest too much."

She shook her head, but there was a hint of pink on her cheeks. So she wasn't so unruffable after all. Good to know. It made her seem more vulnerable—and more attractive.

"He's asked me out a few times," she said. "I've always said no. Look, I'm trying to do a little quid pro quo here."

"You're not offering much quid."

She pursed her lips, narrowing her eyes. "Did anybody ever say you look a little like Harrison Ford?"

"Flattery won't work any better than pity, lady."

"Actually, I wasn't flattering you. You've got that same sort of rugged features and sad intelligence in your eyes. It's a nice combination."

"Right."

"I'm serious! Okay, whatever, try to pay a guy a compliment . . . Listen, I gotta go. But can I assume you learned about her from one of the tattoo artists on the coast?"

"You can assume whatever you want."

"Jesus, you're being a hard ass. Okay, fine. But if I get some more *quid* that's of interest to you, will you be willing to offer up some *quo?*"

He nodded. "I'd certainly consider it. Anything that helps me get to the bottom of her death faster, the better. I honestly don't care who gets there first."

"Unless it's me, of course."

"No, it's not that. And you're smart enough to know it."

He held her gaze. They were less than two feet apart, close enough that he saw the gloss of her lipstick, the few freckles she had on her nose. There had been times when he and Janet had made love in the kitchen, when the mood had overcome them when they were standing just like this. It was mostly because of Janet. She'd told him once that there was something about the presence of food, all those tastes and textures and smells, that was a powerful aphrodisiac.

He felt a warmth spreading up his neck to his ears, and was about to say something to break the tension, when she looked away.

"Okay, then," she said, heading for the door.

She grabbed her jacket and her umbrella. He followed her to the door, opening it for her. She passed so close that he got a good whiff of her perfume again. Definitely jasmine. Cool air streamed in from outside.

"What about you, Carmen?" he said.

"Huh?"

"You must have a reason for moving to Barnacle Bluffs, just like me."

They were inches apart. Her smile never waned, but for just a moment her eyes went dead—gray and flat like the sea on an overcast day. It was there for only a second before the bemused twinkle returned, but it was unmistakable. And it was startling.

"Maybe someday I'll trust you too," she said.

When she was gone, he gobbled up some eggs and toast, then took a shower. Cold. The coffee hadn't fully swept the cobwebs from his brain, and he needed an extra jolt after talking with Carmen. He had to get a hold of himself. It wouldn't help anything if he let himself get confused. There were some roads that had been closed long ago and he didn't see how they'd ever re-open.

After a quick call to Mattie from the payphone at the gas station—they were sending her home that afternoon, and she insisted that Zoe was fine taking her—he set out that morning to visit every art-related store or gallery in Barnacle Bluffs. If that failed to turn up anything, he'd do what he did yesterday and head south along the coast. Saturday was a big tourist day, even in the winter, so he knew he'd find them open.

The sky was a solid gray canopy, and even at ten in the morning the air still had the early dawn haze. Most cars drove with their lights on, the traffic sparse. He visited three art galleries and an art supply store in the span of an hour. His line was that he was a private investigator who'd been hired to find a missing young man and his wife who'd kidnapped his client's nephew, and he had reason to believe they'd come to Barnacle Bluffs. He also had reason to believe the woman loved art, so would it be possible to look through any old job applications they had on file, as well as the guest books over the last two years?

It was a small fib, but he figured if any of them recognized the girl on the news they would have come forward by now, and after the message on his stoop, he was reluctant to be more direct. Maybe he could slow the tsunami of gossip just a little.

All were cooperative. Why wouldn't they be, when it was an innocent little nephew? Neither of the galleries had job applications on file (they were both ma and pa outfits who didn't hire), but one of them had a guest book they dutifully let him examine. There were hundreds of entries in the last two years, and he recorded a couple dozen names on a yellow legal pad he'd brought with him. When the owners raised eyebrows at this, he said that the thieves were probably operating under an assumed name.

The art supply store, which was in the outlet mall, didn't have a guest book, but the tie-dyed manager did have a handful of job applications in a cardboard box in her office. She wouldn't let him look at the applications himself, no matter how persistent he was, but she did agree to give him a list of names, addresses, and phone numbers of everyone who'd applied in the last two years—a total of thirty-nine people, twenty-two of whom were women. All of the women had local addresses, either in Barnacle Bluffs or a nearby city. Of course, that didn't mean the addresses were valid.

When he walked outside, a young man with a blond beard and thick sideburns was sitting on the metal bench. His jeans were spotted with paint and there were holes in the knees. A brisk wind stirred up dust along the sidewalk and sent an empty paper Coke cup skittering across the parking lot. He caught a whiff of caramel corn from the ice cream shop next door.

"Dude, I heard you talking in there," the young man said.

Gage stopped, leaning on his cane. "Yeah?" he said.

"You know, if the girl was really into art, there is another place you should check. It's gonna sound kinda weird, but . . . the public library."

"The library?"

"Yeah. See, maybe five years ago this rich dude who loved art donated all his art books to the library, and there are tons of them. If you're into art, it eventually gets around. They're in this special cabinet. You have to sign them out."

Gage thanked the kid and headed for the library. It was only three blocks from the outlet mall, in a drab concrete building that included city hall and some state and county offices. His knee was acting up, and of course this guaranteed that the elevator would be out. A handwritten sign next to the elevator informed him that if he had a disability he could use the courtesy phone and somebody would help him use the freight elevator, but Gage couldn't bring himself to that level of humiliation. Instead, he winced his way up the concrete steps.

The library was larger than he expected. It only encompassed one floor, but it was the *whole* floor, the air-conditioned stillness neatly packed with row upon row of orange metal stacks, stations of computers, and plush reading chairs the brightest shade of purple he'd ever seen. An elderly black man with white hair and wire-rimmed glasses was perched behind the reference desk, reading a newspaper. He glanced up when Gage approached. He was thin, with slightly effeminate mannerisms, and his brown tweed suit fit so loosely Gage figured he'd slip out of it if he stood too fast.

Upon seeing him, Gage remembered an article a year or two back in the *Bugle*, something about the local librarian celebrating three decades of service. He also remembered that the man had been a widower for over ten years, and that his biggest passion beyond books were his prize-winning miniature poodles. The nameplate on his desk read ALBERT BERNARD. The short glass cases immediately behind the desk were filled with just the sort of massive tomes that might be art books.

"Can I help you?" he asked. His skin was jet black except for a few age spots on his forehead that looked like copper coins.

"Yes, Mr. Bernard—"

"Oh, do call me Al. First time here?"

Gage leaned against the counter, taking his weight off his knee. "Yes, though I can see now that was a mistake. What a marvelous library. Are those the art books behind you I've heard so much about?"

The man beamed with pride. "Why, yes! Are you an art aficionado, Mister . . . ?"

Gage hesitated. Good old Al was just the sort of fellow who would remember, when he eventually saw Gage's face in the paper, that Gage had lied to him. Since this small-town librarian who'd been in Barnacle Bluffs for over three decades might be a valuable asset, he decided the truth was probably best. "Gage," he said, extending his hand. "Garrison Gage."

They shook. The man had a grip like a wet noodle, but his eyes were warm and welcoming.

"Pleasure to meet you, Garrison. Would you like to look at a particular book, or is there a type you're interested—"

"Actually, I have a different kind of request, Al. I'm really hoping you might be able to help me." Gage leaned in a little closer, lowering his voice to a conspiratorial whisper. "I'm a private investigator."

Now he really had Al's attention. The man straightened up in his chair.

"Oh?"

"Yes. I'm looking into the death of the girl who showed up on the beach a week ago Thursday."

"Oh, yes," Al said, "I've followed that terrible business closely. Just dreadful what happened to her. Absolutely dreadful. And to not even know who she is—so awful. You'd think someone would have come forward."

"I have reason to believe she was very into art," Gage said, "so I thought she might have come in here to look at your gorgeous art books."

"It's possible," Al said, "but I'm positive I would remember if she came in. I saw her picture in the paper. However, I do have volunteers who staff the reference desk about ten hours a week, so she may have come in during that time. I could put you in touch with them, but quite a few are on the elderly side, so their memories are not as sharp as they once—"

"Could I take a look at the sign-in book?"

"Oh. Well. Yes, I suppose that would be fine. But if you already know her name, then why—"

"No, I don't. That's just it. I'm looking for names to check with names I've found elsewhere."

Al brought out a black ledger book. With the exquisite care of a curator at a fine museum, he rotated the book and opened it gingerly to the last entry. There were maybe twenty entries per page, no more than a couple a week, in blue and black ink, a name and a state, and over half of them in the same looping handwriting. He assumed that it was Al's, and it was a good thing, because it meant the patrons didn't fill it out themselves. The only part that was the patron's was the signature at the end of the line.

Gage set his things on the counter and opened the spiral notebook to a blank page. He flipped through the pages, seeing how long it was going to take to record every woman's information from the previous year. Before he started, however, one name jumped out at him. ABBY CARSON. It had nothing to do with the name itself. It had everything to do with the tiny doodle next to her signature—so small he had to look twice to make sure it wasn't just an ink smudge.

It was a dolphin.

Chapter 8

AFTER JOTTING DOWN the rest of the potential names he found in the library log—it never hurt to be thorough—Gage thanked Al and headed for his van. Her signature had been dated for the previous March, ten months earlier. While he'd been inside, the sun had slipped out of the clouds and hung there like a yellow marble in a bed of steel wool. It matched his mood. The sun might vanish into all that gray at any moment, but for now he felt a ray of hope. He had a name. It may not have been the right name, it may not have even been a real name, but it was something. She had come to this library and looked at these books. He was sure of it.

The name Abby Carson didn't match any of the names he'd gotten from the art supply store or the galleries, but he refused to let his optimism be dimmed. Driving south, he enjoyed the warmth of the sun on his face. Inside the van, he could almost pretend it was summer. He picked up two turkey sandwiches from the Subway and ended up at Books and Oddities at a quarter to noon.

When he came in, there was nobody at the front counter. He heard Alex's low rumbling voice coming from the back of the store.

"Be with you in a second," he called.

"It's just me," Gage said.

Alex appeared a moment later and Gage held up the plastic bag containing the sandwiches.

"I come bearing gifts," he said.

"I see that. Was helping a gentlemen locate our expansive collection of Louis L'Amour paperbacks. So how goes the battle?"

"I may have just won the battle," Gage said. "The first battle, anyway."

"Really?"

"We'll see. Can I use your computer?"

Alex reached for his sandwich, putting on the face of the pouting adolescent. "Is that all I am to you? A free Internet connection?"

"Hey, that sandwich set me back five bucks."

While the computer was booting, Gage caught Alex up on the message on the doorstep and the dolphin doodle in the library sign-in book. He kept his voice to a whisper until an elderly man with hearing aids as big as Mickey Mouse ears shuffled out of the back, paid for two tattered Westerns, and left. Since Alex said the man had been the only customer in the store at the time, they were able to talk more freely.

"So what do you make of it?" Gage said.

Alex wiped cranberry sauce off his mustache. "I think this is probably going to be a little more complicated than a drunk boyfriend killing his girl in the heat of passion. What do *you* make of it?"

"About the same."

"Any theories?"

"Tons. But first I want to see what the computer tells us."

Gage finished the last bite of the sandwich, polished it off with the rest of the bottled water Alex brought from his fridge in the back, then got to work on the computer. Gage had dropped his own computer out his apartment window after Janet died—along with enough other objects that a few neighbors felt compelled to call the police—but he'd used Alex's computer enough that he still knew his way around them. He did some searches for the names Abby Carson and Abigail Carson, hitting the major search engines as well as the all the popular social networking sites. He turned up hundreds of them. Those that had pictures, none of them matched. Alex watched over his shoulder.

"You think that's her real name?" he asked.

"No," Gage said, "But I want to eliminate the obvious first. Would you mind checking the FBI database?"

Gage scooted out of the chair. With a sigh, Alex took the seat, and with quick, one-finger hunting and pecking brought up the FBI database. He punched in a password and entered her name on a couple different screens. There were several Abigail Carsons with criminal records, but all were much older than the girl. He did bring up some younger Abigail and Abby Carsons searching some related files, and Gage dutifully jotted them down the relevant information.

"You really going to track each one of those down?" Alex asked.

"I will if I don't turn up something another way," Gage said. "Hey, do you have a road map of the western United States?"

Alex slid open the cabinet beneath the cash register and flipped through a stack of papers there. "I think I've got some AAA guides here . . . Yeah, here's one."

He handed it to Gage, who folded open the wrinkled map and set it on the counter. It was so well used it felt like tissue paper. Gage zeroed in on the shop where the girl had supposedly gotten her tattoo, in Kooby, tracing his finger east along the twisting highway.

"That's what I thought," he said. "No reason she would have used this highway unless she was coming from directly east. If she was coming up the Interstate, she would have come west a different way, ending up in another town. Florence maybe."

"You're assuming she always wanted to come to the coast," Alex said.

Gage nodded. "More than that, I'm assuming she always wanted to come to the *Oregon* coast."

"Why? It could have been a spur of the moment decision. Maybe she was heading to Canada and changed her mind."

"Possibly," Gage said, "but I don't think so. Based on what she told the Indian, I think she had her sights set on here. She sounds like she was intent on being an artist and that she wanted to paint dolphins. For some reason, she thought she would find them here."

"That's nutty. It's too damn cold for dolphins."

"Yeah, but she didn't know that."

"How do you know she didn't live in Grants Pass? Or some-place in Eastern Oregon?"

Gage studied the map. "If she lived in Oregon, it's a good bet she'd have been to the coast at some point. Or at least she would have heard there were no dolphins on our coast."

Alex snorted. "You obviously haven't met the same Oregonians as I have."

"Stick with me," Gage said. He traced his finger along the various highways, going east and south. He kept going for a moment, like a mouse hitting a dead end before doubling back, then stopped and leaned in closer. "Carson City," he said, then he looked up at Alex. "Abby Carson."

"You think she was from there?"

Gage shook his head. "Probably not. I think she might have stopped there, maybe had a good time. When she had to come up with a name at the library, it was the first thing she thought of. It's difficult to come up with something truly random on the spur of the moment. She was also probably on the run from some-body. Or didn't want somebody to know she was here."

"Why do you say that?"

"The name," Gage said. "Why else would she go to the trou-ble of writing a fake name in a stupid library log book unless she was afraid somebody might find her?"

"You don't *know* that it's fake."

"My friend, I don't *know* anything," Gage said. "It's just a series of suppositions that I'm hoping leads me to see a greater pattern."

"In other words, guesswork."

He shrugged. "One man's guesswork is another man's investigation. But since we haven't dug up anything so far on her name, it's a good bet, right?" Gage settled back into the computer chair and rested his chin on his hands. "Let's say she ran away from somebody. An abusive father. A controlling husband. We don't know."

Alex leaned against the counter. "She could have been running *with* somebody."

"No," Gage said, "the Indian said she was hitchhiking by herself, remember? She's young, on her own, with little money, and she signs a fake name. No, I'd say she was running. And whoever she was running from never reported her missing."

"Otherwise the police would have turned up something by now." Alex nodded. "Okay, I follow you there. So now what?"

"Now ... I've got to winnow the field. Since no one's reported her missing, let's assume no one's really looking. Do you think you could dig up all the girls raised in foster homes with first names of Abby or Abigail in Utah, Colorado, Arizona, and New Mexico? Focus on girls between seventeen and, say, twenty-two. And towns along this stretch have priority." He pointed at the highways and Interstates that ran from Kooby through Carson City and beyond.

"I can probably get a list together," Alex said.

"Good," Gage said. "Something else is bothering me, though."

"What?"

"Well, she came to Barnacle Bluffs a year ago, right? What was she doing all that time? It's too small a town for somebody to manage complete anonymity. Partial anonymity, maybe, we're big enough for that. But to have *no one* remember her? More likely there are people who remember her but aren't willing to say."

They paused while an old lady pushing a walker came inside, accompanied by a stout middle-aged woman. The old woman placed a stack of romance novels on the counter, and then the two women disappeared into the stacks. Alex counted up the books and wrote a dollar amount on a slip of paper, which he placed inside the cover of the top book.

"Well," Alex said, speaking more quietly than before, "you could say there's only one person who'd remember her—the person who picked her up outside the Indian's store. Maybe he chained her to his bed and it took her a year to escape."

"No," Gage said. "Remember, we're operating under the assumption that was her at the library. She obviously had at least a couple of weeks to get settled. Maybe she was staying at a hotel while she looked for a job, or maybe she was just camping on the beach. It may not be Miami here, but it doesn't get too cold in the spring. Maybe she was still abducted, but not right away. Let's say she did get a job. What kind of job could you get where nobody who knows you is willing to come forward?"

Alex looked at the romance book for a long time. It pictured a buxom woman, her breasts nearly popping out of her dress, being roughly embraced by a man whose chest was more defined than nature would ever allow. "Of course the first thing that comes to mind is hooker," he said.

"It was the first thing that came to my mind too," Gage said. "Do you know if there's an organization running the trade around here?"

"No," Alex said, "but I bet your friend Chief Quinn does."

"I doubt he'd tell me."

"Oh, and here I thought the two of you hit it off so well—as you always seem to do with the local law enforcement. Or is it something else? You saying he's crooked?"

"I don't know him well enough to know," Gage said.

"You know, you could use your leverage against him. Threaten to go to the *Bugle* with that info about his wife."

Gage drummed his fingers on the glass. "I don't want to play that card too often. It's only one possibility anyway. Maybe she didn't fall quite so far. There's that place on the outskirts of town, that strip joint. The Gold Cabaret. Maybe she got a job there. Even if she *did* get into the trade, I can't see her going straight to selling sex in one fail swoop."

"Yeah," Alex said, "and even if The Gold Cabaret knew her, they probably wouldn't come forward. Just the nature of the people who run those places. They're basically just pimps with some vestige of a conscience. And like any pimp, even if they don't think they've done anything wrong, they act like they have just in case."

"It's worth checking out," Gage said.

"What, you think they'll talk if you flash that picture around?"

"I'll be more creative than that. In the meantime, if you could dig up what you can on those foster kids, I'd appreciate it."

"I'll do what I can," Alex said. There was a crunching on the gravel outside, and he looked out at the parking lot. "Ah, here comes somebody we both know."

A yellow Volkswagen Beetle pulled off the highway and parked next to Alex's van, kicking up a cloud of dust. Eve, dressed in a white cardigan and a powder blue dress, climbed out, a wicker picnic basket slung under one arm. From a distance, Gage always thought she looked like a Mediterranean Michele Pfeiffer, with jet black hair and a natural tan. Up close, he knew for a fact that she was prettier.

"What do you think she's got in the basket?" Gage said.

"Oh, lunch I'm sure," Alex said. "She claims the reheated hot pockets I dig out from the little fridge in the back aren't the best thing for my health."

"Too bad you've eaten."

"Oh, I'll eat again."

"Really? You've got a bigger appetite than me."

Alex gave Gage a wry look. "It has nothing to do with appetite. You *do* remember what it's like to be married, don't you?" Then, when he realized what had come out of his mouth, he immediately looked regretful. "Oh, man, I'm sorry. I didn't mean—"

"Don't be," Gage said. "The truth is, I have forgotten."

He tried to make the comment sound nonchalant to Alex, but he knew there was a lot of truth in it, and he felt a quench of sadness. Forgetting wasn't hard. *Knowing* you were forgetting was.

* * * * * *

On the way home, the bright sun lit up the asphalt like a mirror. Mattie wasn't back yet, so Gage hobbled around the perimeter of her house, checking to make sure there was nothing wrong. Ever since Mattie had fallen ill, it was something he'd do once a week. Her black cat, sitting in her bedroom window, alternated between cleaning itself and watching him with the same level of intent it'd focus on a mote of dust. The tall grass dampened the hem of his trousers. He made a mental note to call the yard maintenance company; in the winter, they only came out upon request. He also noticed that a gutter on the north side was coming loose from the house, and he told himself to remember to bring a hammer next time he came down.

When he came back around to the front, Zoe was pulling into the carport in Mattie's beat-up red Cherokee. Plumes of black smoke spitted out of the jeep's exhaust. Mattie herself was asleep in the passenger seat, chin on her chest, but when the car rattled to a stop, she jerked awake. Gage opened the door for her.

"What are you doing skulking around my yard?" she said.

"Madam," Gage said, "I'd suggest you be more precise with your language. A man with a cane is incapable of skulking."

"I thought so too until I saw you. That was skulking as sure as rain."

He offered her his arm, but she ignored it, struggling out of the vehicle with one hand on the door handle and the other on the edge of the seat. Her tattered gray sweater looked like the lint pulled out of the dryer, balled up in some places, full of holes in others. Zoe, as nonplussed as ever, didn't even ask; she simply grabbed Mattie under the arm and guided her toward the house. Gage hefted her suitcase out of the back.

He usually stopped by a couple times a week, but entering the little cottage, he was never fully prepared for the stifling sweat-odor, the stale air, and the lingering scents of the hundreds of incense candles Mattie had burned over the years. The furniture looked like it had been rescued from the dump, but the walls were covered with expensive prints of local artists. She insisted on taking refuge on the plaid recliner in the living room rather than setting up in her bedroom again.

Her face was flushed and she was breathing hard. Zoe got her some pillows and asked her if she wanted anything else.

"No," she said. "You've done more than enough, dear. Didn't you say you wanted to go to the outlet mall and get some jeans?"

"Aw, that can wait, Gram," she said.

"No, you go ahead. You been fussing around me for days. Garrison here can make sure I have what I need. Isn't that right, Garrison?"

"Your wish is my command," Gage said.

"See now? Go on."

Reluctantly, Zoe headed out in the Jeep, insisting she'd be gone only an hour. Gage told her he'd be glad to wait around longer than that, and she returned this offer with a look that would have grown icicles on the sun. After she was out of the driveway, he looked at Mattie.

"You told her," Gage said.

"I did no such thing," Mattie said. "She's just generally inclined to hate you."

"Well, that's a relief."

Two cats, a gray one and a calico, had already taken up their stations on her lap, both of them purring. She scratched them behind the ears. "Don't feel bad. She's generally inclined to hate everyone."

"Except you of course."

"Oh, no, she hates me too. Just not all the time. You thought any more about what I said?"

"About Zoe? I've tried not to."

"The clock's ticking, pardner."

"I try not to think about that either."

She leaned back against the green afghan draped over the headrest, closing her eyes. "Can you do something for me? Bring my suitcase over here."

He fetched it from the bedroom, where he'd put it, and placed it on its side next to the chair. She leaned over and cracked it open a few inches, dug through the top pocket and pulled out a plain brown manila envelope, placing it on her lap. The effort appeared to drain her.

"Is this what I think it is?" Gage asked.

"I don't know," she said, "what do you think it is?"

"I think it's trouble."

The envelope wasn't sealed. She pulled a dozen sheets all stapled together and handed them to him. One glance at the first page was enough to confirm his suspicions.

"Power of Attorney Questionnaire," he read.

"It's from my lawyer."

"Jesus, Mattie."

Now her eyes were open again, but they had a glazed look. "You can fill it out without saying yes. It's not official until you sign the actual Power of Attorney and get it notarized. This is just to help my lawyer get the process started."

Gage shook his head. "I don't know."

"Hey, it's okay. I'm not asking you to leap yet. It's just . . . I got to get the ball rolling so it's ready when you do. *If* you do. I can give you custody of Zoe in my will, which I'll do if you say yes, but these things can get sticky. I've heard horror stories. I've already signed a DNR, but who knows? If I linger on like a vegetable, or my thinking starts to change all of a sudden—it is brain cancer, you know—I don't want nothing undone. I can't leave it to chance."

"Mattie—"

"Nah, nah, it's all right. You don't have to give me an answer now. Just fill it out, okay? This really is the best way to give you custody, and I trust you with all my other stuff too. What little there is. I just . . . I got to do my part while I still can. So it's all got to be good except for your say so. I'm sorry if that's putting pressure on you. I don't mean to. I know you're scared."

"Scared! I'm not scared."

"Sure as shit you are. You'd be out of your mind otherwise. You'd be out of your mind even if Zoe was the sweetest little thing in the entire universe. This ain't no small thing I'm asking you. I know that. I also know you can do it, or I wouldn't have asked."

Gage looked at the paperwork. All those blank boxes literally put her request in black and white, dispensing with any hypotheticals. It made him feel queasy just looking at it. "I'll fill it out," he said.

"Thank you."

He slipped the paperwork into the inside pocket of his leather jacket.

Just as she said she would, Zoe returned an hour later. After swinging by the house, Gage headed to the *Bugle*. An unruly breeze buffeted him from every direction, and the strip of clouds along the horizon was an angry black. There was going to be a hell of a storm that night.

Climbing the stairs in the sheltered alcove, he heard the rhythmic clicking of a manual typewriter coming from within the *Bugle's* office. The door was cracked an inch and he pushed it open. Carmen, sitting at a folding table behind a typewriter in a different corner of the room, looked at him over the rims of her glasses. She wore the same black turtleneck as before. It didn't reveal an inch of neckline, but there was something about the way it molded to her curves that made it seem like it revealed more than a string bikini.

"A manual typewriter?" he said.

"You have something against manual typewriters, Mister Gage?"

"It's not exactly modern technology."

She shrugged. "I'm addicted to the sound. There's nothing more satisfying to me than the clickety clackety of my little Remington Portable. So what do I owe the pleasure? Twice in one day. A woman starts to feel special."

Gage closed the door. His knee throbbed, but he tried to hide his limp as much as possible as he made his way over to her. He realized he was doing this and felt foolish. What was he doing? He was a man with a cane. What could he hide?

"I need some information," he said.

"Ah. "

There was no chair near her, but there was a metal filing cabinet, and he perched himself on this. "You've been in Barnacle Bluffs what, six months?"

"About. Why?"

"You think you know the seedier side of the town pretty well by now?

She smirked. "Seedier. What a nice fifties pulp way of putting it. But yeah, I suppose as well as anyone around here. What are you after?"

"I'm wondering who runs the sex trade around here."

Her eyebrows went up. "Why, you getting a little lonely? Facebook not enough for you?"

"I tried Facebook," Gage said, "but no one wanted to be my friend."

"Hard to believe, with your sparkling personality."

"I know. Actually, I want to know if there's an operation behind the sex trade here or if it's all just freelance stuff."

She took off her glasses and placed them upside down on her typewriter, then leaned back in her chair. "You think she was working as a prostitute?"

"Did I say that?"

"You didn't need to."

He shrugged. "It's just one avenue I'm exploring. You can't tell me you didn't think of it."

"Of course," she said.

"So?"

"So . . . Barnacle Bluffs isn't New York, Garrison. If there's prostitution going on, it's small time. Heck, some of the prostitutes have even been caught advertising on Craigslist. That's how small it is."

"That's what I figured."

She held up a finger. "However . . ."

"I was hoping for that too."

"There *is* somebody you could talk to. He won't tell you anything, but you could try."

"Who?"

She smiled. "Oh, no. You won't get this information for free. I want to know what you've learned about this girl so far."

"Hmm. Soon."

"Ah, so you have learned something?"

"Soon," he repeated.

"Mister Gage, I'm getting the distinct feeling you don't trust me."

"Miss Hornbridge, it has nothing to do with trust. I'm just not quite ready for everything to be public knowledge. But you'll know before anyone else. Is that good enough for you to give me the name of the person I should talk to?"

"Nope. You'll have to do better."

"Like what?"

"You can't think of anything?"

"I'm racking my brains."

"Well," she said, "I guess you'll just have to take me to dinner tonight so you can rack your brains some more."

She said it with laughter in her eyes. It caught him off guard.

"Oh, don't do that," she said.

"What?"

"Go away like that. You're retreating back into your shell."

"I don't know what you're talking about."

"It's just dinner, for god's sake. You have to eat. I have to eat. You tell me some interesting stories, and I'll give you the name of the person who might be of some use to you. I've been wanting to try the restaurant in that new hotel on the south end, The Tidepool. Need to write a review and I hate eating alone. Plus they mostly serve seafood and I hate seafood, so I could use another opinion."

"You moved to the Oregon coast and you don't like seafood?"

"Crazy, huh? So what do you say? Meet me at seven?"

He hesitated. "I don't know if that's a good idea, Carmen."

The wry grin didn't leave her face, but he saw the hurt in her eyes. "What, you have a hot date?"

"No, I just . . . need to stay focused on this case."

"Uh huh. And eating in some way impedes your focus?"

Her tone had turned brittle. He sensed that the conversation was going downhill, and he didn't quite know how to bring it back. "Look, do we really have to make this more complicated?"

"Not really."

"Okay then."

"Fine. How can I help you, sir? Are you wanting to place a classified ad?"

He shook his head. "Now who's retreating into their shell?"

Just for a moment, the look was there on her face again, the one he'd seen right before she'd left his house that morning. The vulnerability. This was a woman who had been hurt, and she wore her grins and her smirks and all her witty remarks as an armor that kept people from seeing the bruises.

It was there and then it was gone. She put on her glasses and squinted at the page in front of her.

"I've really got to get this done," she said.

"Gotcha," he said.

She started typing, the tapping of Remington as loud as thunderclaps. He headed for the door. When he had his hand on the knob, the typing stopped.

"His name is Jimmy Lordenback," she said.

He looked at her. She was still staring at the page.

"I don't know where he lives," she said. "I don't even know if *has* a regular place to live. But you'll find him playing poker almost every weeknight at the casino. He has . . . connections. If you want something, he can usually get it for you. You know the kind of stuff I'm talking about. He wears suits so bright they're practically radioactive. Hard to miss."

"Thank you," Gage said.

Without looking at him, she started typing again.

Chapter 9

THE RAIN STARTED AS A MIST wetting his cheeks. Outside the *Bugle*, the windsocks hanging outside the shops whipped back and forth in the gusts like mad pythons. By the time he pulled the van onto the highway, he could barely see the road through his whirring windshield wipers. Passing his house, heading for the outskirts of town, the downpour became a raging flood falling from the sky, slowing the busy weekend traffic to a crawl.

It was nearly four o'clock when he reached The Gold Cabaret, a stone block building with no windows and a LIVE NUDE GIRLS neon orange sign; the place was right after a gravel pit and before an out-of-business boat repair shop. The gravel and mud parking lot, pock-marked with puddles, was half-filled with dented pick-ups, bumper-crumpled sedans, and other vehicles that looked like the cast-offs from a used car lot.

The crackling on the roof of his van sounded like falling acorns. He slipped the pictures of the girl inside his leather jacket. Clamping his fedora against his head, he bobbled his way to the red metal door. His cane splashed in the puddles. He heard—felt, even—the pulsing beat of a rock song coming from the other side.

When he squeezed inside, a muscular bald white man in a tight black t-shirt was there on a stool. Gage paid him the five dollar cover charge. Led Zeppelin thundered from speakers in each corner of the room, the thumping base hitting Gage like punches to the chest. A Latino woman in garish purple make-up danced on the stage, naked except for a leather outfit that revealed rather than covered. She gyrated her hips in front of a couple twenty-year old-guys who were hooting and hollering and generally making asses of themselves. A few other guys sat a little farther back, tables immersed in shadows. There was no cigarette haze, but the smell still clung to the place.

Gage recognized the attraction of strip clubs, porn films, and the skin magazines. He understood the animalistic urges as well as any man. But for him personally, these things never held much appeal. A woman in a bikini was far sexier than a woman in nothing at all, and a woman in a well-cut silk dress was far sexier than a woman in a bikini. Give him the smoldering look across a crowded room over the fake lip-licking lust of a woman making love to a metal pole any day. Sex appeal was confidence and mystery and allure, none of which had anything to do with clothing—or the lack of it.

The bartender was a broad-shouldered man with a big handlebar mustache and a bad comb over, dressed in the same black t-shirt as the bouncer. He was bent over, murmuring to the only person at the maple counter—a middle-aged woman with a face like dried-up yellow play dough and a bright perm of orange hair that made him think of Ronald McDonald. Gage took a seat on a stool one away from the woman.

The bartender sidled over to him. "What'll it be?" he said. His breath stank of pretzels and beer.

"Actually," Gage said, "I was wondering if I could talk to the manager."

"What's that?"

Gage raised his voice. "Could I talk to the manager?"

"About what?"

"About somebody who may have once worked here."

The man looked like he'd swallowed a lemon. When his face crinkled, his mustache bowed like an inverted V. "Man, it's just hands-off dancing. You want a friend, try one of those 1-900 numbers you see on your TV when you're watching the shopping network."

"Hey, thanks," Gage said. "You think that up all by yourself, or did you get that from the bartender book of one-liners?"

The man stared at him with the intensity of a pit bull. "Who the hell are you?"

"Name's Garrison."

"So?"

It was frustrating shouting to be heard over the music, but Gage pressed on. "So I'm looking into the death of the girl who showed up on the beach a week ago."

"What girl?" he said.

"Come on, man. You're saying you didn't hear about it, in a town this small?"

He shrugged, then pulled out a rag and wiped the counter. "If it's none of my business, I don't pay attention. Don't see how it has anything to do with us."

"I had a hunch she might have worked here."

"Doubt it."

Gage pulled the head shot out of his jacket and placed it in front of the bartender. The man took his time, wiping the counter far longer than the counter warranted, but eventually looked at it. Gage was sure the man intended only a glance, a kind of dismissiveness, but that was actually what gave him away. He actually looked *twice,* before turning his concentration fully to the counter again. The orange-haired woman watched but said nothing.

"Well?" Gage said.

"Don't know her."

"You sure?"

The man stopped wiping and stared at Gage. "You calling me a liar?"

"I'm just trying to find out who killed her, and I'm getting the distinct sense you're deliberately not being helpful."

"Fuck you, man. I think you better hit the road."

Gage slid the photo into his jacket. The pulsing music was giving him a headache. "All right. If you won't talk to me, then maybe you'll talk to the police." He got up from the chair, leaning heavily on his cane. "Wonder how a bunch of cop cars out front will affect business. Maybe they'll check to see if all your dancers are above legal age while they're here."

"I *told* you," the bartender said, "we never seen her."

"Yeah, okay," Gage said.

He started to walk away. He'd only gone a few steps when the expected response followed.

"Wait a minute."

What he *hadn't* expected was that it was the woman, not the man, who'd called after him. Gage turned. She rotated on her stool, arms crossed, her faded jean jacket open. Underneath she wore a white Betty Boop t-shirt, and her rather sizable breasts distorted Betty's face. She looked like the sort of woman who'd spent her whole life in bars. Or behind them.

"Just *who* are you working for, anyway?" she said.

"Nobody," he said.

"Nobody?"

"That's right. I'm doing this all on my own." He took a step toward her, to be heard better over the music. "Can I ask to whom I'm speaking?"

"I don't get it," she said. "What's in it for you?"

"A placated conscience."

"Huh?"

Gage took another step toward her so that they were now only a few feet apart. "I assume you're the manager?"

"The owner, actually. I still don't get why you're doing this."

"Is there somewhere we can talk that's more quiet?"

The bartender, who'd been watching like an impatient parent, finally had enough. "You don't have to talk to this prick, Sue. I'll throw him out of here."

She sighed. "That's all right, Bob."

"But, Sue—"

"Let it go, Bob."

With a snort, he stalked off to the end of the counter. Mercifully, the song finally ended and there was a bit of silence— if you didn't count the assorted snickers, guffaws, and clinking beer bottles. A high-pitched whine lingered in Gage's ears. Sue watched him with world-weary eyes.

"Did she work here?" Gage said.

Sue hesitated, then nodded towards the end of the bar. Under a pink neon clock, there was a hall to the restrooms. She led him inside, and he was careful where he put his cane since the floor was littered with pretzels. The walls were paneled in faux mahogany. Beyond the restrooms was another door, one marked PRIVATE. By the time they reached it, another song cranked over the speakers. She led him into a tiny office, one with a big metal desk, a couple filing cabinets, and framed *Playboys* covering every square inch of wall space—except for a gun cabinet with four rifles inside. The room smelled like burnt popcorn; he spotted the crumpled microwave bag in the trash can.

She shut the door, blocking out the noise.

"Those are my husband's," she explained, nodding at the *Playboys*.

"I'm sorry?"

"I don't want you to get the idea I'm lesbo or nothing," she explained. "I just ain't ever gotten around to taking 'em down. Willie passed two years ago—shot himself with that Smith and Wesson right there." She nodded to the case mounted on the wall.

"I'm sorry to hear that."

She settled into the swivel chair. A boxy 80's era computer sat on the desk next to an adding machine, various papers and receipts piled everywhere. "Don't be. Willie was a rotten bastard. I just ain't found a buyer for this rat hole yet. You interested?"

"It's tempting," Gage said, "but no."

"Yeah, that's pretty much it for everyone. Can't walk away in the middle of the lease, so I'm gonna hold out for at least another two years." She squinted at him, as if remembering the reason she'd brought him inside. "So tell me again, why you want to know about this kid?"

"I'm the one who found her on the beach," Gage said.

"Oh."

He could see that she didn't understand this reasoning but for whatever reason didn't feel compelled to press further. She tapped her hand on the desk.

"Well, she worked here."

"She did?"

Sue nodded. "Only for a week. That's why Bob was acting that way. She just worked a week and then she was gone."

"Do you have paperwork on her?"

She snorted. "What do you think this is, McDonalds? Our girls work for tips. It's a good amount, though. None of 'em ever complains."

"Do you at least know her name?"

"Only her first name. Abby. She went by Dolly on stage, though."

Gage nodded. Dolly, Dolphins —at least he knew he had the right girl. "Do you know anything else about her? She come with anyone?"

"No, didn't come with no one," Sue said. "I think she walked. I never saw a car outside. It was only for a week, you know, and she kinda kept to herself. It's why Bob and me didn't want to say nothing. It's not like we have a whole lot to say, and we didn't want no cops barging in here creating a fuss. Hard enough making a living in this rat hole as it is."

"Had she danced before?"

Sue looked thoughtful. "Hard to say. I think, yeah, maybe. She didn't have any of the usual jitters. But she didn't have a lot of good moves either, so if she had danced before it wasn't for long. Got good tips, though. Guys liked her. There was something about her. It was like . . . I don't know, like you were looking at her inside a cage." She fell silent, staring out blankly into space. "I got this dog once. A stray. He'd been beaten a lot, you could tell, he was all jittery, and I'd kennel him at night because it was the only

89

way he'd calm down. But when I'd open the door in the morning he'd just look at me. He wouldn't come out, even with the door open. That's what this girl was like. The cage door was open but she still wouldn't come out."

"Is there anybody else who might know her?" Gage asked. "How about your bouncer? Maybe a customer?"

"Nah, I don't think so. It's why nobody said nothing."

"When was this, exactly?"

"Oh, let me see. It was right after Jolene left, and I remember her saying she wanted to go get her son before his birthday, which was in May. So April, last year? I think that's about right. Yeah, yeah, it was early April."

"Nothing else?" Gage said.

"I wish I did remember something. It's a shame what happened. You may think I don't care, but I do. I danced once too a long time ago. I could see me in her some. That coulda been me on the beach."

The somber look on her face reminded Gage of when Mattie said the same thing about Zoe. He wondered what it was about these women who saw themselves in this dead girl on the beach, what made them want to project themselves or the people they cared about into that situation.

When he was sure there was nothing more of value she could tell him, he thanked her and left Alex's store number in case she thought of something else. On his way out, there was another girl on the stage, a spiky-haired blond. She swung around the pole and puckered her lips at him. She couldn't have been more than nineteen.

He thought about the girl on the beach, and then he understood. He left a twenty on the dance floor for her.

The bartender and the bouncer were chatting at the bar. Gage nodded to them and headed outside, into moist cool air. The rain had stopped. That was the Oregon coast for you; even a monsoon could pass through as quickly as the tourists. Before the door swung shut, the bouncer called after him. He turned, and the big guy stepped onto the gravel parking lot. His bald dome glistened in the wet air.

"Look," the guy said, and he had a voice much higher and more nasally than Gage expected, "Bob told me you're looking for that girl, the one who showed up dead on the beach."

"Yeah," Gage said. "Why, did you know her?"

"Naw, didn't know her. She didn't talk to nobody. But I do remember something. I don't know if it means much, but I still remember it a year later."

"What's that?"

"Well, it was her last day. She danced a late set, maybe a little after midnight. It was crowded. I think it was a Friday. This dude in a trench coat comes in and sits at the back. I didn't think nothing of it, but man, when she laid eyes on him she stopped dead in her tracks. She just stopped on the stage and stared at him. It was like the music wasn't even playing."

"What happened then?"

"Nothing. She just went back to dancing. It probably only lasted a few seconds, and I'm not sure nobody but me noticed who she was looking at. He only stayed a little while, maybe twenty minutes, had a beer, then left. She finished her set and went home. She wasn't here at close otherwise I probably would have asked her about him."

"You remember what he looks like?"

"Naw. He's just some dude. It was dark and crowded. Only reason I remember it at all was cause it was her last day. We get a lot of creeps in here, so it would have just been one more creep. But then she didn't come back on Monday when she was supposed to and I thought of that guy, wondering."

Gage wondered too. Maybe he was somebody from her old life, who'd followed her to Barnacle Bluffs. Maybe he was somebody she'd met in town. Maybe he was the very person who'd killed her.

He thanked the bouncer and headed to his van. The sky was even darker than earlier, a layered darkness that grew thicker along the horizon. On the highway, he reviewed what he knew so far. She'd arrived in Barnacle Bluffs in late February, coming in through Kooby. She'd gotten a tattoo of a dolphin on her ankle and told the old Indian that she was going to Barnacle Bluffs. She'd signed out the art books at the library in March. In early April, she was stripping at The Gold Cabaret. For a Jane Doe—or an Abby Doe, she did have a first name—there were an awful lot of people already who'd met her.

The question was, what had she done those five or six weeks in between coming to Barnacle Buffs and showing up at the strip club? When he found that out, he knew there was a good chance he'd discover who'd killed her. Books and Oddities was on his way home, so he swung by to see if Alex had talked to anyone at the Bureau. Sure enough, Alex already had a dozen names of foster kids of about her age from the various states east of Carson City, all with the first name Abby or Abigail. There were no missing reports filed on any of them.

He hung out until the shop closed, begged off going to Alex's place for dinner, and took the list with him home. Darkness had fallen, and it was a deep darkness, the cloud cover a veil that swaddled everything in black. The headlights of the passing cars were as tiny as needle heads.

It was after six when he turned off the highway onto the curving road up to his house. He thought about stopping at Mattie's, but he saw Zoe washing dishes in the kitchen and drove on past. He knew he was only avoiding the inevitable, but that was all right. Janet had often said he must have gotten a Ph.D. in avoidance, he was so good at it. Thinking this brought on a sinking loneliness.

When he reached his house, somebody was on his stoop. He saw the person first only as a silhouette—his porch light was off—and it set his heart skipping. But then the van's headlights swept across the person and he saw that it was Carmen, her trench coat billowing about her bare legs. He also saw her black Camry parked right where he usually parked his van, which put him in a foul mood right away.

He parked behind her, half on the bark dust and half on the gravel driveway, giving her just enough room to pull out. When he got out of the car, she stood next to the door, hand on the hood, his weak dome light leaving her mostly shrouded in darkness. Her hair appeared silvery like tinsel.

"Ready to go?" she said.

"Go? "

She chuckled. "To dinner, of course."

"I thought I was pretty clear at your office, Carmen."

"Oh, you were. I just decided to ignore it. Come on, you don't have anything to be afraid of. I've already seen you in your underwear."

He headed for his front door. His damn leg seized up on him, making his limp more pronounced; he must have looked like a drunken pirate with two wooden legs. "My god," he said, "you're a persistent woman."

She didn't say anything while he limped to the door, jangled the lock open, and flicked on the porch light. He thought he might have offended her, but when he turned and looked, she was smiling.

"Persistence is a personality trait that comes in handy in my line of work," she said. "Don't make me get down on my knees and beg. This gravel would be murder on my nylons."

He gaped at her. Not only was she wearing black nylons, but she was wearing patent leather heels, too, the kind a woman only wore when she didn't think she was going to be doing a lot walking. Her lips, bearing a hint of rouge lipstick, glistened in the thick air. There was eye shadow and blush and tiny pearl earrings, all of it subtle, none of it over the top. It was like she was trying to impress him without *looking* like she was trying to impress him.

She was putting him on the spot and it left him in a bind. He couldn't see how he could hurt her again, not so soon. And it *was* only dinner. "All right," he said, "but I warn you, I'm a lousy conversationalist."

She beamed at him. "That's all right. I specialize in getting lousy conversationalists to converse. Your car or mine?"

They took hers.

Chapter 10

IT WAS NOT A DATE. That was what Gage told himself. It was not a date, and if it *was* a date, or at least if she *thought* it was a date, well, then that wasn't his fault. He was just going to dinner. People had to eat, after all.

Without asking him, she chose the popular Romani's, an expensive Italian restaurant next to the most plush hotel in town, the Inn at Sapphire Head. When he asked her about Tidepool, she said that she went ahead and wrote a glowing review based on the opinion of the CPA next door. Gage made a crack about journalistic ethics, and she said she was happy to sacrifice what little journalistic ethics she had so she didn't have to eat seafood.

Both Romani's and the Inn were on the highest point in Barnacle Bluffs, surrounded by both the Inn's golf course and a few hundred acres of national forest which eventually connected with Foggy Creek State Park. When she pulled into the packed parking lot, he told her he didn't like crowds. She reassured him that she'd be his bodyguard. When they squeezed into the restaurant lobby, people everywhere, he suggested they grab a burger from the joint down the street. She said if he left now, she'd write a lengthy piece in the *Bugle* about transsexuals living in seclusion in their hometown and she'd make him the centerpiece.

It went better after that. Twenty minutes later, during which his knee throbbed painfully but he resisted the impulse to dive for one of the few bench seats when it was vacated, they lucked out and got a table for two overlooking the ocean: white cloth tablecloths, separate salad forks, and wait staff in red bow ties, the whole deal. The ocean itself was dark, but spotlights mounted on the restaurant roof shined on the sandy beach below. He could just make out the murmur of the waves over the din in the room.

After they'd given their waiter their drink orders, Carmen tore apart a roll, looking at him over the steam rising from the bread. "So tell me," she said, "how'd you get into the fine art of private investigation?"

"I don't know if I'd call it a fine art," he said.

"Don't dodge the question," she said, and tossed a smaller piece of the roll into her mouth.

She chewed, watching him expectantly, eyes wide. He figured it was a journalistic technique. Start eating and force your interviewee to talk.

"Is this for you or for the paper?" he asked.

"For me," she mumbled.

"I don't know if it's all that interesting."

She waved her hand impatiently for him to continue.

"Well," he said, "it wasn't by choice, I can tell you that much. Originally I thought I was going to be in the FBI. But I was just a kid back then, and I found out real quick that me and the FBI wouldn't get along."

She swallowed. "What happened?"

"I washed out of the program."

"I have a hard time believing that."

He shrugged and took a drink from his ice water. It gave him time to think. He'd already surprised himself with how much he'd already said. There was something about her that made him want to let his guard down. He didn't know where it was coming from.

He thought his taking a drink would encourage her to jump in, maybe take the conversation off on a tangent, but she rearranged her silverware and went right on waiting.

"Maybe it was a mutual understanding," Gage said. "It just wasn't the right fit. I'm . . . not much of a group person. I have a hard time working in a team."

"How surprising," she said.

"You know, sarcasm makes your face look older. It's the wrinkles around the eyes. I just thought you should know."

She stuck out her tongue. He tore open some bread and buttered half of it.

"Anyway," he went on, "it just wasn't my thing. For example, I became a decent knife thrower. Turns out that's not a valued skill in the Bureau. It was always like that. I didn't mind learning to fire a handgun, but their focus was a bit too narrow. I wanted to learn what I wanted to learn whether it was on the agenda or not. I might have still finished, but then my dad died. Almost three years to the day after my mother passed. I went back to Long Island for the funeral. There was a bit of money. Not a lot, but enough to pay off my college debts and still have enough left over that I didn't have to get serious about anything for a while."

"University of Montana," she said, nodding. "Summa Cum Laude."

"You've been reading up on me."

"Surprised?"

"Not really."

"I just never figured out why you went to Montana for school. Me, I pretty much had to struggle just to get into a state school, but it sounds like you could have gone anywhere on a full ride."

He shrugged. "I always wanted to see Montana."

"Yeah, but Harvard, Yale, Princeton—"

"Do I seem like an Ivy League sort of guy?"

"I'm just saying I find it interesting you chose Montana, that's all. So after college, the FBI, and your dad passing, then what?"

"I traveled," he said. "Europe. Central America. Did that for three years, living on almost nothing. When I came back to the States, I stopped and saw an uncle in New York. He had an agency. Three guys, and he said he could use some spot help if I wanted to try it out. No promises, but if he thought I was a good fit, and I liked the work, there might be a full-time gig in it. It was mostly insurance fraud, but I didn't mind. And it turned out I was okay at it."

"Probably better than okay."

"Yeah, well, I worked there for two years. Then my uncle and I had a bit of a falling out, so I decided to hang my own shingle. This was back in eighties, when New York was a cesspool, so there was plenty of work."

"Was your uncle pissed, you competing with him?"

"Sure, but New York's a big town. There was enough work for hundreds of private investigators."

He felt drained. He hadn't talked so much about himself since his early days dating Janet. The waiter returned. She went with the calzone. He had a 12-ounce sirloin and baby red potatoes. She castigated him for not ordering Italian food, and he said that he wasn't in the mood for Italian food, which is why he didn't want to come there in the first place.

When that business was finished, he said, "Now your turn."

"My turn for what?"

He took a sip from the Corona he'd ordered, the beer cold and smooth. He felt it working its magic on him, and he knew he'd have to go easy or he'd be asleep before the meal was finished. That was the bitch about being in his forties. "Your turn," he said, "to give me the condensed version of the Carmen Hornbridge life story."

"Ah," she said, nodding.

"Or the full version. I'm game for either."

There was already a dimming of the eyes. A retreating into the shell. She took her time replying, and when she did, she recited the facts as if she was reading them out of an encyclopedia. "Born and raised in Michigan. Went to school at MSU. Got involved with the student paper, which got me hooked on journalism. Landed a job with *The Detroit Free Press* out of college. Did pretty well for a while, seven or eight years, but saw the writing on the wall. The big newspapers are going under eventually, so I freelanced. Made a comfortable living writing puff pieces for magazines, but I got bored. A colleague told me about the opportunity with the Bugle and I jumped at it." She offered up a smile that seemed carved with a knife. "And here we are."

"You make it sound so exciting," he said.

She shrugged. "I never said it was."

"Why do I get the sense that you're leaving something out?"

"I don't know, why do you?"

"Were there any men in the mix?"

There it was. A flash of anger that swept across her face like lightning. He would have missed it if he hadn't been looking at her.

"None that mattered," she said.

"Really?"

She looked at her water glass. "Yes, really. I was really focused on my work. Not everybody can be lucky in love, you know." She must have remembered who she was talking to because she suddenly looked up. "I'm sorry, that was stupid."

"No, it's true. Not everybody's lucky."

"It was a careless thing to say."

He reached for his beer. "It's all right. I specialize in saying careless things myself."

"It's just . . . There's stuff I don't talk about, you know? It's not a big deal. I just don't talk about it."

"Believe me, I know exactly."

"Maybe you could just avoid that one topic. I know I asked about your past, so I don't blame you, but relationships . . . it's just not something I want to get into. I'll talk about other stuff. My childhood. My favorite color. Why I find men with canes sexy."

"You find men with canes sexy?"

"Most definitely. There must be something phallic about it, I guess."

They both laughed and the tension was gone. He drank his beer too fast and got light-headed. They talked about other things. She talked about growing up in Harrisville, a little town on Lake Huron, the standard happy life with the insurance salesman dad, the kindergarten teacher mom, and two older sisters who'd both found standard happy lives of their own. He talked about his recent addiction to crossword puzzles. She complained about how much work the classified section of the paper was, but how she couldn't get rid of it without creating a small town riot.

Now that they were on comfortable ground, conversation was easy—or at least *easier*. With most people, conversation was a strain. He had a hard time hiding his disdain for small talk, and when a conversation moved to topics that actually interested him, he often said things to deliberately rile people. There was that side of him, the need to poke the nest of snakes with a stick. It was ugly, and he hated that about himself, so usually he said nothing. But with Carmen, talking wasn't work. It was just talking. It still wasn't something he enjoyed all that much, but it wasn't so bad either. There were only a couple of people with whom he'd felt that way. Alex. Janet, of course.

Even the silences were comfortable. On the way back to his place, with their stomachs full and their minds wrapped in the gauzy afterglow of beer and wine, they rode next to each other without saying a word. But it wasn't awkward. A light rain pebbled the windshield. She pulled up his drive, past Mattie's dark house, and parked in front of his door.

"Thank you," she said.

"For what?"

She turned away. Her faced looked wan and yellow in the porch light. The shadows from the droplets of water on the windshield dotted her face like pennies at the bottom of a pond. "For not pushing things back at the restaurant. For not prodding me in a place that was sore."

"Hey, the feeling's mutual."

"I'd just like to focus on the future."

"Sounds like a plan."

"I know it's probably hypocritical. Here I am asking you all these questions, nosing around in your business, and then I clam up on you. It's not intentional. I just . . ." She trailed off.

"Really, Carmen," he said, "you don't have to explain. I understand."

She looked at him. Shadows painted half her face black, but her eyes were wide and bright. He was suddenly aware of this lovely creature across from him, all jagged edges and shards on the inside and curves and gentle slopes on the outside.

"Carmen—" he began.

He didn't get a chance to finish. She kissed him. Her tender lips pressed up against his own, and she cupped the side of his face with her right hand. It had been a long time since he'd kissed anyone, and it wasn't a long kiss, not more than a few seconds, but it still sent a bolt through his body. He tasted tomato sauce and garlic and red wine. He thought of the cold metal bench in Central Park, that spring night so long ago when he'd first kissed Janet.

Then it was over. And she was pulling away, wearing a hint of a smile, eyes lowered demurely.

"You should probably go," she said.

"Yeah," he said. His throat tightened, his voice husky. He cleared his throat. "Listen, I really—"

"Don't ruin it. "

Now she did look at him. There was wanton desire and fear and lots of other things all mixed together. His heart pounded so hard he felt the pulsing behind his eyes. He wanted to ask her inside. He wanted to tell her to go away and never bother him again. He wanted to tell her all the things about the world that were wrong and why it was so. Instead, he opened the door and stepped out of the car. His leg buckled—for the first time in years he'd forgotten all about his bum knee—and he hopped forward a step, catching himself before going down.

"Well that was graceful," he muttered.

"Forget something?" she said.

He turned and saw her holding out his cane. He took it from her, too embarrassed to even say thanks.

"Talk soon?" she said.

"You bet."

He started to close the door, then remembered the list of names in his jacket pocket. "Oh wait, I've got something for you."

He took it out and handed it to her, figuring he could get them again from Alex. He didn't know if he was doing the right thing, but he figured it couldn't hurt at this point. "I think there's a good chance the girl is one of the people on this list."

"Hmm," she said, looking the list over. "A bunch of Abbys, huh? I don't want you to think I kissed you just to get this."

"I don't."

"Though if I would have known," she added with a mischievous smile, "I certainly might have."

It had been the end of the longest day he'd had in years, and Gage slept like it. He didn't wake during the night once, a rarity, and didn't crack open his eyes on Sunday until nearly noon. The last time he'd slept that late had been two years earlier, when he'd had walking pneumonia. That had been a pretty crappy day. Last night had been nothing like that.

The warm glow lasted until he was in the shower, and then it was down the drain and gone as fast as the day's sweat. He couldn't even remember the feeling, it disappeared so fast. He felt cold and alone. He turned up the heat. Kept turning it up. It was scalding now, he knew it was because his skin was turning red, and still he felt cold.

He didn't know how long he was in the shower. It must have been a while because it was only when the water turned cold that he snapped out of his stupor. Wiping the fog off the mirror, he saw that his back and shoulders glowed like a radioactive tomato. Without drying himself, he slipped on his robe, grabbed his cane, and wandered to the kitchen, leaving wet footprints on the linoleum.

He started a pot of coffee. He settled himself into his easy chair. Fog blurred the bushes and rooflines of the houses outside his windows. At first, he wasn't sure if the fog was real or in his mind, and he kept blinking to clear his vision, but the fog remained.

He drank coffee and did crosswords for several hours. Finally, he began to feel better, though he still felt sluggish. Digging through the boxes in the big closet in the spare bedroom, he dug out his old spiral notebooks and found the names and numbers of some of his old contacts in the Southwest, fellow private investigators and various law enforcement types he'd had contact with over the years. Maybe he'd wander down to the gas station and make some calls.

On the other hand, maybe he wouldn't. Maybe he'd drink more coffee and do more crosswords.

The thing that finally roused him to action was Mattie. He sat there on the floor in his robe, surrounded by dusty notebooks, and he wondered about Mattie.

With excruciating slowness, he got out of the chair. With slightly less slowness, he slipped on his clothes, some jeans and an old Coney Island sweatshirt. Momentum bred momentum. Inertia could be overcome. By the time he donned his jacket and fedora, and walked through the thick fog to Mattie's, only the lingering remnants of his trance remained—a dull ache in the chest, a melancholy that was like the aftertaste of cheap wine. He welcomed the thick, wet air against his face, and savored the silence of the fog-swaddled world around him.

Using his cane, he rapped on her door. Nobody answered. He rapped again. He was preparing to rap a third time when the door opened and Zoe stepped outside, eyes hidden behind dark shades. She wore an acid-washed jean jacket with the gray cotton hood up, black leather pants, and ratty sneakers. The facial adornments were gone—no makeup, no nose ring, just pink pale skin that looked like it had been rubbed raw.

"You can watch her for a while," she said.

She pushed past him, heading down the driveway. He watched her and wondered if he should say something, but then Mattie called to him.

"Gage?" she said. "That you?"

Her voice was coming to him from down the hall. He closed the door and headed to her room. The house smelled like chicken noodle soup. The orange tabby darted out of Zoe's room, nearly tripping him. Mattie's door was open, and he found her sitting in bed with an avalanche of pillows behind her, the Wheel of Fortune on the television, an empty soup bowl on the end table. It might have been wishful thinking, but he thought he saw more color in her cheeks, a touch of rosiness.

The right side of her hair was braided, the left side loose. Hands resting on the bedspread, she clutched the remote in one hand and a hairbrush in the other.

"Well, you look like crap," she said.

"I always appreciate your honesty," Gage said. "What's up with Zoe?"

"What do you *think* is up with her?"

"Ah. You told her, then?"

"Bingo."

Her voice sounded off, like a piano slightly out of tune. Gage settled himself on the edge of the bed. Mattie raised the remote and muted the television.

"Stubborn kid," she said, still looking at the television. The wheel was spinning. "I think she pretty much hates my guts right now."

"I very much doubt it."

She sighed. "She was in here doing my hair. It was peaceful. Figured it was as good a time as any. Probably should have turned off the set, cause I know Pat Sajak can be annoying. And Vanna. That woman should sue Mattel—they used her image to make Barbie and she should get her millions."

"There's lots of boys who probably had their first sexual experience with her in mind."

She wrinkled her nose. "That's disgusting. You might as well make it with a mannequin. Pamela Anderson would be better. At least she doesn't pretend to be respectable. She knows what she is and puts it front and center."

"Both of them, in fact."

She looked at him. "I know what you're trying to do. You're trying to make me laugh."

"Is it working?"

"No."

"Okay. I guess I have to try harder."

"I guess you do. You thought any more about what I want?"

Gage hesitated. "Honestly?"

"Why would I want something other than honesty?"

"Good point. Then no, I haven't."

"Hmm. I think I would have preferred a lie."

"Too late now."

Mattie looked away. He wondered if he'd gone too far.

"I *will* think about it, Mattie. Promise."

"Well, that's good."

"It's just . . . my life is complicated."

She nodded. "Whose isn't?"

"Look, no matter what happens, I won't let her end up out in the cold, okay? I'm just not sure about the legal part of it. It's just not a mental picture I've ever been able to form, you know? I just never thought the universe would throw that particular curveball my way. I'm just trying to wrap my head around it, that's all."

"Well, I'm trying to wrap my head around dying, Gage."

"Mattie—"

"No, no, I'm sorry." She exhaled slowly, as if she was counting out the breath. "You don't need that crap. I promised I wouldn't do that sort of thing, the self-pity thing, and I'm not about to break that promise now. I understand where you're coming from. It's okay. Really."

They sat in silence for a while, and as the silence deepened, so did Gage's disgust with himself.

"Maybe I should go talk to her," he said.

"Can't make things worse, I guess."

"Oh, I'm sure I can. Where do you think she went?"

"Who knows. Probably the beach. She's like you that way— goes there to think."

"No, I go there looking for seashells."

She nodded. He patted her hand, but still she wouldn't look at him. Her disappointment hung over them like a dark cloud. He left the room and headed to the beach, holding his fedora as he crossed the highway. The cars were nothing but headlights until they were almost upon him, pale yellow orbs passing through the fog. Down on the beach, he could only see a narrow strip of colorless sand, the ocean hidden behind a gray wall. He saw the dark shape of a person directly ahead, and it made him think of an actor on a stage in front of a curtain.

It was a strange thing, hearing the ocean but not seeing it. A few feet away, he could finally tell that it was her. She had her back to him, arms crossed, her neck glistening from the moisture in the air. He stepped up next to her. She continued staring straight ahead, as if there was something to see rather than just a tapestry of steel wool.

"Quite a view," he said.

She didn't laugh. It was all right. He wouldn't have laughed either.

"Look, Zoe, this wasn't my idea."

"Oh, great," she said, "that makes me feel *so* much better."

"I'm just saying that Mattie's worried about you, that's all. She wants to make sure somebody's looking out after you when she's gone."

"I don't *need* anyone to look out after me."

"Yeah. Yeah, I'm pretty sure that's true."

"I told her what I wanted. She didn't listen."

She still wasn't looking at Gage, but her voice broke a little. Gage didn't know what to do. He was in uncharted waters. Should he pat her on the shoulder? Give her hug? Offer some sort of homespun wisdom? He hated feeling so uncertain.

"Oh, I think she listened," he said. "She knows what you want. And I think she's pretty sure you could take care of yourself if you had to. She just doesn't want you to have to, you know what I'm saying?"

"Not really."

"You're sixteen years old, Zoe. You shouldn't have to be thinking about where to find a good apartment. You should be thinking about . . . prom dresses and college applications."

She looked at him then, eyes cold. "You've got to be joking."

"It's not about me. It's about Mattie."

"Well, she's bonkers then. I don't give a rat's ass about the prom, and I couldn't care less whether I go to college."

"Yeah, well, you just made my point."

"Oh, you going to get all holier-than-thou on me? Tell me not to throw my life away working at the gas station?"

"No. I would never presume to tell someone what to do with their life. I can't speak for Mattie, but I doubt she would either. She just wants you to . . . hold onto your childhood a little while longer."

"Fuck childhood. It's overrated."

"Well, I'd agree with you there. But you've got the rest of your life to be an adult. Why are you in such a rush?"

She shook her head. "What am I supposed to do, go back to playing with My Little Ponies and watching Dora the Explorer? I didn't *want* my life to go this way. It just did. And what the hell do you know, anyway? Why the hell would my life be better living with *you*?"

"It probably wouldn't," Gage said. "It would probably be a lot worse. I know my life would."

"Oh, gee, that makes me feel wonderful."

"Hey, I'm just being honest. You think I want a stubborn sixteen-year-old nihilist living with me who already hates my guts?"

She looked out at the fog. "I don't hate your guts."

"Well, great. That's something at least."

"I just don't want to have to take care of some cripple."

"Cripple?" Gage said, trying to feign irritation but actually feeling it. "You think I'm a cripple just because I have this cane?"

"No," she said. "*You* think you're a cripple because you carry that cane."

Gage was going to say that was bullshit, but as soon as he started to summon the words he wasn't so sure. She'd startled him with her perceptiveness, slicing through all his layers of self-delusion with one comment. He hadn't even agreed to custody yet, and he already thought parenting was a bitch.

"Well, this is going well," he said.

It didn't elicit a laugh, but he did see the first glimmerings of a smile.

"You see?" she said. "You really don't want to sign up for this on a daily basis, do you?"

"Honestly?"

She shook her head. "Why would I want something other than honesty?"

That got Gage to smile. These two were more alike than they probably realized. "Good point," he said. "No, I'm not sure. I didn't tell Mattie yes."

"Maybe if you say no, she'll give up the whole stupid idea and emancipate me."

"I'm not sure I'm going to say no either."

"Why not? If we're both going to be miserable, what's the point?"

"Mattie's the point."

"I don't—"

"It's her dying wish, Zoe. Maybe that's more important than either of us."

It was the thing that finally got through to her. She didn't answer, but she blinked a few times, eyes shiny and bright. He knew if he was going to make any sort of connection with her, it was going to be now.

"Look," he said, "I'm just being upfront with you here. No matter what happens, I promise you I'll always be honest, okay? I don't know if you living with me is a good idea. I'm pretty much an asshole and I know it. But here's what I do know. A week ago Thursday, I was walking on this very beach and I found a girl not much older than you, dead as can be. I'm trying to find out who killed her and so far I'm not even sure what her name is. It's like . . . nobody was looking out for her, you know? I think that's all Mattie wants—somebody to look out for you. Whether you live with me or not, I want you to know I'll be looking out for you, okay? If you don't want it, well, I'm going to do it for Mattie anyway."

She said nothing for a long time, then finally shrugged. "Whatever," she said.

"That's it?" Gage said. "I give you that whole Hamlet impression and the best you can do is whatever?"

She gave him a sour look. "Don't flatter yourself. It was closer to Falstaff than Hamlet."

"Ah! A Shakespeare fan. That's one thing we have in common, anyway."

She sighed. "Okay, look, I get it. I want Mattie to be happy too. So if you want to tell her yes, you'll be my pseudo daddy or whatever, fine, I'll act like the meek little girl and tell her I'll go along with it. But I'm not living with you, and if you force me, you'll never hear from me again, got it? I'll check in with you once in a while, though. And I won't ignore your calls."

It wasn't exactly the sort of thing that would make Mattie happy, but Gage figured it was the best they could do under the circumstances.

"So you want to lie to her?" he said.

"You have a better idea?"

"No. Not really."

"Well, there you go."

With that, she headed down the beach—not back up the steps, but down toward where there were rocks and tide pools. He wasn't sure how much they'd really accomplished, how much *bonding* had really taken place, but it was the longest conversation he'd ever had with her so that had to count for something. When she'd gone a dozen paces, she turned back, already mostly faded by fog, a slender figure that could have been any girl.

"Hey, Gage," she called.

"Yeah?"

"Who looks after you?"

He didn't have an answer. She shook her head and turned away, disappearing into the fog.

* * * * *

Mattie was sleeping when Gage returned to her house, all five cats curled up around her. She was so still that for one dreadful moment he thought she might have passed away, but then he saw the telltale rising and falling of her chest, so subtle that he stood watching for a time just to make sure.

He took out the documents from inside his coat, where they'd been ever since she'd given them to him, and smoothed them on top of her dresser. Using his own pen, he filled out all the blanks, the little boxes that reduced his whole life to numbers, dates, and addresses, then folded the paper back up.

Her hands were clasped on her chest. Carefully as he could, he slipped the paper under them. She stirred but did not wake. One of the cats batted playfully at his hand.

Leaving her sleeping, he slipped out of the house.

Chapter 11

QUINN WAS NOT HAPPY. That much was obvious. The police chief looked at the handwritten list of names again, his brow furrowing, his enormous eyebrows curling downward along with his frown. The blinds behind him were only partially open, but the angle of the sun shined directly into Gage's eyes, forcing him to shift his head a little to get a better look at him.

The secretary scurried in, dropped a stack of papers on a mound of other papers, and scurried out. A plate containing a half-eaten cinnamon roll teetered on the edge of his desk.

"You gave them to *who* first?" Quinn said.

"Carmen Hornbridge," Gage said.

"Yeah, that's what I thought you said. You really don't like me, do you?"

"Whether I like you or not is really immaterial."

"But then why drag a *reporter* into this, for god's sake?"

"It was part of the deal."

"Deal? What deal?"

"That's between me and Carmen."

Quinn dropped the names on his already cluttered desk. "Yeah, well, your deal with me is that you would keep me in the loop."

"I am," Gage said.

"But you gave them to her on Saturday! That was two days ago!"

To Gage, Quinn's voice sounded petulant and childish, like a sibling demanding that his lollipop be exactly the same size as his sister's. His instinct was to say as much, but he let it go. It wasn't because he liked the chief. It was only because he didn't want the extra hassle that particular Monday morning.

He looked at the chief with the well-it-is-what-it-is sort of resignation, as if events had merely unfolded without his control.

"Okay, fine," Quinn said, "I'll give it to my detectives and they'll check them out. Anything else?"

Gage thought about telling him about the message on his doorstep, but he didn't like how it would make him sound. He also didn't want the cops traipsing around his property looking for clues. "Nothing that comes to mind."

"You got any theories yet?"

"A few."

"You mind sharing?"

Gage thought about it for a moment—or at least gave the appearance of thinking about it for a moment.

"No," he said.

"God damn it, Gage—"

"I'm not holding out on you. I just need a little more time to mull it over."

Quinn tore off a piece of the cinnamon roll and plopped it in his mouth. "I've got a couple detectives on staff who could mull it over too. Maybe the more people mulling it over, the better."

"Oh, and I'd be too afraid they'd laugh at me, since the caliber of my mulling obviously won't be up to the caliber of their mulling."

"Gage—"

"But I will tell you this much. I've come to believe she was an aspiring artist."

That got Quinn to look at Gage with a more curious expression. "Really? Why?"

"Let's just say it came to me in a moment of mulling."

Quinn sighed. "I should never have made that remark."

"Here's what I'd like to know," Gage said. "If you were an aspiring artist, and you were looking for other like-minded artists, where would you go in Barnacle Bluffs? Are there popular hangouts where artists go?"

Quinn nodded and looked off into a corner of the room. "Well," he said, "I'm not really into the art scene, but three places come to mind. They might wander up to the community college in Newport. They might go to the Barnacle Bluffs Community Center. Or maybe they'd go just north of town to the Northwest Artist Colony. Of course, they might just end up on the beach smoking pot. That seems the most popular destination for kids, whether they're artists or not."

"Tell me about the Northwest Artist Colony," Gage said. "What is it?"

"What am I, the Yellow Pages?" Quinn said. "Find out yourself. Until I get more info out of you, that's all the help you're going to get."

He picked up his phone, Gage's signal to leave. That was the problem starting off a relationship on the wrong foot—it forever dictated how things proceeded from that point. Of course, he almost never started a relationship on the right foot, but it was something he'd gotten better at over the years. Threatening to tell the press that Quinn's wife was once a stripper, though, was most likely not the best way to break the ice. But it was what it was.

The kindly old lady at the Barnacle Bluffs Community Center was far more helpful. The little octagonal building was on the west side of Big Dipper, next to the hospital and Ocean Waves Retirement. That should have been sign enough that the community center would be filled mostly with gray hair and walkers, which it was; the five rooms were packed with toothless Bridge players, liver-spotted knitters, and other wrinkled occupants engaged in the sorts of crafts and hobbies that a spry nineteen-year-old wouldn't have been caught dead doing.

One room that the old folks used focused on water colors, painting based on the photos they'd taped to their drawing easels, and that's where Gage stopped.　He asked who came the most and was directed to a wizened old woman with bright purple hair, a white shawl draped over her bony shoulders.　She was painting a blooming yellow rosebush.

"You come here a lot?" Gage said.

She leaned over, cupping her hand behind her ear.　Her skin made him think of a piece of paper someone had crumpled into ball and then done their best to straighten out again.　"You'll have to speak louder, dear."

"I said, do you come here a lot?"

The woman smiled, flashing several gold-capped teeth.　"That sounds like a pick-up line, honey.　If you want to ask me out on a date, you should just say so."

"I'm afraid you'd be too much woman for me."

She laughed.　"And you'd be right.　What's on your mind, then?" Gage pulled out the glossy headshot of the girl and showed it to the woman, asking if she'd ever seen her.　The woman picked up the glasses hanging around her neck, hands visibly shaking, and studied the picture.　She did so for only a moment before cringing.

"Oh, no," she said, "never seen her.　That was awful what happened to her."

"You heard about that?"

"Well of *course* I've heard about it, honey.　Get the paper every day.　I may be old, but I can still read."

"I was led to believe she may have been an aspiring artist."

"Oh.　Well.　That's even sadder, then.　The world not only lost a beautiful girl, but an artist too.　Don't think she'd come here, though.　Who'd want to hang out with all these fuddy duddies? Honestly, the only reason I come here is I look good next to all of these wannabes.　My ego needs the boost."

"Somehow, I doubt that," Gage said.　"What about this Northwest Artist Colony I've heard about?　Think that might be a place a young artist would go?"

"That's where *I* would go if I was young," the woman said. "You can stay up to two weeks in one of the cabins, and if you don't have much money, it's no problem, you just have to do some chores. Most of the funding comes from donations. I go to their annual show every year and they do some wonderful things." She beckoned for Gage to lower his ear, and he did, allowing her to whisper the rest. Her breath smelled like peppermint. "I also hear that if you want to get laid, it's not a bad place to go."

Gage feigned astonishment. "Is that so?"

She nodded. "That's what I've *heard*, anyway. I don't have direct experience. But the action has to better than here. The only man interested in me lately is this guy Phil, and he can't keep his mouth shut. I don't mean he talks too much. He's just old and has a problem with his jaw—hangs open all the time, by God. I do have my standards, you know." She squinted at him, her eyes bright even through her cataracts. "What about you? You don't have a ring on your finger. You committed or on the prowl?"

He wrote Alex's bookstore number on a scrap of paper and handed it to her. "If you think of anything else, call this number. He's a friend of mine. And I wouldn't exactly describe myself as on the prowl."

"It's one or the other, honey. All right, you got that panicked look in your eyes, so I won't be holding you any longer."

"You kidding? I could hang out with you all day."

"Liar. Anyway, if you go talk to those kids at the Colony, you tell 'em if they want to sneak any grass down here, tell them to ask for Agnes Clayborne. They'd have at least one buyer."

"Okay. Are you sure that's a good idea at your age?"

"Honey, at my age everything's a good idea. Oh, and I like your cane, by the way. My second husband, god bless his soul, he had one just like it."

Using the pay phone outside the community center, Gage placed a call to Carmen to see if she'd dug up anything from the list of names. Right after he asked her, a man in an orange blazer across the street started up a jackhammer, tearing into a roped-off portion of the hospital parking lot.

"Nothing yet," she said, "but I'm working on it. Where are you anyway?"

He cupped his hand over his free ear to better hear her. A breeze cutting into the covered patio area where he stood, whistling into the receiver, made it even more difficult. When he told her, she laughed. When he told her who he'd spoken with, she laughed even harder.

"Oh, I know Agnes. Did a feature on late-blooming artists a few months back and interviewed her. She's a kick. Good one to have in your Rolodex. Knows just about everybody in town."

"Good to know. Do you know how to get to the Northwest Artist Colony?"

"Those crazy hippies? Sure. Why, you think this girl was a Van Gogh-wannabe or something?"

"Or something. How do you get there?"

She told him. It seemed simple enough, just look for a certain mile marker north of town, and right after that there'd be a gravel road and a wooden sign with the letters NAC painted on it in white.

"Let me know if you find out anything from the list of names," Gage said.

Carmen laughed. "How? By carrier pigeon?"

"Sure. Isn't that how everyone communicates these days?"

"I hate to break this to you, Gage. But if you want to keep up with a woman like me, the least you could do is get a phone."

"Should I be trying to keep up with a woman like you?"

"Probably not," she replied. "So when are you going to return the favor and take me out to dinner?"

"You don't waste time, do you?"

"Why would I want to waste time? My biological clock is ticking. If I'm going to have a baby, I need to get going on it."

He was speechless.

"I'm kidding, Garrison. Jesus. I think I heard your heart stop."

"Maybe it did. How about this weekend?"

"Yikes. A girl might start to think a guy isn't interested, waiting that long. How about tonight?"

"I'm going to play a little poker tonight," Gage said.

"Ah. I assume you're looking to sit down with Jimmy Lourdenback. All right. Wednesday then. You can pick me up at the office at eight."

"You're something else, Carmen."

"Yeah, that's what all the boys tell me." She laughed, but it sounded a bit forced. "I keep telling myself it's a compliment."

Despite how straightforward the directions had seemed, Gage still drove by the gravel road three times before finally spotting the sign.

It had been nicely carved, but it blended in a little too well with the scotch broom bushes crowding the road. The scotch broom—and this was something Gage had learned from reading one of Carmen's articles—was a transplant from England many years back. With no natural enemies in Oregon, they ran amuck, choking off all other vegetation. Crowds of volunteers came out every summer to hack them back, but they always returned the next year even stronger. Most of the first timers to the Oregon coast thought the yellow-flowering bushes were pretty—until they saw exactly how prevalent they were.

After ten minutes driving up a rutted gravel road, tires sloshing through puddles, each bump and jostle going straight to his knee, Gage knew he was getting close when he spotted a couple of tie-dyed kids alongside the road, sketching a fire-blackened oak. They smiled at him and, true to form, flashed the peace sign. Two minutes later, the road ended at a big brown building that might have once been a church, with wood shake siding, stained glass insets on the front doors, and a white steeple with a bell tower. The gravel parking lot was packed with at least two dozen cars, mostly VW vans and beetles.

A dozen kids perched on the wooden steps, a few sketching but most of them talking animatedly, a collage of dreadlocks, grizzled faces and paint-spattered overalls. Gage parked the van in the dappled shade of a mossy live oak. Douglas firs crowded all around; steeped in their shadows, nestled into the forest, were dozens of cabins. Well-trodden trails lead from their doorsteps to the main building.

When he got out, the air was rich and full of life. The gravel drive was so deeply rutted, it was hard to find solid ground with his cane. Pine cones crunched under his boots. A guy and a girl at the top of the steps were smoking, and as he got closer, he smelled that it was pot. A spindly white guy with a big brown afro and wisp of a goatee was insisting that God was dead, just as Friedrich Nietzsche had said, and that religion was a mind-controlling device created by the rich and powerful to keep the poor oppressed. He ended most of his sentences with *per se*. "Well, it's not exactly a moral equivalency, per se." Gage waited until the guy finally took a breath before asking who was in charge.

"Hey, man," the spindly guy said, "I'm making a point here."

"Oh, I'm sorry," Gage said. "I thought you were done. Who runs this place?"

"Why you want to know?"

"I'm with the Friedrich Nietzsche Appreciation Society," Gage said, "and I'm selling tickets to our bake sale. You want one?"

Everybody but the spindly kid laughed. His eyes turned into petrified wood.

"Oh, ha ha, very funny," he said. "You're quite the riot. So, tell me, what do you think about Nietzsche? Was he right about religion or not?"

The kid smirked. Most of the others seemed embarrassed by his behavior, a few looking away or at their shoes.

"Well," Gage said, "the first thing is that Nietzsche didn't technically say 'God is dead.'"

The kid snorted. "I think—"

"A character in his book *The Gay Science* said it, a character who was in fact a madman. Most scholars believe he wasn't talking about god personified, but instead about the shared cultural belief in god, something that bound people together until the

Enlightenment. He was mostly concerned that that shared belief helped create a moral foundation for mankind, and without it, something would have to take its place or man's worst nature would run rampant. He was never overly concerned about religion . . . *per se.*"

The kid looked dumbstruck. The rest of them weren't much different, gaping at him the way Gage imagined a group of Elvis impersonators would gape if the real Elvis suddenly walked into the room.

"This way?" Gage said, pointing up the worn path.

They nodded. When he walked around the corner, he heard the spindly kid finally pipe up, "Well, that's *one* way of looking at it."

Ivy strangled most of the north half of the building. Moss-covered steps lead down to a red door, and next to the door was a sign that read, "N.A.C.—Director's Office." Gage knocked. Nobody answered, so he tried the door. Unlocked.

Inside was a fairly large room, cool and musty, original artwork on the walls. Nobody was there. The room was divided into two parts—the front area, with a number of mismatched couches and chairs on a beaded Native American rug, art books piled on the bamboo coffee table. The back corner had been turned into an office, cordoned with the type of dividers usually found in corporate cubicles; they would have looked more out of place except that they, too, were completely covered in artwork—everything from oil paintings to pencil sketches to photography. A short, wood-paneled hall led from the back around a corner.

"Hello?" Gage said.

Nobody answered. Gage noticed a large oak plaque, immediately to the right of the door. The top read, "The Northwest Artist Colony Kindly Thanks Our Sponsors," and beneath were dozens of gold-tinted plates engraved with names. There were three categories, with the top category, "Benefactor," having only four names—Martin Jaybee, Sapphire Holdings, John Blackstone, and Seacrest Hatchery. Martin Jaybee most likely owned the supermarket chain, Jaybee's, that ran up and down the coast, and the Sapphire Holdings obviously owned the Inn at Sapphire Head. The other two he didn't know.

"Can I help you?"

A grizzly middle-aged man emerged from the hall. His amber-tinted glasses made his eyes look large, and his green Hawaiian shirt was buttoned halfway down his chest, revealing a carpet of gray hair. He was round without being fat, and his watery blue eyes twinkled as if he was about to burst into laughter. His gray-blonde bangs were sweat-plastered against his forehead.

"How much money does someone have to donate to be a Benefactor?" Gage asked.

"Why, are you thinking of donating?"

"Maybe."

The man stepped next to Gage. He smelled like beef jerky. "A hundred thousand dollars."

Gage looked at the list again. "Wow. That must buy a lot of paintbrushes."

"But you only need to donate a thousand dollars to make the list as a contributor. Every little bit helps."

A redheaded girl emerged from the same hall, adjusting her bra beneath her one-piece tie-dye dress. Her mussed-up hair stood on end. She had her head down, and obviously hadn't expected Gage to be there, because when she looked up she reacted with a bit of a start. "Oh, hi," she said.

"Hi," Gage said.

"I'll talk to you later, Jill," the man said quickly.

She blushed and left without another word.

"She's—she's a good painter," the man explained. "Very talented."

"I imagine she benefits greatly from your one-on-one tutoring," Gage said.

The man looked at him, doubt blooming in his eyes. "Um, yeah. Now, about that donation, Mr. . . .?"

"Oh, I'm not here about a donation. I'm here about the girl who showed up dead on the beach a couple weeks back."

"Oh," the man said. He looked confused.

"Did you know her?"

"Know her? Why would I know her?"

"I don't know," Gage said. "I thought, you know, maybe you gave her one-on-one tutoring."

The man's already pink cheeks darkened considerably. "What are you saying? I've never even met this girl! I—I don't even know what she looks like!"

Gage pulled out the girl's photo and handed it to him. The slick paper trembled in the man's hands.

"No, I don't think I've seen her before."

"You don't think?"

The man shoved the photo back to Gage. "Do you know how many people come through this place just in a week? Hundreds! Some of them stay an hour, some stay weeks. I—I can't keep track of them all."

"I don't want you to keep track of them all," Gage said. "I just want to know if this girl—and her name might have been Abby—was ever here."

"What, you with the fuzz or something?"

"The fuzz?" Gage said. "What is this, the seventies?"

"I just—I just want to know who I'm dealing with."

"The name's Garrison Gage. I'm a private investigator. Can I ask your name?"

"Who are you working for?"

"An interested party," Gage said. "Do you have a name, or should I just call you The Tutor?"

The man's gaze smoldered. "Man, you really are an asshole, aren't you?"

"It's a chronic condition. But at least I'm not exploiting an authority position over teenage girls. I believe that would be a worse offense."

The man pointed at the door. "Out!"

"Not quite yet. I have a few more questions. Unless you'd like me to go find out how old that girl is, maybe see if her parents know what's going on here . . .?"

The man said nothing for a long time, and when he did, all

the anger and energy had gone out of his voice.

"No," he said.

"Good. I'm glad we see to eye to eye. What's your name?"

"Ted. Ted Kraggel."

"Nice to meet you, Ted. So you're not sure if this girl was ever here. Fine. How does this place operate? What's its business model? How long has it been around?"

In a low monotone, Ted gave him a brief history of the Northwest Artist Colony. At first the words came haltingly, but he began to warm up after a while, and by the end he had most of the twinkle back in his eyes. The NAC had been formed twenty-seven years earlier, with a generous grant from an art-loving widow of a timber baron, and it relied heavily on the donations of other art-loving benefactors to keep it going. They had guest speakers, free art supplies, and a full-time staff of five people. There was a tuition for room and board, but that could be waved based on an artist's financial hardship. They'd had a little trouble with the law with the rather common drug use on campus, but otherwise they had a pretty good reputation in the community, and their annual art show was becoming internationally recognized.

"So as far as you know," Gage said, "there's no way to know for sure whether she was here or not?"

"No," Ted said. "Can't say there is. Not anymore."

"Not anymore?"

"Well, a number of years ago, we used to keep guest book logs and other records, but the Board told us to do away with all of that a couple years back."

"The Board?"

"Yeah. The Board of Directors. Couple of the richest donors, a couple children of the founder, a couple other prominent art people in the community . . . I guess the thinking is, a lot of these young people, some of them are really misunderstood. You know, being artists and all. They may not all *want* a record that they're here."

"Right."

"Some of them, you know, their parents don't exactly approve. We don't want artists feeling like if they come here, Mom or Dad can show up and find out that they were here painting when maybe Mom and Dad would rather they be doing their chemistry homework."

"Or find out that little Johnny or Suzy," Gage said, "is here when they're supposed to be in college."

Ted shrugged. "Look, we don't tell kids to skip class. But some of them, this is the only place they find peace of mind. It's the only place where they feel accepted. And anyway, it's not like we're talking everybody. Probably ninety percent of the people are 18 or older."

They talked for a little while longer, then Gage thanked him for his time. Before leaving, he wandered around campus and showed the girl's photo to a couple dozen people. Only one person, a black guy with dreadlocks, said she looked familiar. But he said if he saw her around, she must have stuck to herself. That was common too—a lot of them said there was a certain kind of artist who just came, lived there, ate the food, and pretty much did his or her own thing.

On his bumpy drive back to the highway, Gage thought that a loner was exactly the sort of person that a predator would single out, somebody with no friends or family to miss them.

Since it was going on noon, Gage headed to his house. The sky looked like crumpled aluminum, and the ocean was as flat as a steel blade. He popped in on Mattie, who thanked him profusely for filling out the questionnaire. She insisted she hadn't felt better in weeks, so who knew, maybe it was all for not, ha ha, but he could see it was false bravado. She told him she would let him know when he would really have to make a decision, and he told her that was fine, knowing full well he had pretty much made a decision when he signed the document. He wasn't quite ready to admit it to himself— he was still hoping some other, better alternative for Zoe would emerge spontaneously—but it still felt like he'd boarded a train that was well out of the station.

Back at home, he made himself a tuna fish sandwich and ate it at his kitchen table along with a glass of ice water, absorbing the latest *Time Magazine*, *Newsweek*, and *The New Yorker*. He subscribed to dozens of magazines and they'd been piling up lately. When he was finished, he took out a yellow legal pad and recorded everything he thought he knew about the girl on the beach:

Name = Abby ???
Age = 18-20?
From = Southwest?
Details = Traveling alone. Wants to be a painter. Not incredibly well-schooled, since she thought there might be dolphins on the Oregon coast. Checked out books from the library, so she does think about books when she wants to learn something. Worked as a stripper a couple weeks and probably did it before. Keeps to herself.
Abducted? Might be others.

It wasn't that great of a list. After all the people he'd seen, and all the leads he'd gotten, he felt like he should know a lot more. It wasn't like she'd lived as a shut-in, for God's sake. She may not have been the life of the party, but she'd talked to people. She'd interacted with them. How could nobody know who she was?

Then he got to thinking. What about him? He'd lived in Barnacle Bluffs for five years. Until a couple weeks ago, who besides Alex would have been able to identify him if he washed up on a beach? Would people remember him? Would people say, yeah, he kind of looks familiar, I think he bought groceries here, I think I saw him walking on the beach, but you know, can't be sure, could be anyone. He kept to himself. A loner. That's what he was.

He took out her head shot and placed it on the desk next to his list. Maybe he was more like her than he cared to admit. Maybe she hadn't been all that interested in other people. Maybe something had happened to her, something awful, and she just wanted to be left alone.

The question was, what was that awful thing?

Mulling this over, Gage didn't feel much like going out, but eventually the windows darkened. He had to keep looking for puzzle pieces. He owed it to Abby, after all. If he was the one lying in the morgue, wouldn't he want somebody to keep going until it came out who'd put him there?

Maybe not. But he wasn't like other people.

There were also the other possible girls. If nothing else, that had to keep him going.

It was a quarter after six when he arrived at the casino. The last wisps of red light graced the horizon, the sky above a deep black. The parking lot was full, forcing him to park at the back, near the bevy of motor homes lined up like the Great Wall of China. When he got out of the car, a fine mist wet his cheeks. He smelled the salt water on the breeze. The three domed buildings that made up the casino resembled big circus tents. He'd crossed three rows, cane clicking on the asphalt, when someone called to him.

"Gage."

It was Carmen. He scanned the parked cars and didn't see her until she flashed her dome light. The Camry was parked one row up and five cars to his right. He sauntered over to her, glancing around to see if anyone was watching. Nobody was. She had the window down, and the angle of the pale yellow lamplight cast the top half of her face in shadow, her grin floating in darkness like the Cheshire Cat's.

"Miss me?" she said.

"Carmen, I'm not sure we want Jimmy Lourdenback knowing we—"

"Pipe down now. I'm not staying. I just couldn't wait to give you this."

She handed him a piece of paper. It was a printout of a newspaper article, three columns, a grainy black and white photo at the top. The headline was, "Santa Fe Teens Finish Grand Theatre Mural," and the picture was of a dozen or so gangly boys and girls sitting on a curb in front of mural of three knights on horseback fighting a fire-breathing dragon.

"Recognize the girl on the left?" Carmen said.

Gage looked at her closely. The picture was from across the street, making the faces quite small, but there was still no mistaking her.

It was definitely the girl from the beach.

Chapter 12

THE GIRL PICTURED in the newspaper article was a year or two younger than the one who'd washed up on the beach, but she had the same high cheekbones, the same milky white skin, the same dark blonde hair—though longer, and tied behind her head. The overalls were folded up to her knees and the sleeves of the red plaid shirt were rolled up to her elbows. The slash of dark paint on her forehead looked like a knife wound. She was the only one not smiling, and the only one not looking at the camera. Instead she was looking at the paintbrush in her hand, a big one, the kind a person would use to paint a house.

"Abigail Heddle," Carmen said.

The name was listed below the photo, along with the names of the other girls. There was also a copyright that placed the photo two years earlier. Gage looked at Carmen. She was smiling like a kid who'd found the golden Easter egg. Tired of seeing only half her face, he bent down, wincing at the stab of pain his knee. He gripped his cane as if it was a wizard's staff, leaning his cheek against the cool wood.

"How'd you find her?" he asked.

"Beauty of the Internet, my friend. Most newspapers are now part of LexisNexis. I zeroed in on the states you mentioned. We got real lucky. One of the first searches I did was using the words Abby, Abigail, and art. This one popped up. If they hadn't put her name in the caption, I wouldn't have found anything at all."

"What else did you find out about her?"

"What makes you think I found out anything else?"

"You're a reporter. Once you had her name, I'm sure you started digging."

She pursed her lips. "Hmm. What makes you think I'd tell you? You haven't exactly been forthcoming about what you've found out."

"All right, you have me there. I'll tell you everything I know tomorrow."

"Promise?"

He nodded.

"All right," she said, "but I'm going to hold you to that, buddy. I did make a few more calls. I have an old classmate who works for the Santa Fe Reporter, and she put me in contact with the right person in Children's Services down there—somebody who was willing to divulge some information as long as it was off the record. You were right. She was a foster child, or at least she was since the age of twelve."

"What happened to her?"

"The person I talked to only knew what was in the file, which was that her parents were deceased. She bounced around for a few years and eventually ended up with John and Becky Larson, who officially adopted her a year later at fifteen. Their records stopped at that point, because she was no longer a ward of the state."

"Did you find out anything else?"

"Only that nobody ever reported her missing. She would have been nineteen when you found her on the beach. Nineteen and three months to be exact, according to their records."

"So she was probably eighteen when she came out here," Gage said. "Legally an adult."

"Right."

"Have you called the parents yet?"

"No. But I wanted to."

"Please don't. Let the police do it first. You'll have your crack at them, I'm sure, and I can use it as a bargaining chip to get access."

"I could say the same thing."

"Doubt it," Gage said. "It's one thing to have a burned out old detective present when they interview the parents, and another thing to have the press. But I'll make sure you get your interview, believe me."

She looked about to say something, then frowned.

"What?" he said.

"The police," she said. "In my experience, whenever they get involved in a story, they screw it up pretty good."

"Well, I'm sure you know they say the same thing about reporters."

"Oh, sure. But it's this police chief, Percy Quinn. I've dealt with him a couple of times. I'm not sure if he's dirty or not, but he's definitely hiding something."

Gage marveled at her instincts. He thought about telling her about Quinn's wife, then thought better of it. It would have been like dangling fresh meat in front of a lion. He'd already weakened his relationship with Quinn; he couldn't take a chance on severing it completely.

"Oh," Carmen said.

"What?"

She pointed. A portly man in a bright yellow suit and matching bowler hat was strolling along the sidewalk in front of the casino, making his way toward the entrance as if he wasn't particularly in a hurry. Gage couldn't make out much from across the parking lot, but he did see that the man wore an eye patch over his left eye, and that his silver hair fell below his shoulders.

"It's Jimmy Lourdenback," Carmen said.

"You've got to be joking," Gage said.

"I told you he's a character. He's got connections you wouldn't believe, though."

"It looks like he needs a connection with a good tailor."

She made a *tsk-tsk* sound. "Don't say that to him. One thing about Jimmy, he's got an ego the size of Montana. And he's vain as hell. So you're still going in?"

"Sure, why not? We may know her identity, but that might not tell us what happened to her."

She nodded. "Well, you've only got one chance of getting anything useful out of him—suck up to his ego big time. The few times I've managed to get something out of him—and they've been very few—that's what I did. The thing is, he doesn't see himself as a bad guy. He sees himself as a good guy who sometimes operates on the wrong side of the law out of necessity. Maybe you can use that. I don't know. I think your chances are better at the roulette wheel, personally."

Walking into the casino, Gage figured he had one thing going for him as far as Jimmy Lourdenback was concerned. Jimmy didn't know who he was. It was a card Gage could only play once, and probably only for a limited time. Gage could pretend to be anybody.

The problem with playing that card, though, was that it was risky as hell. Gage hadn't exactly been keeping it quiet as he asked around about the girl—Abby Heddle. He reminded himself that it was better to think of her as having a name, a real person, rather than just an anonymous girl.

News traveled fast in small towns. Jimmy may have already known all about Gage, and if he didn't, he would probably know soon enough. No, his best bet might be to come straight at him with the truth, but in a way that gave Gage the edge. He wasn't sure what that way would be, or whether that was the approach to take, but his instincts had always been one of his best assets.

It'd been a long time since Gage set foot in a casino, but as soon as he walked through the revolving glass doors into the echoing outer hall, the familiar sounds brought all his old memories back—beeps and whistles, rhythmic clicking of slot machine handles. The excited murmur of the crowd was behind it all, infectious in the same way laughter was. Even he felt the urge, and he'd sworn it off long ago. The smell wasn't quite the same; gone was the heavy cigarette stench, replaced by only the faint whiff of cigarettes that still clung to the walls, like the way the smell of a three-pack-a-day smoker clings to his clothes long after he's given up the habit.

Gage remembered the casinos lobbying hard against the anti-smoking ordinances when they were on the ballot, but now that they were law, the change hadn't dampened people's enthusiasm for gambling in the slightest. The place was packed. Most of the people were of the silver-haired variety, wearing fanny packs and thick glasses, the kind of people he'd expect to find behind the wheels of the behemoths in the back of the parking lot.

After leaving the lobby and its big ceramic tiles, he passed the slot machine zombies, the bingo room with its oversized checkerboard monitors, and made his way across the low nap carpet to the card tables. There weren't a lot of people at the blackjack tables, but he saw the poker room up ahead and it was crowded. Sure enough, when he walked inside, he found ten green felt tables, each seating five or six people.

He was in luck: the card room boss, a weasely fellow in a black suit, was explaining how the night's Texas Hold-Em tournament would go. It was winner take all, ten rounds, the blinds doubling every other round. There were still spots, so Gage paid the fifty dollar entry fee to the young lady in the casino uniform by the marker board and took a seat. Jimmy Lourdenback was seated a few tables away, his one good eye hidden behind mirrored sunglasses with only one lens, the other side revealing his eye patch, looking all the world like a pirate in the witness protection program. He didn't even glance at Gage, which was probably a good sign.

As his dealer—a dark-skinned kid who definitely had Native American blood in him—dealt out the cards, Gage felt a flood of memories come rushing back. How many nights had he spent in rooms like this one? Too many to count. His playing days had spanned less than three years, while he was in college and realized that poker could help him to pay his way. But in those three years, he'd played almost every night, both casinos and private games. Why had he given it up? He couldn't quite remember. It coincided with his leaving for the Academy, but he didn't think that had anything to do with it. One day he had just woken up and didn't want to do it any more.

He was rusty at first, nearly bombing out in the third hand when he went all in against the tattooed kid across from him, a heavy better Gage figured for a bluffer and was right—just at the wrong time. That was the thing about Texas Hold 'Em. Winning required two things: patience and timing. You had to be willing to fold a lot of hands, your chips slowly dwindling as you played the blinds, watching the cards, calculating the odds, reading the players, and then choosing the best moments to strike. You would still lose a bunch, but if you didn't get impatient and go on tilt, and if you had some skill, you would end up on top a good portion of the time.

Fortunately, it was one of those nights, and after a couple hours he was sitting at the final table with Jimmy Lourdenback. Jimmy had no obvious tells; his expression never changed whether he was up or down, bluffing or betting with real cards. Then the other players were out and it was just he and Jimmy, Gage with a slightly larger stack. It was a good thing, too, because if they had been even, Jimmy most likely would have beaten him. As it was, Gage bluffed him twice with junk, then bated him into going all in when Gage had a King high flush and Jimmy had an Ace high straight.

When Gage raked in his chips, the card room boss announced to the few remaining people that they had a winner. Light applause followed. Jimmy sighed and rubbed under his eye patch, briefly giving Gage a glimpse of the scarred flesh. Jimmy took his time shuffling out of the room, waddling like an old walrus. Gage hurried, claiming his winnings—the princely sum of three hundred and twenty-five dollars—and hustled after Jimmy.

Turned out he didn't have to. Jimmy was waiting for him outside the door, leaning against the wall next to the restroom.

He was no longer wearing sunglasses. In his bright yellow suit and bowler hat, he could have taken a second job as a road sign. Stopping next to him, Gage caught a whiff of Jimmy's aftershave, a pungent, lime-tinged smell that reminded Gage of the hair tonic his childhood barber had used.

"Hey," he said, "good job in there. You nearly took me out."

"Nearly," Jimmy said, curling a long strand of gray hair behind his ear. "But you, you're a hell of a player."

"I was a little rusty, but I did all right."

"Rusty? Shit, I hate to see you when you're not rusty. I've got a hell of a headache today, otherwise I would have probably done better. Where'd you learn to play like that, anyway?"

Gage realized this was Jimmy's vain side rearing its ugly head. He knew he had a decision to make. He was either going to have to bluff Jimmy—in other words, come up with a lie that would give him the best chance to find out what he needed—or come at him with the truth.

The lie would have given him more options, but it was one of those moments, just like in the poker game, when Gage sensed something in his opponent that suggested a lie wasn't the best way forward. Maybe it was the fact that Jimmy was waiting for him, or maybe it was the look Jimmy was giving him with his one good eye, a wary apprehension that seemed to be more than just one card player sizing up another, but Gage's intuition told him to go all in.

"Just practiced," Gage said. "Lots and lots of games. Of course, that was back in college. When I decided to I wanted to get into the FBI, I thought it wouldn't look too good if somebody spotted me at a casino." He laughed. "Of course, I decided the FBI wasn't for me either, but that's another story."

Jimmy looked at him for a long time. His eye did dilate, the hazel vanishing into black, but otherwise he showed no reaction. The other thing that made reading him tough was his doughy face; the slight shifts in facial muscles obvious on most other people were invisible on Jimmy.

"I heard about you," he said.

132

"Oh yeah? What have you heard?"

Jimmy dropped his voice to a conspiratorial whisper, leaning in a little closer, his long gray hair draping over his shoulders. His breath smelled of garlic and onions. "I heard you was a private dick."

"You heard correctly."

"I knew who you was the moment you walked in the door."

"I'm not surprised," Gage said. "That's why I didn't figure there was a point in trying to hide anything from you. You'd see right through me."

The direct appeal to Jimmy's vanity worked like a charm. As cool and as unreadable as he'd been before, he became as obvious as a puffed up peacock now—straightening his back, smiling like a kid who'd just been patted on the head by the teacher. One of the casino workers carrying a tray full of Cokes and 7-Ups asked if they wanted a drink and Jimmy waved her off.

"You got that right," Jimmy said. "I don't miss much."

"Well, that's why I've come to talk to you," Gage said. "I'm hoping you might be able to help me."

"About that dead girl on the beach?"

Gage smiled. "You really are on the ball."

"Got to be," Jimmy said. "I don't stay on top of things, I'm out of the loop quick. And once you're out of the loop, you're out. You know I can't help you none, don't you?"

"I was afraid you'd say that," Gage said. "Carmen told me you probably wouldn't."

Jimmy's thin eyebrows arched, the creases in his brow disappearing under his bowler hat. "Carmen? You mean that cute little blonde runs the newspaper?"

"That's the one."

"She's a looker. You two an item?"

"Oh, I wouldn't say that. Just friends."

Jimmy blew air through puckered lips. "Ain't no man alive that would be just friends with that one unless he couldn't get more. So she's either putting you off or you're lying to me."

"Or I don't know myself," Gage said.

"Ah. Right. On account of your wife and all. I bet that messed you up pretty good."

The conversation was veering in a direction that made Gage uncomfortable. He didn't want to talk about Janet with anyone, and he especially didn't want to talk about her with someone like Jimmy Lourdenback.

"You could say that," he replied. "Hey, you want to get a drink?"

Jimmy scratched his chubby chin. "Man, I'd like to, but my sponsor would kill me."

"You're in AA?"

He grinned. "Surprised? Almost two years sober. Nearly ruined my liver, but finally realized I had to do something about it."

"Impressive."

Jimmy shrugged. "I just want to live, that's all. But I'll have a piece of pie with you. Come on, they got a banana cream in the deli that you won't believe."

The deli was a cozy place in the back corner of the casino, with a black and white tiled floor and an Elvis clock on the wall. Somebody had burnt some grease; the smell still hung in the air. They got their banana cream pies from a glass case and sat in the corner next to the neon jukebox. Nothing was playing. Nobody else was in there except the clerk, a gray-haired woman who was busy sweeping. Next door was the bingo hall, and now and then Gage heard the muffled sounds of the announcer calling out the latest numbers.

Jimmy took a bite, then closed his eyes and savored it. "Like a little piece of heaven."

Gage tried it too. It was a little sugary, but it wasn't bad. "That's a decent piece of pie."

"You kidding? You can't find pie like this anywhere. That's the thing about pies. You never know who's going to have the good stuff. The fanciest restaurant could have crap. Some little hole in the wall that burns their food and insults their customers might have the best pies in the world. You just never know."

"You sound like a man who knows his pies."

"Yeah, well, it's my last guilty pleasure. I may have given up smoking and drinking, but I ain't ever giving up pies. My dietician tells me I'm high risk for diabetes, but I don't care. A man's got to have something to live for you, you know?"

Gage tried to visualize Jimmy Lourdenback talking to a dietician. He was finding this strange little man who had one eye, who was in Alcoholics Anonymous, and who was a pie fanatic to be defying all of his initial assumptions. "So you're probably wondering why I've come to you," he said.

Jimmy forked up another bite. "I got a pretty good idea," he said, before shoveling it in.

"I know you said you can't help me, Jimmy. I respect that. But this girl, her death's been gnawing at me. One thing about me is I'm stubborn. Once I'm on a case, I never let it go. I'm going to keep digging until I found out who killed her. It may take me a week or a year, but I'll never stop. If you read up on me, you know that."

Jimmy didn't say anything, eating his pie, fork clinking against his plate.

"So here's the deal," Gage said. "I already know her name. I know—"

"What's her name?" Jimmy said, looking up.

"It'll be in the papers soon enough," Gage said. "I know her name. I know where she came from. Pretty soon I'm going to know a lot about why she came to our little village by the sea. I know she worked briefly as a stripper at The Gold Cabaret, and I know somebody came in there that scared her so bad that she never came back. What I *don't* know is what she did for the year before she worked as a stripper. I have my guesses, of course. I have my suspicion that maybe she worked for you."

Jimmy finished up his pie, scraping up the last bit of cream and savoring it. Gage had been hoping for some kind of reaction and he wasn't getting one.

"The thing is," Gage said, "I'm going to find out. You can be sure about that. And when I do find out, it would be unfortunate if your name got dragged into all of this."

Jimmy wiped his mouth. "Huh. Didn't figure you for trying to strong-arm me."

"I'm just stating a fact."

"Right. Let me tell you something, Gage. You think I survived this long being an idiot? There ain't nothing out there you'll ever find that will be solid enough that any respectable paper would print it with my name attached—and that even includes your girlfriend's little rag. I'd sue her ass so fast for slander she wouldn't know what hit her. I run a cleaning service that just so happens to employ a lot of attractive women. They get paid to clean houses. What they do outside of that is their personal business."

"I imagine your rates are a little on the high side."

Jimmy shrugged. "When you want the best cleaning service, you gotta be willing to pay for it."

"I bet."

"So quit trying to pressure me. It won't work."

"Then you won't help me?"

"Even if I could, I don't know why I'd want to now that you're being an asshole about it."

"I'm just determined, Jimmy. Maybe that makes me get a little carried away. You already said you wouldn't help me, so I was just trying to find an angle."

Jimmy was quiet a moment, staring at Gage with the same intensity he'd looked at him back at the poker table. "Why the hell you care so much about this kid anyway?"

"I found her on the beach."

"That all?"

"It's enough."

"Huh. You been out of this kind of thing so long, it seems strange that just finding a dead girl would want to make you rush back in. What, you want to get your other leg busted up too?"

"Are you saying that's what'll happen to me if I keep digging into this?"

"I'm not saying *nothing*," Jimmy said.

He finished his pie, Gage watching him, neither of them saying a word until Jimmy pushed his plate away.

"Good stuff," he said.

"I guess my appetite is gone," Gage said.

"You should never let anything get in the way of a healthy appetite, friend. No matter what you do, a man's gotta eat."

"Did you get that from Ann Landers?"

"Hey, now, no need to get surly." He studied Gage, pursed his lips, then got to his feet. He tipped his bowler hat back on his head, revealing the gray bangs sweat-plastered to his forehead, and smiled down at Gage. "You're a pretty good poker player. It's not a bad skill to have, you know?"

"Gee thanks."

Gage drummed his fingers on the table, looking at his half-eaten pie and waiting for Jimmy to go away. But he didn't. Then he bent over and dropped his voice to a whisper—not that it mattered, because there was no one else in the diner.

"Tell you what I'm going to do," he said. "I got a game I play Wednesday nights down at Sapphire Head. A lot of fat wallets. They know me pretty well, know all my moves, so I never score much. But you? You could come in there and clean house. I'll help you, and we'll split the take fifty-fifty."

"No, thanks."

"You sure? I really think you should be there, Gage."

Gage looked up. There was something in Jimmy's tone that suggested this was about more than poker. "Are you saying I might learn something?"

"There's always plenty to learn, friend. They might not have that much to teach you about poker, but they might have plenty to teach you about Barnacle Bluffs."

"I see."

"All I'll say is this girl, she wasn't anybody in my circles, know what I'm saying? I'm not even saying I know what circle she was in, but whatever you learn from these folks, it can't hurt. Interested now?"

"Maybe."

"Okay, go to the front counter at nine o'clock on Wednesday

and say you're there for Mr. Moore's chess club. They'll direct you to a room. It's different each week. Say you heard about the game from Harry Malaki. He moved to Phoenix last April, but he had a heart attack a month ago, so nobody would be able to check. I'm going to throw a bit of a hissy fit, because I'm going to ask how the hell you found out about it, and then I'm going to tell them you played a pretty good game at the casino."

"Wouldn't it be better if they thought I was a sucker?"

Jimmy shook his head. "Nah. Not these guys. They're going to take it as a challenge. It's just important that they think we hate each other."

"Ah."

"So in about thirty seconds, I'm going to curse at you out and storm out."

"Is that really necessary?"

Jimmy smiled wryly. "You don't know these guys, Gage. Not only are they good, they're some of the most powerful people in town."

"Some of the most powerful people in Barnacle Bluffs, huh? That's really saying something."

"Hey," Jimmy said, "this may not be New York, but don't underestimate these guys. It's a good bet that most of them know exactly who you are, and exactly what you're up to. And that's what I'm offering you—the chance to get inside that circle." He smiled. "And a hefty cut of your winnings, of course."

"Of course."

Jimmy shot a glance at the waitress, then over his shoulder. The waitress was wiping down one of the glass cases. A casino worker pushed a hand-powered vacuum past, and an elderly couple shuffled behind her.

"I told you," Jimmy cried, "the answer is no! And that's final!"

He stormed out, playing his part well enough that Gage actually felt a flash of adrenaline even though he'd been expecting it. His little act also elicited the expected reactions from the people around—lots of staring without trying to *look* like they were staring.

After appearing to stew in his own anger for a moment, Gage got up abruptly and stormed out himself. He didn't know if Jimmy's poker game would lead anywhere, but he hoped it did—and only partly because he might learn something to find out who killed Abby Heddle.

The other part was because he was enjoying himself, and he hadn't enjoyed himself in a long time.

Chapter 13

I
T WAS NEARLY MIDNIGHT when Gage called Percy Quinn at home—looking up his number in the gas station phone book—but he didn't want to wait another day. A semi rumbling out of the station coughed up a cloud of diesel. Quinn, his voice froggy, put up quite a fuss when Gage told him the terms for the names of the girl's parents—namely, that Gage be present when they were questioned—but there was more relief in Quinn's voice than irritation. When Gage called him back a hour later, just as they'd agreed, there was even more relief in Quinn's voice than before.

Quinn told him John and Becky Larson were indeed Abigail Heddle's parents. They'd been devastated to learn about her death but not all that surprised, since she'd run away at seventeen and they hadn't heard from her since. They'd booked an early bird flight to Portland and planned to be in the police station at two Tuesday afternoon. They wanted to bring Abby home for burial in Santa Fe, but they'd agreed to answer questions. They didn't even ask for a lawyer.

A quarter after two the next day, after checking on Mattie and finding she was no worse but no better, Gage found himself tapping his fingers on the wide walnut table at the station and watching the leafless maple saplings swaying in the breeze. The sun had burned off the last of the morning fog, and the shadows from the blinds striped the table with horizontal bars. Irritated at waiting, he was about to get up when Quinn entered, accompanied by a rumpled middle-aged man with only a scattering of gray hair, liver-spotted cheeks, and deep bags under his eyes.

"Gage," Quinn said, "this is Detective Brisbane. He's the lead on this case, along with Detective Trenton. You want coffee? Alice should have gotten you—"

"Where are they?" Gage said.

"Coming back from the morgue with Trenton, I imagine. Should be here any minute. We had to get that formality out of the way."

Gage was sitting in the corner, facing the door. Quinn took a seat on the same side farther down. Brisbane sat next to him. He'd walked in wearing the facial expression of someone who had just eaten something sour and it hadn't changed.

"So you're the guy going around stirring up trouble," Brisbane said.

"Excuse me?" Gage said.

"Easy now," Quinn said. "We're all friends here."

"What do you mean, stirring up trouble?" Gage said. "All I'm doing is inviting folks to the policemen's ball. Having a hard time, though, because people heard how Brisbane got drunk last year and sang Moon River in his underwear."

Brisbane's sourpuss face remained, but a hint of red crept into his cheeks. The door opened and a lanky redhead so tall he actually had to duck under the doorframe entered. His gray trench coat was six inches too short. Right behind him was a man and a woman, practically midgets in comparison. The man was mildly overweight; she was morbidly obese. The man wore a blue suit and red tie that looked like they'd been driven over in the parking lot. Her gray wool sweater was big enough to cover a boat, and her makeup was so thick he wondered if she'd applied it with a trowel. Her eyeliner was badly smeared. Her long auburn hair was remarkably pretty, and would have been the first thing

Gage would have noticed had she not been so large.

Introductions were made, hands were shook. When they were seated, it was the woman, Becky, who spoke first.

"So you're the one who found her?" she said to Gage. There was a quaver in her voice.

"That's right," Gage said.

"Thank you," she said.

"For what?"

She tried speaking, got choked up, and slumped her head. John glanced at his wife only briefly, but there was a look of such disdain that it actually startled Gage. Sometimes he could tell a lot about how people felt about each other from a single look.

She started crying. Since no one moved, Gage offered her the handkerchief from his jacket, which she accepted.

"What do we have to do to take her home?" John said. He didn't sound like a man who'd just lost his daughter. He sounded like a man who'd bailed his daughter out of jail too many times.

"Well," Quinn said, folding his hands on his table, "first off, now that you've ID'd her and we know there's no mistake, I just want to say how sorry we are for—"

"When can we take her home?" John repeated.

"We're going to make it as easy for you as possible, but you know that she *is* part of a murder investi—"

"Murder?" Becky said. She dabbed her eyes with the handkerchief. "You didn't say anything about murder on the—"

"I'll handle this *dear*," John said. He looked at Quinn. "You made us a promise, Chief Quinn. You said we could take our daughter home if we cooperated."

"And you will," Quinn said. "I'm just not exactly sure about the timing. Most likely it'll be in the next day or two."

John banged his fist on the table. "This is insufferable! We can't just hang around this podunk town. Abigail wasn't murdered. Why would anyone murder her? She tried to kill herself three times when she was living with us, and this time she managed to do it right."

Though he'd raised his voice, his facial expression never

changed, giving Gage the impression it was all an elaborate charade. It was the tall Trenton who answered.

"I understand your frustration," he said, in the soothing tone of a practiced psychologist. "You've had a long day. We're just trying to make sure things are done right, that's all."

"What would be *right*," John said, "would be to let us take Abigail home."

"Wait a minute," Becky said, sniffling, "when you say murder . . . We're not suspects, are we?"

"Don't be ridiculous," John snapped. "They don't think . . ." He trailed off, looking at their faces. "No, really? You can't honestly think something so stupid!"

"Hold on now," Quinn said. "Nobody said you're suspects."

"We were a thousand miles away!"

"I said *hold on*." Quinn raised his voice. "Let's not make this an unfriendly conversation. You have a lot of information that might help, that's all. You're not suspects."

"Well," John said, "when you go around pointing the finger—"

"We're not pointing the finger at anybody. That's just it. We don't have anybody to point the finger *at*. No suspects, no motives. But she had some bruises and lacerations on her wrists that make us think she was bound. It also makes us think suicide is less likely."

John shook his head. "I saw those marks a few minutes ago. The last year she was with us, she had marks like that on her wrists all the time. She was into some of this . . . this kinky stuff with her scuzzbucket boyfriends." He made a sour face.

"Bondage?" Gage said.

Everybody looked at him, like fraternity brothers who'd just noticed somebody crashing their party.

"Yeah, that's the word for it," John said.

"How many boyfriends did she have?" Gage said.

"A lot. Hundreds."

"Oh, not that many," Becky said with a nervous laugh. "John exaggerates. There were probably a dozen."

Her husband snorted. "You really weren't paying attention. She had a guy up in that bedroom of hers every night of the week, and it was always a different guy."

Becky looked teary-eyed. "Oh, John. I wish you—I wish you wouldn't."

"Wouldn't what? Tell the truth? That's what these guys are after. You don't want them to know she was a slut? Well, she was."

"John! Please."

"I don't know why you beat yourself about it, honestly. By the time she got to us she was damaged goods. Nothing we could do about it. I told you that at the time, but *you* wouldn't listen."

Becky didn't speak. Everybody looked uncomfortable. Quinn scratched his chin. Brisbane was scribbling in a little notebook he'd pulled out of his pocket.

"You said she tried to kill herself three times before," Gage said. "Can you tell us more about that?"

"You know," Brisbane said, looking up from his notebook, "this really is a police investigation. We don't mind you being here, but—"

"It's all right," Quinn said.

"But Chief—"

"It's all right," Quinn said more curtly. "I was about to ask the same question."

They looked at John and Becky. Her whole face trembled, as if all that anguish would coming pouring out at any moment, her layers of makeup crumbling like a soggy avalanche. John shrugged.

"I don't know what there is to tell," he said. "They happened in the last year she was living with us. She was never very happy. We did everything we could—bought an old Datsun pick-up, converted the attic above the garage to her bedroom so she had more privacy, gave her plenty of allowance. None of it mattered. She hated us from the first moment she lived with us, and even adopting her didn't make one damn bit of difference."

"That's not true," Becky said.

"Oh yeah? I warned you not to spoil her, that it would only

make it worse, and look what happened."

"How did she try to kill herself?" Gage asked.

Brisbane shook his head. "What does that have to do with anything?"

"Maybe nothing," Gage said. "Maybe everything. Humor me."

"Humor you?" Trenton said. "What, is this some kind of game to you? These two lost their daughter. The least you could do is show a bit of sympathy."

"What, are you Dr. Phil now?" Gage said. "I don't need any cheap pop psychology, thank you very much. And I doubt that either of these two need it either."

"Watch your mouth," Trenton said.

"Or what? Or you'll pop me in the face? Go ahead. Of course, you only get one swing. I'm charitable that way. It gives my conscience a pass. After that, I'll drop you."

"Stop it, you two!" Quinn said.

"I think the Larsons just want to get this thing solved so they can get their daughter out of here," Gage said. "If you could solve it without me, I wouldn't be here."

"All right, all right, " Quinn said. "Let's not start pissing on the floor to mark territory. I'd like to hear what the Larsons have to say."

John ran his hand over his wrinkled tie. "Well," he said, "the first time—"

"Maybe we should get a lawyer," Becky said.

"Don't be ridiculous. We've got nothing to hide."

"I don't like these questions."

"I don't like them either," he said. "But do you really want to drag this thing out?" He waited for her to answer, and when she didn't, he pressed on. "I didn't think so. So let's see. The first time was right after Christmas. I remember because she had all her gifts from us piled in the corner, not even touched. The second time—"

"But how did she try to do it?" Gage said.

"Okay, well, it was a bottle of Becky's antidepressants, prescription stuff. She swallowed the whole damn thing. If Becky hadn't gone up to say goodnight—"

"Do you always go up to say goodnight?" Gage asked.

Becky nodded.

"All right. How about the second time?"

"Well, let's see," John said. "She cut her wrists—"

"That was the third time," Becky said.

"Right. That was the third time. The second time she was going to jump off the bridge near our house, but a policeman talked her down. When she cut her wrists, she did it at school in the girl's locker room and the gym teacher found her. She didn't quite manage to cut her veins, though, so all she did was make a mess of herself."

"When she cut her wrists," Gage said, "did she do it in an area where it was likely the gym teacher would find her?"

"I guess. It was in the main showers. Why?"

"Well," Gage said, "it's hard to say for sure without knowing more about her, but many people who attempt suicide are doing it as a cry for help. They don't have any intention of going through with it. In all three of these cases, she had to know that it was likely someone would find her right away."

John shook his head. "So you're saying she *didn't* really want to commit suicide?"

"I'm saying that's a possibility," Gage said.

"You know how many times the school called because they found some note or something she wrote where she said she wanted to off herself?"

"That would fit the pattern too," Gage said.

"What pattern?"

"The pattern of crying out for help."

Becky teared up again. "But we did everything for her! We tried to get her help—we did! We—we took her to counseling—"

"I'm sure you did everything you could," Gage said. "Just because someone's crying out for help doesn't mean they know they're being heard."

"Just because she was crying out for help before," Brisbane

146

interjected, "doesn't mean she wasn't serious about committing suicide here in Barnacle Bluffs."

"Exactly my point," Gage said. "We're just talking about odds here, that's all."

The woman made a gurgled sucking noise. "My girl, my little girl."

"Oh, god," John said, "she was in our lives for like three years. She wasn't your little girl."

Nobody said anything for a moment. Who could say anything after something so callous? Gage had to suppress the desire to crack the guy on the side of the head with his cane.

"I worked on a missing person case once," Gage said. "The woman's only child had been abducted. The mother had been trying on a dress at Macy's, and when the woman wasn't looking the little girl crawled under the dressing room door. It was maybe twenty seconds before she noticed. When she went looking for her, the girl was gone."

"Your point?" John said.

"The girl was only two," Gage said. "By your standards, the mother shouldn't have been very attached. And yet, when they found the girl's body in a culvert, I don't think anyone doubted how much she loved her. I'd say she was pretty upset."

"That's not the same—"

"Hey, hey," Quinn said, shooting Gage an angry look, "we don't need to get into a philosophical question here about love. We're just interested in finding out how she died, okay?"

John nodded, but his unruffable demeanor had finally been broken. He looked like he wanted to kill Gage. It was what Gage had been hoping to see. He also wanted to accomplish something else, and he got that too: a look of gratitude from Becky Larson.

They talked for another hour and a fuller portrait of Abigail Heddle emerged. Her parents had died in a car crash when she was twelve. She was tight-lipped about them, but John and Becky had learned that they were traveling hippies of sorts, selling beaded artwork and other crafts at county fairs and art shows across the country, living out of a tiny Toyota motor home. They were in Santa Fe at the time of the accident. Abby spent the next two years bouncing around foster care.

She was apparently the worst kind of problem child. She lied. She stole. She tried to get other kids into trouble. When Becky Larson turned thirty-nine, she had something of a midlife crisis. She'd never been able to have children, and at her age didn't really want to start with an infant, but she suddenly wanted to make a difference in a child's life. She didn't want any child, either. She wanted a child who needed her.

Child and Family Services had just the child for her. John tried dissuading Becky, but when he couldn't, he figured it a passing phase. He thought maybe having a difficult foster child would get it out of her system. It didn't. In fact, the more awful Abby treated Becky, the more resolved Becky became. In the end, despite a lot of protesting from John, they eventually adopted her.

She smoked. She slept around. She failed all of her classes. She came home in the middle of the night, stoned out of her mind. They were pretty sure she had at least one abortion, maybe two. As far as goals, she really didn't have any except for a vague idea of maybe being an artist. Becky tried to encourage this interest by buying her art supplies and enrolling her in classes at the community center, but the art supplies never left their package and she never once attended the classes.

About a year after first moving in with them, Abby started disappearing for days at a time. They'd ground her, but she only laughed. She stumbled into the house in the middle of the night looking like she'd hadn't changed her clothes or showered since they'd last seen her, scrounge around in the fridge, and curse them when they asked where she'd been. Usually, she was gone in the morning.

The absences changed from days into weeks. She moved in with a boyfriend twice her age, a toothless jerk they were pretty sure was a drug dealer, and moved back a couple months later. Then she disappeared one night a year ago last September and left a note on the dining room table: "Dear Becky, I'm going to do some traveling. Don't come looking for me. Thanks for everything. I know you were trying to help, but some stuff's just too broken to fix, you know? Love, Abby."

It was the only time she'd ever used the word love. Becky cried for weeks, but they followed her wishes and didn't go looking for her. When six months passed with no word, Becky hired a private investigator to see if they could track her down, just to placate Becky's worries, but he hadn't been able to find anything. Then they got the call from Chief Quinn.

When they were finished, Becky said she wanted to go back to the hotel and to lie down. John demanded to know by the end of the day whether they could arrange to have Abby's body sent to Santa Fe. Becky wanted her buried next to her parents. Quinn said he'd do everything he could to make that happen.

On their way outside, John disappeared to use the restroom, leaving Gage and Becky to walk out together. Gage had been hoping to catch her alone. Even though it was sunny, the wind had an icy bite.

"I'm really sorry about this," he said.

She turned. The sun was in her eyes, and she held up her hand, the shadows of her fingers falling across her face. "Thank you," Becky said. "I really . . . really do miss her. I know it's silly—"

"It's not silly."

"Well, John thinks it is."

"That says more about him than it does about you."

"I guess. He just . . . He handles things differently, that's all. He has a harder time showing that he cares."

The breeze rippled her hair around her neck like a scarf. His shadow on the pavement was tiny compared to hers. It made him wonder what kind of childhood she'd had, being so big. Or was it a condition that came on late in life? Either way, she couldn't have had it easy.

He stepped to her side, so she didn't have to look into the sun. "Look," he said, "there might be more we can do. I'm a private investigator. If you'd like—"

"I don't think we can afford a private investigator."

"Well, you can afford me," Gage said, "because I'm not going to charge you anything."

She looked taken aback. "Why?"

"Don't need the money."

"But you must have better things—"

"No, I don't."

"But there has to be a reason . . ."

Gage shrugged. "I found her, that's enough. Plus my joints were starting to rust here in this weather, not moving around much. Listen, I'm going to keep on working on this whether you hire me or not, but I'd prefer to say I'm working for you."

"Oh. Well, I'm sure John—"

"Not him," Gage insisted. *"You."*

"Oh. Okay. I guess that's fine. Do I need to sign something?"

"Your word is good enough. But I was wondering if you might be willing to do one thing for me. Would you mind talking to a reporter friend of mine?"

"Reporter?" She looked worried.

"I know. Talking to the press is probably the last thing you want to do. But there comes a point when getting the press involved may not be a bad thing. It can shake things up a little. And this reporter—she'll make people know the real Abby, you know? It'll be a way of making something meaningful out of her life, sharing her story."

"I don't know," Becky said. "She did some awful things—"

"There are other girls out there living the same way. Reading her story might make them feel less alone. If we save one girl, it's worth it, don't you think?"

The door to the police station opened and John emerged. When he saw them talking, he acted perturbed. Becky watched him coming, then glanced at Gage.

"I think you're right," she said. "We're staying at the Inn at

Sapphire Head. Room 223. Have her give us a call."

"Thank you."

She took a strand of her hair and curled it around her finger, staring down at it. "I just keep wondering if there was something I could have done differently," she said. "I keep wondering if I could have done something that prevented all this. Do you know what I mean?"

Despite her size, in that moment she didn't seem large to him at all, but small, a child in a cruel and lonely world. He thought about that dreadful surprise, five years earlier, when he'd pushed open a bathroom door. At that moment, he'd felt like a child too. John walked up to them, only catching Gage's parting words.

"Unfortunately," he said, "I know exactly what you mean."

Chapter 14

WHEN GAGE WALKED into Books and Oddities with two coffees and a couple of donuts, he found Alex reading a yellowed copy of the *Enquirer*, the front page picturing Ronald Reagan standing next to a bug-eyed green alien. A circular blue stain, like one from a paint can, marred the back page. Alex's feet were up on the counter, bits of sand embedded in the soles of his deck shoes. He wore no socks.

His already dark skin appeared a shade darker, his bald scalp tinted pink. His glasses rested at the end of his nose, and he read with his head tilted far back, as if cringing from an unpleasant smell. A cardboard box in about the same condition as the paper rested on the counter.

He glanced at Gage, and in all seriousness said, "Did you know that Ronald Reagan wanted to shut down Area 51, but Nancy told him to keep it open because visitors from Alpha Centauri would be landing by Christmas to tell him what to do about the Iran Contra scandal?"

"I didn't know that," Gage said.

"You learn something every day," Alex said, tossing the paper into the cardboard box.

Gage took a seat on the other stool and leaned his cane

against the counter. "Find some good books?"

Alex shrugged. "Picked up ten boxes at the auction the other day for a buck a box. Mostly old magazines and Reader's Digest condensed books, but I did find a first edition of an early Robert B. Parker that made my day."

"Good for you. You been out in the sun?"

"Painting that south side this morning. Eve demanded it. I wanted to put it off another year, but she still wants to open the B&B this summer."

"And Eve told you not to wear sunscreen?"

"I'm a Spaniard. I don't need to wear sunscreen."

"Uh huh. And how many pre-cancerous moles have you had removed now?"

"My god," Alex said, "you're worse than Eve." He snatched the donuts away from him. "What do you have here? Nothing but old fashioned? A man can't pick up a chocolate bar with raspberry sprinkles?"

"The aliens took them all," Gage explained.

They drank their coffee and ate their donuts. A woman in the back was helping her toddler pick out Dr. Seuss books. After she'd made her purchase, Gage caught Alex up on everything that had happened since they'd last talked—finding out who Abigail Heddle was, the poker game with Jimmy Lourdenback, and meeting the girl's parents. Alex listened intently, stroking his mustache and saying "mmm" or "ah" when Gage said something of interest. When Gage was done, Alex patted his lips with a napkin.

"I have to say," he said, "that was a pretty damn good donut for being just an old fashioned."

"That's it?" Gage said. "I give you all this great information and you make a comment on the donuts?"

"Well, it *was* a good donut. The coffee, however, could have used a little more cream."

"Take it out of my tip. Come on, I want to hear your take on this."

"No, what you want is for somebody to act as a sounding board for *your* take on this. But fine, here's my thoughts. John

Larson sounds like a good candidate, but it sure doesn't make a lot of sense. What, he flies out here, kills her, then flies back and pretends she's gone missing? Plus his wife would notice. Unless he and his wife were in it together."

"He *is* a traveling salesman," Gage said.

"Still pretty risky. And what about a motive?"

"If my hunch about him is right, it might have been as simple as trying to blot out the guilt he felt for what he'd done. A sexually repressed domineering guy with a sexually confused teenager in the house—it's not hard to connect the dots."

Alex wrinkled his nose. "Do you really think something like that happened?"

"Honestly? No. Why not sooner? Why wait so long? But maybe he was going to, but then she disappeared. Maybe he found out where she was, and thought, hey, I can kill her and pretend I never even knew where she was. Maybe that's why she wrote down "Abby Carson" in that library book. He was the one she was running from."

"It's a stretch," Alex said.

"Yeah, that's why my gut says no. But I'm going to press Becky a little about it when I see her later. If something was happening, she would have been aware of it, even if she was denying it to herself. Her little "he's really a good man deep down" routine was a bit too earnest. Maybe I can provoke a reaction. It probably won't be a fun lunch. I hate making women cry."

"You jest," Alex said. "You like it and you know it. What about that director of the Northwest Artist Colony. What was his name? He seemed a possibility."

"Ted Kraggel," Gage said. "He's definitely on the list. Maybe they had something going for a while, then she wanted out. Somebody came in to The Gold Cabaret that night and scared her. Might have been him."

"Might have been John Larson too," Alex said.

"Might have been John Wayne, back from the dead. That's the problem—could have been anybody and everybody. Could have been somebody who saw her dance a few times, creeped her out because he touched her ankle once or something, then grabbed her in the parking lot. A total stranger."

"But you don't think so?"

Gage shook his head. "There was nine months between that meeting in the strip club and when she showed up on the beach. Something more complicated happened than a stranger raping her and tossing her off the bluffs. There was also the message left for me."

"*There are other girls,*" Alex said, nodding. "I've seen and heard a lot of creepy stuff, but that's right up there. Any idea who wrote it?"

Gage wadded up the paper bag and leaned over the counter, tossing it in the wastebasket. "If I knew that, you think I'd be here with you adding to my waistline?"

"Okay, okay. Just wondering if you had suspects."

"Half the town," Gage replied. "If I could find that person, I'm pretty sure I could crack this wide open. How somebody had time to lay all those stones without being seen is beyond me."

"If this was an episode of CSI, we'd bring our crack investigative team and they'd find human hairs on your driveway and match it with DNA in some database."

Gage nodded. "Who needs CSI? Sherlock Holmes didn't have any of that fancy equipment, and he could solve a case just by noticing the color of mud on someone's boots."

"We've had this conversation before, haven't we?"

"How long has that CSI show been on?"

The Inn at Sapphire Head was just around the next bend, but Gage was still twenty minutes late meeting Carmen and Becky Larson.

It was the poshest hotel in town, with a dozen stories and a hundred rooms all nestled into one of the steep cliffs that gave Barnacle Bluffs its name, each one with a stunning ocean view. In addition to the award-winning restaurant and the twenty acres of professional caliber golf course, the hotel also contained an

Olympic-sized indoor pool, spacious meeting rooms, and impeccable catering that attracted conferences related to everything from the American Dental Association to National Kite Flyers Club. The oceanside view of the hotel had graced the cover of *Architectural Digest* three times.

Gage knew all this because he'd read it in the in-room binder the one time he'd stayed there, when he'd flown out from New York to close the deal on his house. It was one of the few times in his life he'd decided to treat himself; afterwards, he'd decided the experience didn't suit him. He just wasn't a treating himself sort of guy, regardless of the circumstances.

He flipped his keys to the valet, a scrawny Asian kid who wrinkled his nose at Gage's van. Five minutes later, Gage limped his way to Room 223. Becky answered and directed him to the rattan couch, where Carmen was sitting with a notebook in hand and a digital audio recorder beaming its read light from its place on the glass coffee table. On the deck, John slouched on one of the white lawn chairs, smoking a cigarette in the purple twilight.

"Took you long enough," Carmen said. She wore a two-button navy blue jacket, matching pants, and brown sandals.

"Sorry," Gage said, "forgot I was having my legs waxed."

Only Becky laughed. It was the kind of too-hearty laugh of someone especially nervous. Carmen, sitting on the love seat, scooted to make room. He navigated his way toward her, but the tight space between the coffee table and the wooden arms of the love seat made for tough maneuvering, and his cane came down on her foot. She let out a yelp that would have woken a coma patient, and in his surprise he stumbled into her. Making matters worse, he found that his right hand was cupping one of her breasts.

"*Well,*" she whispered into his ear, both of them cheek to cheek, "you certainly know how to make your intentions known."

"Sorry," he said, climbing off her. It wasn't all that easy. He got his hand off her breast right away, but it required him to put all his weight on his left, which meant he had to make a herculean effort to propel himself off that one arm to the other side of the couch. Which he managed to do, barely.

All the while, Becky was giggling. In other circumstances, her reaction might have annoyed him, but he was glad to have somewhere else to focus his attention. What *was* annoying was that his brilliant move was the one thing that finally caught John Larson's attention, who was staring at Gage through the glass like he might gape at a monkey in a zoo.

"Well, really," Gage said, with mock seriousness, "you do understand that it's not at all kosher to make fun of a cripple. Especially today, on Disabled Person Day."

Becky's face sobered. "Oh, I'm sorry," she said, "I didn't know—"

"He's joking, dear," Carmen said. "He's just trying to cover for the fact that he went to all that effort just to cop a feel. And there's no such thing as Disabled Person Day."

"I can't help it if you put your chest where I'm falling," Gage said.

"Mmm, I'm sure," Carmen said. She turned to Becky. "Now that we've got that little business taken care of, can we talk about your daughter? Don't bother explaining anything to him. I'll fill him in later."

They talked for over an hour. In the end, Gage wasn't sure how much "filling in" there would be, because it was obvious Becky didn't know this girl who'd lived under their roof for a couple of years very well. What he *did* learn was really just an elaboration of what he already knew—that she loved art, that she hung out with too many guys, and that she walked around with a lot of anger.

Gage kept trying to nudge Becky into revealing something about John that she might be hiding, but either there was nothing there or she'd done such a good job of hiding it from herself that even she wasn't aware of his true nature. At one point he bluntly asked if John had ever had an affair, or if she suspected he'd had one, thinking this would break through her walls, but even that didn't faze her. She said he'd never do that, that he had many faults but he'd always been loyal to her.

When they finished, Gage and Carmen walked out together. Once they were safely ensconced in the elevator, only the two of them, he said, "Sorry about that in there. I really am a damn klutz."

"It's okay," she said. "In fact, I think it's the most action I've gotten since moving to Barnacle Bluffs."

"Come on, be serious."

"I *am*," she said. When he didn't say anything, the amusement drained from her face, and she said quickly, "Well, what did you think about our little interview?"

"Was there anything I missed?"

"Nope."

"Well, it's like they had a stranger living in the house."

"My take too," she said. "You pick up anything that makes you think more about John as a suspect?"

"Still not ruling him out, but I wouldn't place money on it at this point."

In the confined space, it was hard to ignore the jasmine scent of her perfume, or the way she had curled her blond hair behind her ear. She glanced at him, and there was a shared look, an awareness of their proximity and their mutual attraction. He found himself staring at her lips. The doors opened and they walked past the fountain and over the ceramic tiles to the covered drive. He was aware of the way her body moved inside her clothes, the way her breasts swayed gently inside her jacket. They handed the two valets their keys the kids scurried to retrieve their cars.

The sky was black, the mist in the air wetting their faces. Under the pale yellow lights, he watched how the moisture glistened on her cheeks.

"Well," he said, "let me know if you find out anything else."

"Likewise," she said. And then, after a moment, she added, "Aren't you forgetting something?"

He looked at her.

"We have a date tonight," she explained.

"Oh, right."

"Well, gee, *that* reaction just makes me feel all warm and fuzzy inside."

"Sorry. I've just been focusing so much on this case—"

"It's okay. We're still on, though, right?"

He saw that look again, the vulnerability. She put up a tough front, but she wasn't fooling him. She was someone who bruised easily, who obsessed about little things, who worried and fretted and wrapped all this anxiety in the useful but burdensome cloak of modern womanhood. She had to be strong. She had to be tough. In her line of work, she spent a lot of time swimming with the sharks, after all, and weakness was not allowed. But it was there in the eyes. There was never any hiding it from the eyes.

"Of course," he said. "Pick you up at eight?"

"On the dot," she said.

His van pulled up first, spitting out a nice plume of black smoke. It was a different kid than before, one who was wise enough not to sneer at Gage's dilapidated ride, and so Gage handed him a five. As he stepped inside, Carmen called to him.

"Garrison?"

He turned. "Yeah?"

"Aren't you forgetting something else?"

"Uh . . ."

She smiled. "My address?"

Chapter 15

THEIR SECOND DATE began much better than their first. Gage was now resigned to calling it a date, even if he still wasn't quite comfortable yet with the *idea* of dating. He was getting more comfortable with Carmen as a person, but the thought of being intimate on any level with a woman other than Janet was enough to cause flurries in his stomach—and not the right kind of flurries, the nervous kind. These were darker and full of dread. Instead of butterflies, he'd have to say he was full of hornets.

Yet when he pulled to a stop in front of her little cottage on the north side of town, and she opened the door to her house before he'd even put the van in park, his heart did a little jig at the sight of her.

Even through the mist that dotted his passenger side window, even in the weak porch light, she looked resplendent in a black leather jacket and a hip-hugging black skirt. When she stepped into the van, sliding in one long tan leg, and then another, he found himself staring. She noticed his staring and smiled.

"You're on time," she said.

"You sound surprised."

"I am, pleasantly. What's this on the radio? Sounds like John

160

Coltrane."

"Right you are. You a jazz fan?"

She was. In fact, she was more than a casual fan. She could have practically taught a course on the subject, making her one of the few people whose knowledge of jazz surpassed his own. She knew the difference between Miles Davis and Dave Brubeck, and when a new song came up, she could say who played it, wrote it, and any bits of trivia associated with it. Even Gage could only name the composer two thirds of the time. To top it off, she'd played the saxophone for nearly twenty years, and in high school even flirted with going pro until she got bit by the journalism bug.

Turned out jazz wasn't all they had in common. He took her to a Greek restaurant, one of the few restaurants he went to on the rare occasions when he felt like eating out, and was surprised when she said she was a big fan of Greek food and Greek culture in general, and had even gone on a ten-day cruise through the Mediterranean. This got them off on a tangent about the Roman Coliseum, a place he'd visited in his own youthful travels, and he discovered that, like him, she was something of a history buff. At one point, while eating their *sofrito* and sipping their white wine, they found themselves arguing about whether Aristotle or Plato was the greater philosopher.

Even their arguing wasn't unpleasant, a playful banter that was more like teasing. She was no wilting flower. This was a woman with a formidable intellect. She tried to come off as average, denigrating her education by calling it "state-level smarts," and saying she was just a small town hick at heart, but he didn't buy it. It was a way to disarm and befriend, to put others at ease.

She wasn't really much like Janet, but the smartness of her, the intelligence, now that was everything like Janet. It was enough to get him thinking about her, remembering their own playful arguments over the dinner table, a half-empty bottle of red wine between them, the candle nearly burned down to the nub. It was something she'd loved, a candle at dinner time, and the surest proof of their love for one another was the number of candles she'd had to buy to keep up with their conversations. She must have bought hundreds over the years. So many candles.

"What's wrong?" Carmen said.

They were on their way home, having finally gotten the hint from empty tables and the waitress who kept glancing at her watch. He hadn't been aware that anything was showing on his face. The earlier mist had turned into a steady drumming of rain, the windshield wipers squeaking at full speed.

"Ah, nothing. The weather." He attempted a smile, but the glumness was too heavy.

"Thinking of Janet?"

He looked at her in amazement. He hadn't wanted to confirm that was what he'd been thinking, but his expression was enough. She placed her hand on his leg and squeezed it gently.

"It's okay," she said. "It doesn't bother me."

He could see that there was more that she wanted to say, some bridge she was thinking of crossing, but instead she looked forward. They drove the rest of the way to her house in silence, her hand remaining on his leg. The van felt smaller, warmer. He wanted her to take her hand away. He wanted her to leave it there. There was something unraveling within him. It was both the best and the worst he'd felt in years.

When they reached her house, he put the van in park. She still hadn't taken her hand away, and her face, with the light of her porch behind her, was lost in shadows. He caught just a hint of the whites of her eyes, saw the way they were wide and expectant. His heart beat faster.

"You want to come in for a drink?" she said.

He gazed out the rain-streaked window at her doorstep, then back at her. Not sure. Hesitating.

"You won't melt, Garrison," she said.

"Okay."

They were instantly drenched. She ran, laughing, to the doorstep. He stumbled after her with his cane, tripping on the step and bumping against her, making her laugh even harder. The rain on the back of her leather jacket looked like diamonds. She fumbled with her keys, her breath fogging. When she turned the lock and opened the door, she smiled at him mischievously. She walked inside, saying she had to get the light. He followed her into a dark living room.

He felt as if he was playing Russian Roulette. Except he was a bullet in the gun, spinning, spinning. Something was going to happen. Five years was a long time to spend in a spinning gun. He hadn't even known that's where he'd been until now, but it was true. He'd been there ever since Janet died.

He closed the door, sealing them in darkness. The rain pebbled the roof. He smelled dust and old books and a hint of lemon.

"Carmen?" he said.

"I'm over here."

"I thought you were getting the light?"

"We don't need a light."

Her hand pressed down on his arm. She took his cane and dropped it; it landed on a rug with a thud. She guided him across the room, him following in the wake of her jasmine perfume. His eyes started to adjust; he saw street light rimming the living room curtains, a faint glow coming from down a narrow hall, and the outline of her hair. Her heels clicked on a hardwood floor. His own soggy shoes squished and squeaked.

She pushed open a door.

There was a pink nightlight in the corner, next to a bedside table. A four-post bed dominated the room, barely enough space to squeeze around with dressers on the sides and a hope chest at the end. Lace curtains billowed, a cool breeze flitting through the cracked-open window. He smelled wet grass and fecund earth and a hint of the ocean three blocks away.

"Carmen—" he began.

She kissed him. His pounding heart, the rain tapping on the ferns, even the smell of her, so close, all vanished into that kiss. Her lips were soft and moist. She leaned into him. Even through their leather jackets, he felt the pliable flesh pressing against him. He found his hands on the swell of her hips, just below the hem of her jacket. Her fingers started working on the buttons of his own leather jacket. He felt his body responding.

"Wait," he murmured.

She didn't stop, her kiss turning desperate. She was working on his shirt now, the first two buttons undone.

"Wait," he said, pulling away.

"Please—I just—just want to make you happy—" she said.

She tried kissing him again and he grabbed her wrists, holding her at bay. It was comical, because she continued leaning in, trying to get closer, and he had to use a fair amount of strength to keep her back.

"Carmen, stop!" he said.

It was the shout that finally broke the spell. She seized up, frozen as if hit with a stun gun. She blinked a few times, then, looking utterly ashamed, dropped her head. Her hair fell down over her face like a curtain coming down on a play. He let go of her arms and they fell to her sides, limp. She stared vacantly at the floor, unmoving.

"Carmen—" he began.

"It's all right," she said, defeated.

"It's just—I haven't even known you a week."

"It's okay," she said.

"Carmen—"

"No, really. You don't have to explain. I'm rushing things. Jesus."

"Carmen, don't."

"You must think I'm a floozy. Or a slut. I'm—I'm sorry." She looked away. He could still see her eyes, and there were tears brimming. He reached for her, and she spun away, awkwardly, bumping against the bed and bumbling a little on her feet, then finally going down, slumping against the bed. She buried her face in the bedspread, cupping her arms around her head as if trying to blot out the world.

"Oh, God," she said.

Her body shuddered, but she couldn't contain it. She sobbed, the sound muffled by the bedspread. Gage was stunned. He wasn't sure what had happened. Where had the smart, formidable woman gone? He didn't know what he'd done to cause this.

"Things are just moving too fast," he explained.

His voice sounded pitiful—plaintive, small, and worst of all, cold. He hated himself for it. Was that the best he could do? Was that all good old Garrison Gage had in the way of human empathy? Her crying continued unabated. He crept through the dim light, afraid that his bum knee would decide this was the time to give out and he'd go sprawling at her feet.

He made it to her, extended his arm, touched her back.

"Hey," he said.

The crying slowed. The shuddering turned to trembling. She looked at him, sniffling. In the near-darkness, the room a tapestry of black and white, the tears streaking her cheeks looked like icicles in the snow.

"I'm sorry," she said.

"You don't have to apologize," he said.

"I'm quite a piece a work, aren't I?"

"Well, I don't know if it's the appropriate time to comment on how attractive you are, but yes, you are definitely a piece of work. A knockout, I'd say."

She laughed. It wasn't much of a laugh, more of a spasming hiccup, but he was still glad to hear it.

"Now you're just trying to cheer me up," she said.

"Just stating the facts. You make a man weak in the knees just looking at you, and that's a dangerous proposition for someone who has only one good knee."

"Uh huh. All right, don't lay it on too thick."

He helped her up. She hunched on the edge of the bed and let out a deep sigh. He sat down next to her, the mattress sagging under their weight. The cracked open window was directly across from them. The breeze picked up, the curtains rippling against their legs.

"Can you hand me that box of tissues over there?" she asked.

He retrieved them from the nightstand. She dabbed at her eyes and blew her nose. She'd gone through three tissues before she looked at him.

"Sorry you had to see that," she said.

"I like a little spontaneous sobbing in a woman. Keeps things interesting."

"So I haven't totally scared you off yet?"

"Far from it. It's all I can do to keep myself from ripping those clothes off of you right now."

She chuckled. "I think that's the nicest thing a man has ever said to me."

"Well, I mean every word of it." He swallowed, trying to think of what to say, how to put things right. "Carmen—"

She silenced him with a finger on his lips. He didn't know what surprised him more—the finger to his lips, or that he could taste her tears.

"It's okay," she said. "I know I was moving a little too fast."

"A little?"

"Okay, a lot. I don't know what got into me. I—well, I do. Kind of. I just—well . . ."

"It's okay," he said. "You don't have to explain."

"No, I want to," she insisted. "You're the first person I've ever wanted to talk about it since coming to Barnacle Bluffs and if I don't say it now, I never will. It'll probably scare you off permanently, but that's okay. If we're honest here, I've probably already done it."

"Impossible," he said.

That got a smile out of her. "Yeah, well, you say that now, but where will you be on Valentine's Day?"

"Probably at Hallmark's with all the other poor schmucks buying you the most expensive card in the place."

"We don't have a Hallmark's in Barnacle Bluffs."

"Well, then I'll be wherever poor schmucks go in Barnacle Bluffs. But I'll be looking for a card. Probably end up with one of those stupid ones that sings a song. I never know what to do when I'm picking out cards. There's always so many of them."

She arched an eyebrow. "Finished?"

"What do you mean?"

"If you're trying to make me feel like I don't have to say what I'm about to say, then it's not working. I'm still going to say it."

"After all that build-up," he said, "you *better* say it now. Okay, what is it?"

The truth was, he hadn't been trying to change the subject so much as to drain some of the tension. To make it seem like less of a big deal. It worked for a moment, too, but now the curtains fell over her eyes again. She stiffened her back and offered up a wry smile, like she was going to veer off in another direction at the last moment, but then she sagged back down. It was like watching a sheet on a clothes line flutter to the grass.

"It's about a man, of course," she said.

"Okay."

"A man I loved."

"All right."

She swallowed hard. "It really does sound kind of lame when I say it out loud. I don't know. You're probably going to laugh."

"Love is never lame, Carmen. And I promise I won't laugh."

She searched his eyes, and he could see her thinking: was this someone she could trust? He wanted to be that person for her. But he didn't want her to confide in him something she wasn't ready to confide. Outside, the rain tapping on the ferns faded to a murmur, like a conversation happening in another room.

He squeezed her hand. "Carmen, you *don't* have to say anything. It's okay."

"No, I have to. If I don't, I'll never do it." She took a deep breath. "It was when I was at the Detroit Free Press. First year out of college . . . I thought I was big stuff. I was assigned local color stories for the entertainment section, which was pretty disappointing, but I thought I'd make the most of it. Wrote lots of stuff about Girl Scout troops and bingo nights at the senior centers. Then a few months in when I went trolling for stories, I heard about this new band playing some of the clubs around town called Rock Eyed Angles. Lots of buzz. So I listened to them play." She stopped for a moment, her eyes wide and bright.

"And?" he prodded.

"When I walked in, I heard his voice," she said. "The lead singer. I still remember the song, too. It was called 'Something in the Snow,' and it was about this girl who built a castle in the snow where she lived until the spring came. It was . . . amazing. He was amazing. His voice was like Ray Charles at his very best. And then when I squeezed my way into the packed bar, I saw him. And—Gage, I know this is stupid. I know intellectually that these things don't happen. But he looked at me. And it really was love at first sight." She glanced at Gage, challenging him to defy her.

"You don't have to explain it to me," Gage said. "I still remember the first time I saw Janet." And he did, vividly: walking out of her office at the Museum of Modern Art, high heels clicking on the shiny hardwood floor. He'd been ready to ask her some questions about one of her employees, but when he saw her the entire case went right out of his mind.

"So you know then," Carmen said, nodding. "You know how your life can go a whole different direction with one look. It was like that. I mean, he wasn't the *best* looking man. Tall and thin, brown hair tied back in a pony tail, scruffy. His denim jacket had holes in the arms. He had cigarette burns all over his t-shirt.

"But he looked at me the whole time he was singing. I know it's corny to say he was singing just for me, but this time he really was. So when he was done with his set, I told him who I was and asked whether he'd agree to an interview. He said he would so long as I agreed to dinner. I wrote a real glowing piece in the paper about him. Six weeks later we were living together. Six weeks later he got down on his knee and proposed."

"Wow."

"Yeah, it seems fast," she explained, "but at the time it was totally natural. Like we'd known each other for years. But here's the thing. Here's where things started to go wrong. I said no. I said I wasn't ready."

"That's not wrong, Carmen."

"It is when you loved someone as much as I loved John. John Coller, that was his name. I loved him more than life itself. Seems crazy for how long we were together, but I did. I told him I needed to get settled in my career. I wanted to focus on me a while. I wanted to keep things the way they were just a little bit longer, so I could move up the career ladder a bit."

"Seems logical."

"Well, it is if it were *true*," she said. "But really, deep down, it was because I was afraid."

"I think you're being a little hard on yourself."

"Not really. I wanted to spend the rest of my life with him. There was no doubt about that. I was just afraid ... I don't know, maybe of jinxing it or something. As long as we didn't get married, then we couldn't get divorced."

"Let me guess," Gage said, "your parents were divorced?"

She looked at him. "You're not making light of this, are you?"

"No. Of course not. I'm just—"

"Because yeah, they divorced when I was twelve. At the time, it was the worst thing that ever happened to me."

"Carmen—"

"It was bad, too. A really bad divorce." Her voice turned brittle. Her pupils flashed wide and dark, and her back stiffened. "Did your parents divorce? Do you have any idea what's it like when you're at that age when you're trying to figure yourself out and then your whole world is turned upside down? Do you have any idea what it's like when you're trying to understand how your father could actually be spending his nights in some other woman's bed?"

Gage felt his own defenses rise. It wasn't like he'd asked to play the role of therapist—lay down on the couch, ma'am, and tell me all your troubles. Book your next appointment with the receptionist on the way out. But he had been careless and he knew it. This wasn't about him.

"I didn't mean to mean to come off that way," he said. "Tell me about what happened with you and John."

She bore into him a moment longer with tigress eyes, then it was gone, and he was peering into the cracked shell again.

"He seemed fine with it," she said. "He said things would happen in time. So for the next three years, we settled into a routine. I worked my ass off at the paper, really trying to make a name for myself. He threw himself into his music. We weren't spending a lot of time together, especially since John started touring with his band. He was also getting interest from L.A. to put a record together. I finally got a promotion to Features Editor. Do you know how hard it is to get promoted in a dying industry? It's damn tough."

"I believe it."

"When I got the news," she said, "he was out on the road, hitting some clubs in Chicago. I thought I'd surprise him. Got there late. I found one of the band members in the hotel bar, drunk off his ass, and he told me which room John was in. If he'd been sober, I don't think he would have done that. You can probably guess where this is going."

"I have an inkling," Gage said.

She shook her head. "Stupid. I was so stupid. So young and naive. I even changed in the restroom into this little black nightie. God . . . Walked in into his dark room and dropped my trench coat on the floor. Could barely make out a shape on the bed. Said . . . said his name . . ."

"Hey, easy now."

"Jesus, this was like three years ago and I can still barely talk about it. So . . . The shape moved. There was a cough. When you've been with someone a while, you even know how they cough. It wasn't him. I knew that right away. Then she let out a yelp and flicked on the light. It was this young naked kid, this girl, maybe eighteen but that would be pushing it. She was alone in bed, and she looked up at me all terrified, her big breasts just hanging there. I still remember how big those stupid breasts were. God, the things you notice at a time like that."

"I'm sure I would have noticed them too."

Carmen snorted. "I was still so stupid. I stammered that I was sorry. Told her I must have had the wrong room. I started to back out, but then the curtains covering the doors to the patio pushed aside and John rushed in. He had a bottle of beer in his hand and he was just as naked as her." She lapsed into silence.

"What happened then?"

"I don't really remember. There was some shouting. He

pleaded with me. He said she didn't mean anything to him, and of course this girl started crying. I rushed out of there and drove home crying. I didn't answer his calls, and by the time he got back into town the next afternoon, I'd already put his things on the curb and changed the locks. He kept calling, both at home and at work, and I'd always hang up on him. He left long rambling messages. He wrote me letters. Emails by the dozen. I didn't even look at them until later. After a couple weeks, he only called once a day. After a month, it was every couple of days. Then, about six weeks in, he showed up at the apartment. I wouldn't answer, but he talked to me through the door. He said he was going out to L.A in a week, just him. He was going to record some songs. He wanted me to go with him. Said . . . said it would be a good opportunity to see if we still had something left. If we could patch things up. He—he—he—

"Hey, Carmen, it's all right."

She took a deep breath. "He said he loved me. He made a terrible mistake and he loved me. I didn't say anything. It was the last time we talked. He headed for L.A. for bigger and better things and I just let him go."

"What happened to him?"

"He died."

"Oh, man, I'm sorry."

"It was just one of those freak things. He was driving across country to L.A., and I guess he had a woman in the car. They were . . . fooling around while he was driving. He must have been distracted, I guess, because he didn't see the van driven by some drunk guy who was veering into his lane. Everybody ended up dead in that one."

"Jesus."

"Yeah," she said. "That's what I said when I saw it come across the wire. Then I went in the bathroom and threw up for half an hour."

"Man, I'm sorry."

She nodded. "That was a bad day. You know, the worst thing? It wasn't hearing that he was dead. I mean, don't get me wrong, that was bad. But the worst thing was that when I heard he had this woman in a car, I felt—this is awful, but . . . *relieved*. I thought, okay, well, I was right. He didn't really love me. He was with another woman. If he could move on that quick, it must have meant he didn't really love me. He probably never did. I'd just been stupid all a long."

"You weren't stupid."

"Oh, I was. But not for that. You see, it gets better. I decide to torture myself and do a story on it. Local musician on the rise tragically killed. Everybody in the office thought I was nuts, that I should pass it off to another reporter. But I was Features Editor, and this was my penance. I find out this woman was really just another girl, some kid he met at a bar the day before he left. I talked to the other band members. Every last one of them said he never stopped talking about me."

"He still made his choice, Carmen."

"Oh, I know," she said. "But so did I. And the more I thought about it, the worse I felt. You see, I think I drove him away. If I hadn't been so scared, if I hadn't been so afraid to say yes, I love you, I want to spend the rest of my life with you, if I'd been willing to take that leap, well, maybe he wouldn't have gone looking. I was so afraid he'd just end up being a man who disappointed me and then he did. If I'd—if I'd really given him all my love, he'd still be a live today."

"There's always a lot of what-if's," Gage said. "Believe me, I know. But he did make his choice, Carmen. No matter what you would have done, he very may well have done the same thing."

"Maybe," she said, nodding, her voice quiet. "Maybe."

But she didn't sound convinced. She didn't say anything more and he didn't know what else to say. Sometimes there wasn't anything to say. It was a tragic story. It wasn't a unique story. It happened to thousands of people every day. But it was *her* story. Something had been lost in her, never to be regained. All she could do was what everyone could do. Put the pieces back together the best you could so that what remained could still pass as a whole person. Carry on. Smile. Step around the land mines if you saw them coming, because one more of them and you knew there wouldn't be enough pieces to patch into anything any more.

He put his arm around her and pulled her against him. She felt tiny and fragile, a hummingbird in his arms. He waited for her to cry, but she didn't. They sat there listening to the slowing rain, until even that sound was gone and all that remained was the distant murmur of the ocean.

Chapter 16

THE NEXT MORNING, Gage went for a walk on the beach. The clouds lay low over the ocean. He felt this creeping sense of anxiety, worsening by the day, growing into panic. It was that warning on his stoop. If there really were other girls, were they alive? If so, what was he doing going out on dates? If he felt it necessary to sleep with his Beretta by his side, maybe he shouldn't have been sleeping at all. Maybe he should have been doing more.

But what? He couldn't think of anything for now other than going to that poker game at the Inn.

On the way home, he stopped at the gas station and called the *Bugle*. Carmen was there, hard at work on the Abigail Heddle story. She sounded pretty chipper. She didn't bring up the previous night and he didn't either. He didn't know what that meant, or whether it meant anything, but when he put the phone down he felt strangely depressed. On the way up to his house, he stopped at Mattie's. Zoe answered, headphones on, deep circles under her eyes. She didn't bother to take them off, barking at him in a voice fit for a crowded bar that Mattie was sleeping. Then she shut the door, leaving Gage in an even fouler mood.

He spent most of the morning and a good part of the afternoon at his dining room table, drawing diagrams linking possible suspects, jotting down every clue he'd learned, trying to make connections. It was something he liked to do with most cases, a way of free associating to see if it would stir up something new, but this time it only made him more frustrated.

When the daylight in the bay window was starting to fade, easing into late afternoon, he headed to the bookstore. A couple of families were browsing the children's books, though the children themselves seemed more interested in climbing the shelves. When Alex saw Gage, he immediately took Gage by the elbow and led him into the cramped storeroom, one hardly wider than their shoulders and packed on both sides with books. There was also a bucket with a mop, and the place smelled strongly of disinfectant.

"I'm glad you stopped by," Alex said. "I was going to go see you if you didn't."

"What is it?" Gage said.

"It's that new girlfriend of yours over at the Community Center. Agnes. She called a little while ago."

"What?"

"She said she was at the hospital visiting a friend of hers. When she came out, she saw the director of the Northwest Artist Colony sitting in a car at the back of the parking lot. Ted Kreggle."

"She sure?"

"She said she'd know that hairy fellow anywhere."

"Sounds like him," Gage said. He remembered her saying she'd attended some of the Colony's shows. "Is that it?"

Behind his glasses, Alex's eyes were beaming. "No. This is the good part. She said Chief Quinn drove up in a cruiser and parked right next to him. Then he got out and had Kreggle roll down his window. It was all the way across the parking lot, but she said it looked like the Chief was shouting at him, like Kreggle was in trouble. Then the Chief got in his car and drove away. She didn't know what it was about, but she said since you'd asked about the place, you might want to know that the guy might be in trouble with the law."

"Interesting," Gage said. "She was sure it was Quinn, huh?"

"Hey, I'm just you're answering machine," Alex said. "Which, by the way, you should probably pay me for."

"I'll keep that in mind. So what do you think?"

Alex took off his glasses and rubbed the bridge of his noise. "Hard to say, but I think it's more complicated than Quinn just telling the guy he was parked illegally."

"That's what I'm thinking too," Gage said.

Though what it meant, exactly, Gage wasn't sure. It certainly was a new wrinkle. He thought about doing a little stakeout of Quinn, but it would have to wait. He had a poker game to attend.

After heading home, he had a quick bowl of chowder with too much salt, then it was time to head out to the Inn at Sapphire Head.

The headlights of the oncoming cars wore golden crowns. The tires of the van whispered over wet asphalt. He pulled into the covered drive a few minutes before nine and got the same crap from the valet. He went through the song and dance at the front desk, saying he was there for Mr. Moore's chess club, and a bright-eyed brunette with nice teeth told him to go to Room 313. The elevator was taking forever, so he took the stairs, and regretted it by the time he reached the third floor. His knee was on fire and he was sweating like the out-of-shape middle-aged bastard that he was.

The inside of the Inn was just as posh as the outside: lavender carpet with taupe trim; gold-framed mirrors; mouse quiet, not a soul around. Standing outside 313, he wished he didn't have the damn cane. He knocked. When the door opened, releasing a cloud of cigar smoke that smelled like ripe oranges, the person who greeted him wasn't someone he expected.

Percy Quinn.

He was dressed in an obnoxious yellow and orange Hawaiian shirt, not his usual drab button-up dress shirt and thin tie, but it was definitely Quinn. Gage gaped at him and Quinn gaped back, those big eyebrows arching.

"Gage?" he said.

Gage's mind raced, trying to understand what this meant. First the news of him meeting Ted Kreggle, now this. He saw no shame on Quinn's face, just surprise and suspicion. With the door only cracked open, Gage couldn't see anyone else in the room, just the corner of a cherry wood cabinet, thin blue carpet, and a bit of white laminate flooring to what must have been the bathroom. He heard the rumble of voices, some laughter.

"In the flesh," Gage said.

"What are you doing here?"

Before Gage could answer, the door opened wider and there was Jimmy Lourdenback, dressed in a bright purple suit instead of a yellow one, hat tipped back on his head, a bead of sweat running down the front of his eye patch.

"Who's this?" he said. "What? *This* guy! This is a private game, pal. How'd you find out about it?"

Quinn looked at him. "You know him?"

Jimmy leveled one of his puffy little fingers at Gage. "He was at the casino on Monday. Won the damn thing, too, but he doesn't play like a normal player. It's—well, I don't know what it is. But he don't belong here."

"Easy now," Quinn said. "How *did* you find out about this game, Gage?"

Gage glanced at Jimmy, but there was no panic in his eyes. If Jimmy was worried about Quinn being there, he didn't show it.

"If I'm not wanted, I can leave," Gage said.

"I didn't say you had to leave," Quinn said.

"I just got to talking to this guy down at my friend's bookstore, Books and Oddities, a few months back. I think his name was Larry. Maybe Barry. He had a funny last name. He was buying a poker book, and we got to talking. I gave him a few ideas he hadn't thought of, and he told me about this game. Said if I mentioned him, they'd try me out for a night. I just finally got in the mood to play some poker."

Someone shouted from within the room: "Oh, hell, guys, just let the man in! If Harry thought he was good enough, then he's good enough."

"I'm not playing with him," Jimmy declared flatly.

There was something on Quinn's face, a growing suspicion, and he held the look a few extra beats as if he was deliberately sending a message to Gage. Then he cracked a smile and held open the door.

"If Jimmy doesn't want to play," he said, "then it's our gain. Come on inside."

There were three guys gathered around a circular kitchen table, one of them in a wheelchair. A pitcher of ice tea, a bowl of popcorn, and a pile of chips graced the shiny oak surface. The man on the left was enormous, pushing three hundred pounds at least, with a cascade of chins and oily black hair pulled back in a pony tail. He tapped a cigar burned nearly to the nub over a glass ashtray.

The man in the middle—thin and gangly, with a buzz cut of bright white hair—was shuffling the cards. The man in the wheelchair looked shrunken, like a wax figure too long in the sun, his head tipped down as if the glasses he wore were too heavy for him. His cream-colored vest dwarfed his body like a life preserver on a small child. He was hairless except for his brown beard, trimmed into a jutting triangle in a style once fashionable in the nineteenth century. In the back of the room, the air conditioner hummed like a barbershop quartet.

"Welcome to our little club," the man in the wheelchair said, his voice high and reedy, refined in the way of an English butler. "I'm Winston Hamlin. Pull up a chair. I'd offer you mine, but as you can see, I'm somewhat attached to it."

His eyes twinkled in a way that reminded Gage of his own grandfather, who used to like to make kids laugh by pulling coins out of their ears.

"Garrison Gage," he said, offering his hand.

They shook. The man had a grip like a wet sponge. Gage resisted the urge to wipe his hand on his pant leg.

"Gage?" Hamlin said. "Why does that name sound familiar?"

"He's the detective I was telling you about," Quinn said. "The one from New York."

"Ah," Hamlin said, smiling broadly. He had the small, pointy teeth of a ferret. "My son would *love* to meet someone like you. He's really addicted to those New York cop shows. Sit, sit. I own this fine establishment, so if you need anything, just let me know."

Gage leaned his cane against the wall and took a seat next to Hamlin. Quinn sat across from him, and Jimmy stood with his arms crossed and a petulant look on his face. Gage watched the other two to see if his chosen occupation provoked any reaction, but if it did, he didn't see it. The man with the white hair and the pony tail went on shuffling his cards, and the big guy stacked up the chips he'd just won, his cigar smoldering in his left hand. Judging by their stacks, they hadn't been playing long.

"I'll sit this one out," Jimmy said.

Nobody paid him any attention. Hamlin motioned to the big guy.

"This fellow here is Charles Logan," he said. "He prefers to be called Chuck. You remember the Power Potato Peeler? Well, that was his invention. He's invented all kinds of clever devices like that. He's one of the smartest inventors in the country."

"Used to be," Chuck said. "Now I do nothing but lose money at cards. And get fat. That's retired life for you."

"Oh, pish posh," Hamlin said, waving his hand as if clearing smoke. "We've talked about this before. No jests about your weight."

"Whatever," Chuck said. He took a puff from his cigar and looked glum.

"And this distinguished gentleman," Hamlin said, "is Martin Jaybee. He owns—"

"Let me guess," Gage said. "The Jaybee grocery stores."

The man nodded. "Half. My brother owns the other part."

"Your brother," Chuck said, shaking his head. "Don't know why you even mention that bastard. He hasn't lifted a finger to help you in years."

"Family's family."

"Not mine," Chuck said. "I left those pricks back in Texas when I was fifteen and they can rot there for all I care."

Martin shrugged and started dealing the cards. Hamlin laughed nervously, like a pastor's wife whose children were cursing in front of the tea club. He looked at Gage.

"The game is seven card stud, deuces wild," he said. "We play something different every week. I assume you're good for a thousand dollars? That's the stack we start with and we play until someone's got all the chips or we're too tired to play further—which often happens."

"Or until Marty gets mad and turns the table over," Chuck said.

Martin sighed. "I only did that once."

"Well, it made quite an impression," Chuck said.

"Now, now," Hamlin said, "we all have piques of anger now and then. I seem to recall you having a few fits yourself over the years."

"I never turned any tables over," Chuck said. "But then, I'm not an artist like Martin. Artists are bound to be emotional."

Martin sighed. Gage doubted there was any real bad blood between them. He'd seen this kind of thing all the time, when one player was trying to get into the head of an other. The comment made Gage remember the plaque he'd seen at the Northwest Artist Colony, the one that bore the names of both Martin Jaybee and Sapphire Holdings.

"Artist, huh?" Gage said, reaching for his wallet. "Do you paint?"

"Sculpture," Martin said. His dour expression brightened considerably. "Mostly with metals, though I do some ceramic now and then."

"He's quite good," Hamlin said. "The hotel has a number of his pieces."

Gage reached for some cash—he'd stopped by the bank earlier in the day—but Hamlin put out his hand.

"Oh, no, we don't exchange any currency here," he said. "Of course, this is a purely social game. The numbers are all entirely imaginary."

Chuck laughed. "Unless you end up in the hole. Then you

get a nice little bill at the Inn at Sapphire Head that's not imaginary at all."

"Well," Hamlin said, "*that* bill would be for staying at this fine establishment, of course. An entirely different matter."

Chuck snorted. "Right . . . Can't even tell you how many times I've stayed here over the years." He made the sign for quotation marks around the words *stayed here*. "I live just down on the beach a block away, but hell, I just love sleeping in these comfy beds."

"And the Inn *does* pay some nice consulting fees, of course, should the need arise," Hamlin said. "You've gotten a number of those checks in the mail, Chuck, I seem to recall."

"Not *that* many."

"If you do get a bill," Hamlin said, "you just pay on your way out. I make the call at the end of the game, telling the front desk the appropriate room charges. All major credit cards are accepted, of course."

This got them all to laugh. The cards were dealt. The first hand, he ended up with a pair of jacks on the board but junk in his hand. He decided to play it out and lose some money, spending his energy watching the others. His mind was clicking the pieces around, trying to make sense of why these particular people were here. Jimmy Lourdenback had called them the movers and shakers, the people with connections, and Gage could see that. Even Percy Quinn fit that description, though Gage had been surprised to find him there.

"I'll see your twenty and raise you fifty," Gage said on the turn. He still just had junk. "You know, I'm guessing there's a number of art lovers here. I was down at the Northwest Artist Colony a few days ago and I saw a couple of your names on the donor's board."

Martin, who'd already folded, glanced at Gage. It wasn't so much surprise Gage saw but curiosity. Chuck glowered at his cards, and as far as Gage could tell, Hamlin hadn't even glanced at his hole cards. He sat with his hands folded, slightly hunched, grinning at Gage.

"You're quite a perceptive fellow," he said. "I'll have to remember that. Yes, I do have a soft spot for the arts. Well, in a way it's second hand. My wife, bless her soul, was a great lover of art. I'm just trying to carry on her memory."

"I'm sorry," Gage said.

"Oh, don't be. She died over twenty years ago, when my son was just a toddler. A terrible car accident that also left me in this wheelchair. *That* was a rough time. But it still makes me happy to write checks to causes she believed in. I'll see your one fifty and raise you a hundred." He pushed in his chips.

Groaning, Chuck tossed in his cards. "Not this time. But watch out, I'm going to bluff you next time and win."

"You always say that," Martin said.

"And when I do, don't I always win?"

"I don't remember." Martin was still looking at Gage. "I give a little money to NAC too. It's a nice place to go when I want to be around other artists."

"That's pronounced *artistes*," Chuck said.

Gage and Hamlin had a showdown, and of course Gage lost just like he predicted, but not by much. Hamlin only had a pair of kings.

"Thank you," Hamlin said, sweeping in his chips.

"For what?" Gage said.

"For letting me have that one. You weren't going to bet at all, but you wanted to show your appreciation for us letting you be here. It's duly noted."

"It's pays to be nice to your hosts," Gage said without missing a beat.

It was from that point on that Gage knew he was playing against a formidable player. In fact, the other two were great players too—even Chuck, despite the woe-is-me act. Gage didn't care if he won any money. In fact, he thought it'd be better if he lost a little. The key word was little. He didn't want to lose his shirt. He was really going to have to stay on his toes or that's exactly what would happen.

It was Quinn's turn to deal the cards, and while he did he

said, "So, Gage, how's that case coming? You solve it yet?" He smiled wolfishly.

"You'll be the first to know," Gage said. Then he decided to throw a hand grenade into the conversation and see what happened. "Actually, Carmen's going to run a hell of an article about Abigail Heddle. A real nice piece about her life."

"What?"

"I figured it was time to shake things up a little," Gage said.

"You could have told me."

"I *am* telling you."

"You could have told me *before* you decided to let her all the way in on this."

Gage shrugged. He was watching all of them, judging their reactions. They were studying their cards. Of course, these were top players. They may have come across as angry, irritated, or bored, but the truth was, they could show any emotion at any time based on what they were trying to accomplish. All top poker players could. He didn't know if they were all at that level, but he had to assume they were.

Quinn, for his part, looked about to explode, then it went away and he shrugged. "Well," he said, "I guess the genie had to get out of the bottle eventually."

"It really was terrible what happened to that girl," Hamlin said. "I think we can all agree on that. Just terrible. Have they found the girl's parents, then?"

"They're in town," Quinn said. "I guess now that it's going to be in the paper, we might as well talk about it. She was adopted. A real screwed up kid. Ran away from home real young, who knows what she got mixed up in. Still no real leads." He shot Gage a glance.

"Adopted, eh?" Hamlin said. "Well, it doesn't matter. A parent's love is a parent's love. I imagine they were quite heartbroken. Do you have children, Garrison?"

"No," Gage said.

"A pity. You strike me as a man who would have been a great father."

Gage laughed. "You've known me, what, twenty minutes, and you can already say that?"

"I have a way of reading people. There are lots of people who shouldn't have been parents. And others who should be. You fall into the latter category. It has to do with a sense of responsibility and empathy that you're either born with or you're not. Myself, my son is one of the best things to happen to me. If it wasn't for him, well, after Beatrice died, I don't know what I would have done. Focusing on him was the only thing that kept me going."

Chuck took a cigar out of his jacket and bit off the end, spitting it on the floor. "You still spoil that kid rotten, Ham."

"Oh, I know," Hamlin said. "I just can't bear to deny him anything. Not after what he's been through." He looked at Gage. "I think you understand what I mean. From what Percy told me, you know what it's like to lose someone. How that changes you."

Gage said nothing. That wasn't a place he was willing to go. Not now. Not with them. They played a few hands. He won some and he lost some. They made small talk and Gage got a better sense of who they were. They seemed like good guys. Of course, people said the same thing about Ted Bundy. Some monsters were just better at hiding it than others.

Over the next two hours, Gage lost about half his stack, but he was determined not to end the evening more than a hundred in the hole. At some point, Jimmy Lourdenback drifted out, but nobody really noticed. So much for his grand exit. Later, someone needed to make a phone call and another person wanted to hit the head, so they decided to take a break. Gage ended up following Hamlin out onto the deck, helping the old man by pushing the wheelchair over the metal threshold.

A strong breeze him them full in the face, but it was an oddly humid breeze for winter. No rain. The lantern-shaped porch light illuminated white plastic lawn chairs, a glass table, and an iron railing. The night sky and the ocean below it stretched across the horizon like a curtain over a dark stage. "Thank you, sir," Hamlin said. "I'm not so proud that I refuse the kindness of others. But I'll have you know, I wasn't always this way. I was once a young strapping lad like yourself."

"I'm not all that young, sir," Gage said.

"Well, you *seem* young to me. And I seem old. I guess that's what I mean." He gazed out at the ocean, his pointy beard blown back like a scarf thrown over his shoulder. "There's something about the sea, isn't there?"

"What do you mean?"

Hamlin contemplated the darkness. Down at his height, he could barely look over the bars. "It draws people from all over. Some people come to remember. Other people to forget. Still others come to start over. For some people—maybe for most people—it's a little bit of all three. It has that power."

Gage thought about himself. Had he come to forget Janet? To remember her? Or was it to start a new life? He thought of Carmen and her own issues. How many other people did he know who came to Barnacle Bluffs for at least one of those reasons? Alex? Mattie? It was true that the sea had power. There was no denying it.

He was about to say something about this when the door slid open and a tall, lanky young man with long black hair and bad acne leaned outside. His tinted orange glasses reminded Gage of John Lennon. His goatee was so light that at first glance it just looked like a smudge of dirt, though it had been shaved and trimmed to perfection.

"Hey, Pop."

The old man wheeled around, his face brightening. "Nathan! Gage, this is my son, Nathan. What are you up to, son?"

The kid didn't even look at Gage. He was sucking on something, something that smelled of strawberries. "Got any cash on you? I was thinking of going to the movies."

"Oh. Sure. Let me see." He fumbled in his jacket for his wallet and pulled out a twenty. "Will this do?"

Nathan frowned. "Can you make it forty? I'm thinking of taking a date."

"Oh. Yes. Of course."

Hamlin gave him another twenty, and without even a word of

thanks, the kid retreated. When he was gone, Hamlin leaned forward in his chair, straining so far that Gage was sure he was going to fall on his face. At first Gage had no idea what he was doing, but then he saw it: a candy wrapper on the concrete. Gage picked it up—careful not to put too much weight on the bad knee—and handed it to Hamlin. It was from a Jolly Rancher candy.

"Oh thank you," Hamlin said. He tucked it into his pocket. "Nathan is terribly addicted to these little things. Harmless enough, I guess. What are you addicted to, Garrison?"

It was such an unexpected question that for a moment Gage simply stared at him, trying to understand if he meant something else.

"Excuse me?"

"Addicted. What's your addiction?"

"I don't have one."

Hamlin smiled. "In my experience, we're all addicted to something. Percy's addicted to his job as police chief. Chuck's addicted to food. Martin's addicted to his art. Maybe for you it's misery. Who knows. Shall we go back inside? There's a bit more playing to be done."

Chapter 17

THERE WAS INDEED more playing left to be done, and after another two hours Gage finished two hundred in the hole. He had to work not to go any deeper. He probably would have lost all of it, too, if Hamlin—who had the biggest stack—hadn't finally yawned and said he was ready to call it a night. If Gage was really interested in getting back into poker, he'd definitely want to play with them—not to try to beat them so much as to learn. When you reached a certain level, it was hard to find players who could challenge you and keep you sharp.

Of course, he had no interest in playing poker for poker's sake—or at least he had no interest until Percy Quinn caught up with him in the lobby.

"Gage," the police chief called.

He was just walking through the outside doors, parking slip in hand. He slowed but didn't stop, turning to greet the chief. None of the others were with him. The night felt thick and warm, more like a June night than a December one, the breeze whispering through the Douglas firs crowding the back of the parking lot.

"Chief," Gage said, handing his slip to the valet.

"Say, I just wanted to tell you," Quinn said, "you're quite a player. I don't say that about everybody."

Quinn wore a navy blue trench coat over his Hawaiian shirt, and Gage could see the bulge of the man's revolver.

"Thank you."

"I mean that. And, well, I was wondering if you were planning on coming back?"

Gage felt groggy and tired, and he really he just wanted to go home, but there was something in Quinn's voice that got Gage's hackles up.

"Maybe," he said. "Depends on my schedule, I guess. I'm a busy man."

"Okay," Quinn said. "I deserve that. But listen, unless you're really here to play poker, this isn't the place for you. I just say that in case you're here fishing for information. These guys, they trust me. We trust each other. If you're wanting to be part of that, maybe it might work for you. But if you're here for other reasons . . ." He trailed off.

Gage met his eyes. There was something there—a challenge, a hidden menace, a predator waiting for the prey to cross his path. Maybe none of that. Maybe he was an honest man with a mean streak. Maybe he was a mean bastard who was good at coming across as a nice guy. Whatever he was, he wasn't simple, and they were engaged in some kind of contest Gage didn't yet fully understand. It may have had nothing to do with Abigail Heddle. It may have been as stupid as a pissing contest, but whatever it was, Gage wasn't going to back down.

This wasn't the time, though. The time would come soon enough.

"I just wanted to play some cards," Gage said, and then turned and waited for the van.

It was a still night, and hotter than it should have been for December. The inside of Gage's house felt stuffy and confining; he had the sense he was in the cabin of an old fisherman's boat moored at a marina. He wanted to stay up, maybe do some thinking about the case, try to fit Quinn into the puzzle, but he hadn't been home two minutes when an extreme fatigue overwhelmed him.

His eyelids felt like lead. He'd had a beer during poker, so that made him a little fuzzy, but it was more than that. He figured it was because he'd been going all-out on the case and he wasn't used to it any more. Or maybe he was just getting old. His collar was damp with sweat. Why was it so damn hot? Shuffling to bed, he cracked open his bathroom window to circulate some coastal air across the hall to the bedroom. This turned out to be a stroke of luck.

If that window hadn't been cracked, then he might not have woken to the sound of murmuring voices.

As it was, he still struggled to swim up out of unconsciousness. He was sure that the voices were his parents discussing how Garrison was getting into fights at school again, how the school was going to suspend him if he bloodied just one more lip, and it was only the faint click of the front door opening that cleared away just enough of the fog for the warning bells to start ringing in his head.

Someone was breaking into his house.

More than one someone. Two someones.

Even so, getting himself to actually *move* was another matter. He felt as if someone had taped his eyes shut and chained his body to his mattress; every movement took enormous effort. He was rolling a boulder up a hill. He was pushing a freight train.

There were footsteps in the hall—they were coming.

Finally, he managed to pry his eyes open—just in time to see the shapes of two men appear in his doorway. With the only light coming from the kitchen, that's all he could make out, though he *could* see that one was much bulkier than the other. The thinner one was taller. Lanky.

They stood motionless for a long time, watching. It could have been a dream, except the acid taste in Gage's mouth and his heart pounding in his ears were both so real. He kept willing himself to lunge for his Beretta, but he couldn't do more than wiggle his fingers. The Beretta was on the nightstand. Only inches away. He felt a tingling up his arm. The power to move was coming back.

"It's over there," one of them whispered.

A hoarse voice. It sounded familiar, though Gage couldn't say who. He was having a hard time even keeping his will intact. He wanted to fall back into the comfort of sleep. Give up, go away, die a peaceful death. The thinner of the two moved into the room, heading for the nightstand where his Beretta was perched on a stack of *New Yorkers*. He saw that the man was wearing a mask. They were both wearing ski masks.

Gage's arm moved ever so slightly. Or had it? He couldn't tell.

Then the thinner of the two, the one who hadn't spoken, had the gun in his hand. The bigger one leaned over Gage, his breath smelling of beer and pretzels. Gage closed his eyes.

"You awake, pal?" the guy said.

Gage knew his only chance now was to play dead. No movement of any kind.

"Hey," the man said, and slapped Gage hard on the face with a gloved hand.

The blow stung like hell, but Gage managed to remain silent. The pain wasn't such a bad thing; it got some blood flowing, gave him another jolt of tingles in his fingertips.

"He's out," the bigger one said. "Come on, you take one arm and I'll take the other."

The voice, the voice—where had he heard it? Now they were lifting him out of the bed, one on each side, the leather gloves digging into his armpits. He went as limp as a rag doll, letting his chin droop and his feet drag. Gage was not a light man, too many late night bourbons the last few years, and the two of them were really huffing as they dragged him down the hall.

His sense of self-preservation was screaming at him to do something, to flail or scratch or kick his way to freedom, but he tamped it down. Not yet. He focused instead on offering no resistance; he was a lump of slumbering flesh, nothing more.

He stole a few glances through cracked open eyelids, but all he could make out were black ski masks and black sweatshirts. He fully expected them to veer towards the front door, to drop him in a trunk, and was surprised when they headed instead toward his kitchen table. When they angled him into one of the wooden chairs, it dawned on him what they were going to do.

Suicide, baby. The great detective decided he just couldn't take it any more and offed himself with his own gun.

His suspicion was confirmed when he felt the cold handle being pressed into his palm. This was it, then. He had to act now or he was dead.

But his body wasn't behaving. He could barely twitch his fingers.

"Wait a sec," the bulkier man said. His voice came from slightly behind and to the left, which meant it was the thinner of the two men pressing the gun into Gage's hand. "Wait. Hold on."

The gun was removed from his palm. Gage held still. There were footsteps, heading back down the hall. Bathroom? Wherever he was going, it bought Gage a few extra seconds. He focused on his hand—the tendons coming to life, the blood flowing through all those little veins. He focused on what he was going to do, the exact motion of his fingers and his arm. Rehearsing it in his mind. Seeing it happen again and again. The feeling was coming back fast now, the tingling all over his body. It was going to be close.

More footsteps. Since they were both behind him, Gage cracked open his eyes. He saw the black glove come into view, holding something; there was a clatter on the oak table. His vision was mostly blurred, but he saw that it was rectangular. He saw the glint of metal, the shine of glass. He knew what it was: Janet's picture, the one he kept by his bedside.

"Nice touch, eh?" the bulkier one said. "Okay, do it."

The gun was pressed into his palm. Fingers were maneuvered into place, one gloved hand holding his arm, the other positioning the gun. Even as his mind raced, Gage still didn't resist. The ants were dancing on his hand, thousands of tiny pinpricks. The gun was pointing down, so he couldn't act now. He had to wait, wait until he had the best chance of hitting them before they could react.

He heard movement behind him; the big man had shifted, but where? He wouldn't be able to get the taller one, because he was holding the arm, but the bulkier one might only take a slight jerk of his arm. His gun hand was lifted, coming up, pointing at his temple. The cold barrel of the gun pressed against his skin.

The tall one's gloved hand reached for his finger. Through slitted eyes, Gage looked at the picture of Janet—graceful as a swan in her white business suit, her wide, glimmering eyes like passageways to another world. It would have been easy to let go. He was one trigger pull away from joining her, wherever she was.

All he had to do was . . . nothing.

It was a fleeting whim, but it didn't take hold. It wasn't Gage's way. There was also Mattie and Zoe and Carmen and Alex and all the other people who'd wonder: why, why this way, why now? Oh no. He might take a dive into the deepest of deep ends one day soon, but it wouldn't be like this.

An idea came to him. He let his head slump forward, as if he'd fallen into a deeper sleep. Just as he hoped, a hand took a fistful of his hair and jerked his head into place. The rough grip made his eyes water, but he stayed limp. Two hands on the gun meant this hand was the bulkier man.

"Do it," the man said.

It wasn't as good as a bat's echolocation, especially in Gage's stupor, but the voice gave him a pretty good sense where the bulkier man was. The gloved finger closed on his trigger finger, starting to push. Gage summoned his strength, slowly tightening his grip on the handle. The key was to put all of the effort into pushing his whole arm upward—keeping his wrist firm, no wasted energy, the whole movement directed at getting the Beretta aimed at the man's chest.

An instant before the trigger was pulled, Gage felt the man holding the gun recoil ever so slightly. Away from the blast. Face probably turning away. It was a normal human reaction, and it was what Gage had been hoping for.

He shoved his lower arm upward with everything he had.

The gunshot was like an earthquake inside his head. His vision went white. The recoil snapped his hand back, his wrist rolling, but he managed to hold fast to the Beretta. There was an anguished scream. The man holding his arm let go, and Gage rolled to the left—off the chair and toward the floor.

Something heavy thudded against his chair just as Gage slid off it, toppling it forward, slamming it into the table. Gage went down hard, rolling, ears still ringing like church bells. His forearm banged against one of the oversized table legs. His vision faded in out of black. He willed himself to stay awake, still rolling, rolling completely over, bringing the gun up.

Just as he managed to turn, he saw a huge shape descending on him—a boulder in an avalanche—and fired the gun into it. Fired it again and again.

It was a man. He saw that an instant before the body crashed into him, slamming his head against something hard. Then everything went dark, cold and dark, and he thought to himself stay awake stay awake stay awake . . .

Chapter 18

GAGE WOKE WITH A START, a great pressing weight on top of him. His body was crumpled awkwardly, his bad knee screaming in agony. The room was pitch dark, and the moaning of the wind and the bustle of the pines were so loud he thought he was outside. There was a moment of disorientation— Was it an earthquake? Was he buried under a house? —and then he smelled the musky sweat of his attacker and the leather jacket and the gunsmoke still hanging in the air.

Gun smoke. If he still smelled gun smoke, it couldn't have been too long.

The other man might still be in the room.

A door banged as loud as a gunshot and Gage tensed. Front door. That was why the wind was so loud. His right hand was still firmly entrenched on his Beretta. A good sign.

With a great heave, he pushed the big man off him. It wasn't so dark after all—his oven light, a pale bubble in the darkness, spread a net of shadows over everything. Down as he was under the table, it took a bit of doing to untangle himself, wincing when he unfolded his bad knee. Sweat broke out on his brow and he felt himself fading out again, but he didn't let himself go. He was alive and he wanted to stay that way.

His racing pulse felt more like a fluttering of wings than a heartbeat. When he managed to pull himself into a sitting position, his breaths came in short gasps. The table leg pinched his back. He lifted the Beretta, holding it close, blinking away the sweat. It took a moment for him to get his bearings.

Sandwiched in the space between his kitchen counter and the table, the big man was sprawled on his back, one leg bent under him in a way that no living person would tolerate. In the shadows, the blood pooling on Gage's carpet was as black as ink. There was so much blood—buckets of it. The man's clothes were so dark that the whites of his eyes, visible through the cloth ski mask, hovered ghost-like in midair. Gage thought that the mask covered the man's neck until he realized that the reason the neck was dark was because of all the blood.

He reached out and took hold of mask and yanked it off the man's face. Swollen eyes stared upwards, unblinking. Pasty-faced, a big handle mustache, a wispy comb over—Gage recognized him immediately.

The bartender from The Gold Cabaret.

"Somebody drugged me," he said. "I'm sure of it—something was put into something I drank at that poker game. One of those date rape drugs, probably."

The gas station was deserted, the mini market dim except for the lights inside the coolers. The Budweiser sign glowed neon red in the window. The air was as thick as cotton, damp on his face. Above him, the street lamp wore a golden crown; the rest of the night was painted black. He couldn't see the ocean over the houses across the quiet highway.

"Quinn?" Carmen said. She'd sounded groggy when she answered moments ago, but not any more. It was well past three in the morning.

"I've got no proof of anything, but that's where I'd place my bet."

"It could have been one of the others. Or somebody who

spiked something in your house."

He picked up the dangling phone book and paged through it. Sure enough, Percy Quinn was listed, just as he hoped. Dorfang Road. He supposed a small town police chief with political aspirations *would* want to be listed. "Well," Gage said, "I guess we'll find out soon enough."

"What do you mean? Garrison? You're not going to do something stupid, are you? Maybe you should wait until the morning when things seem a little more—"

"Don't call it in," he said. "I plan to report this one myself."

She was still talking when he hung up.

Driving south along Highway 101, Gage clenched the steering wheel with one hand and his Beretta with the other. In the foggy murk, the road seemed like a tunnel to nowhere. When he reached the end of town, just past a sand and gravel pit, he turned east into the hills. Once he was into the pines crowding the narrow road, and with no streetlights, only his headlights penetrated the darkness. He passed a few paved roads, then a few unpaved ones, until he finally came to Dorfang.

It was a gravel road, deeply rutted. A wooden sign listing Quinn's address, the only one, was nailed under the street name. Gage parked on the muddy shoulder, the right side of his van brushing against a thicket of ferns. He shoved the Beretta into his leather jacket and reached for his cane—and found, in his haste, that he'd forgotten it.

Didn't matter. Trudging up the slight incline, his heart racing, his knee didn't bother him at all. Within the forest, the air felt cooler. Without a flashlight, he had only what little moonlight managed to squeeze through the thick air and the dense canopy—a patchwork of shadows, a contrast of dark and darker. He was glad when he spotted a flicker of yellow ahead, guiding him like a lighthouse.

The gravel road widened into a circular drive, inside a clearing in the trees. The porch light shined on a wrap-around porch attached to bright blue manufactured home, dolled up with a white picket fence and a garden at least twice as big as the little house, crowded with dozens of lawn ornaments. To the right was a blocky metal building as big as an aircraft hangar. A late 80's Ford pick-up was parked in front.

Gage wiped the moisture out of his eyes with the back of his hand. Other than the porch light, the little fluorescent bulb over the kitchen window was the only light on in the house. To the right of the storage building, two squares of light lay like yellow blankets on the gravel. He started for the house until he saw a shadow pass briefly over the squares of light.

He froze. When it didn't happen again, he crept toward the light. Rounding the building, he saw the window, the glass splintered and dusty. There was a metal door, a sliver of light where the door was cracked open. He stepped up to it. Held his breath.

There was a clatter that made him jump, something thudding on wood. Then a gnawing—a chisel? Gage moved to the window, taking his time, easing his head down to the glass. Peering inside, he saw a tall man leaning over a workbench, his back to Gage. A silver motor home, an aluminum fishing boat, and rusted-out old Chevy filled most of the space; the L-shaped workbench was nestled in the corner. The man wore a knitted wool hat tucked low over his ears, so Gage wasn't sure it was Quinn until the man turned, and Gage got a good look at the bushy eyebrows and gaunt face, thick glasses with black frames resting low on his nose. Quinn, all right. He wore oil-stained gray sweatpants and a brown flannel shirt.

Gage eased out his Beretta and undid the safety. Carefully as he could, he eased open the door. It made no sound. That gnawing—it was definitely a chisel. Quinn was so engrossed in whatever he was doing that he didn't notice Gage slipping into the room. A space heater whirred near Quinn's feet.

Gage leaned against the flat front end of the motor home, about a dozen paces from the workbench.

"Couldn't sleep?" he said.

Quinn spun around, brandishing the metal chisel like a

knife. Turned as he was, Gage could see what Quinn had been working on—a wooden block he'd been carving into a sleeping cat, half-finished.

"Gage!" Quinn said.

"More lawn ornaments?" Gage said.

"What're you doing here?" And, after noticing what was in Gage's hand: "Are you out of your *mind?*"

"Probably," Gage said.

"What happened to you?"

The way Quinn scrutinized Gage's face, Gage realized that he must have had blood on his forehead. It probably would have been a good idea to check himself in a mirror before leaving, but what did it matter?

"I want some answers," Gage said.

"You better put down that gun, pardner. If you don't—"

"Shut up."

When Quinn advanced towards him, Gage raised the Beretta. Quinn froze, face darkening. Behind the thick glasses, his eyes were enormous.

"What the *hell* is going on?" he demanded.

"Tell me right now," Gage said, "was that you at my house a couple hours ago?"

"What?"

"It was pretty sneaky of you, putting something in my drink like that. Did you do it when I was on the patio talking to Hamlin?"

"Are you nuts?"

"Would've worked, too, except I've always had a fast metabolism. Either that, or you didn't use enough. What, afraid it would've knocked me out right there in the apartment? That wouldn't do, would it? Not if you wanted to make it look like suicide."

The police chief stood as still as one of his lawn ornaments, confusion reigning on his face. "What are you *talking* about? Someone broke into your house?"

"I figured you'd play dumb," Gage said.

"You're making a mistake, Gage."

"Uh huh. Then tell me, why were you meeting with Ted Kreggle yesterday in the hospital parking lot?"

There was a pause—a brief one, but still there. "What?"

"Is it because you both like teenage girls?"

A flare of pink appeared on Quinn's neck like a collar. "You better watch yourself, mister!"

"So you don't deny it, then? You met him?"

"Who told you that?"

"Why'd you meet him?"

"None of your damn business!"

"He your fuck buddy? Do you do him too or just the girls?"

"You're an asshole!"

"Are there others, Chief? Where are they? Tied up in your motor home?"

"Get out!"

"I'd think that having a hooker wife would be more than enough—"

With a scream, Quinn launched himself at Gage. He may have been tall, lanky, and on the downside of fifty, but he charged forward like a guy who'd played some linebacker. Gage had a split second to make a decision on firing the Beretta, but something made him hesitate. Something wasn't quite right.

The hesitation cost him the upper hand, and then the chief was plowing into him, a battering ram into his gut. Gage managed an uppercut to Quinn's chin with the handle of the gun before his back slammed into the motor home. It was like getting pancaked between two brick walls.

The impact knocked the wind of him. He slumped to the floor, knees jarring against the concrete. Fortunately his uppercut had done the same to Quinn, who was staggering backwards like a boxer seeing stars. By the time Gage was getting to his feet, using the motor home's bumper for support, Quinn had shaken the blow and was running at him again. The look on his face—he was like some kind of mad dog.

This time, Quinn came at Gage with a fist straight to the

face. It was a good punch, powerful, lots of shoulder behind it. The kind of punch that would have taken down most men. The advantage Gage had in these situations is that people always underestimated his reflexes. Even before he was hobbled by the knee injury, he tended to lope from place to place, giving people the mistaken impression that he was also *slow*. But he wasn't slow. When you were the type of guy who tended to say things that pissed people off, you needed some speed to get you out of trouble. Gage never would have lasted in this business otherwise.

At the last second, Gage shifted his head six inches to the right. It happened so fast that Quinn didn't have time to adjust his aim. All that force and weight behind his punch plowed his fist straight into the motor home's metal siding.

The bang was like a thunderclap. To Quinn's credit, the impact didn't stun him for long, just an instant while his face screwed up in pain before he was turning to go at Gage again—but it was long enough. It gave Gage the chance to knee Quinn in the groin.

With a loud guffaw, Quinn doubled over, but now it was Gage who underestimated his adversary. He figured a knee to the groin like that, the chief would be down for the count, but Quinn threw himself onto Gage like a wrestler grapping for position.

In his surprise, the Beretta flung from his hand and clattered to the concrete.

Quinn had his arms wrapped around Gage, and Gage had Quinn's head in an elbow lock. There was some screaming and huffing and then both of them went sliding down the side of the motor home—shoulders slammed against the floor, sweat flying, and both of them flailing and jerking and pummeling, neither of them able to get the advantage. Gentlemanly combat was out; survival was in. Quinn's wool cap went flying. With his head locked in his Gage's arm, Gage could see the liver spots within the tufts of thinning white hair.

"Percy?"

It was a woman at the door, blocked from their view by the motor home. They both froze as if they'd just been whistled by the ref. Gage thought it was an old woman's voice because of how frail she sounded.

"Go back to the house, honey!" Quinn shouted.

There was the shuffling of slippers on the concrete. Quinn let go of his lock on Gage's legs and tried to scramble toward the woman. After briefly resisting—and seeing that the Beretta was in the other direction, by the back tire—Gage let him go.

While Quinn staggered towards the woman, who was just now coming into view, Gage stretched and groped for the Beretta. When he'd gotten it in his hand, he spun over, pointing it at Quinn. The chief was moving to intercept the woman, trying to steer her to the door.

For a moment, Gage thought she *was* old, because she was thin and stooped, bony and slight in a worn flannel robe. But then he saw her face and realized that she probably wasn't even as old as Quinn—forty-five maybe. Her red hair was thin, but the color was vibrant—too vibrant, really, a candy shop red. As bright as her hair was, though, her skin had a washed out look, like weathered granite.

"Who's here?" she said.

Quinn folded her into his arms, pressing her against his chest with a hand on the back of her head. He tried to steer her away, but she managed to turn her head and look at Gage. Her eyes were dead. They saw him but didn't see him. It was a look that froze Gage in his tracks.

"Is he the dealer?" she said. She was resisting being turned. As small and frail as she was, she was doing a pretty good job of holding her ground.

"Shh," Quinn said. "No, no. He's no one. I just—let's go back into the house."

"Dealer?" Gage said.

Now they both looked at him. Quinn saw the Beretta still in Gage's hand and grimaced.

"So what, you going to shoot me now?" he said. When the woman started to speak, Quinn shushed her, pressing her head against his chest. "Go ahead, Gage. Nothing I can do to stop you."

Gage lowered the Beretta. "What did she mean, dealer?"

"Who is he?" the woman asked, her voice taking a frantic edge. "Who's this man? What does he want?"

"Shh. It's all right, Ginger." And then, to Gage, he added: "I'm taking my wife back to the house. We're done here. I'm going to pretend none of this ever happened and so should you."

"No so fast," Gage said. "I want to know what she meant. You dealing drugs?"

"That's right, Gage. I'm dealing drugs. Why don't you call it in, okay? You can even use my phone. I know you don't have one of your own."

Then Gage put it together. Ted Kraggel. The smell of marijuana that clung to his clothes. "Oregon has a medical marijuana law. Why didn't you go that route?"

Quinn snorted. "The doctors, nobody can diagnose her. All we know is she gets migraines something fierce. The weed—it's the one thing that helps."

"Still, even migraines—"

"Why you arguing this with me, Gage? I could only press so hard. I mean, think about it. A man in my position. Busting growers during the day, lighting joints for his wife at night. You were the one who dug up that stuff about Ginger's past. All that stuff would come out too once people found out my wife was smoking pot. The details would be lost in the smear campaign. I mean, Jesus. I thought you were this great detective. I'm starting to wonder."

With Gage's adrenaline subsiding, shame took its place. How easy it'd been to strap himself into roller coaster of his emotions. It never used to be that way. Reason and logic prevailed. What had happened to him? He was only a shadow of the man he once was. Shame turned to disgust. Disgust turned to self-pity. He steeled himself against it, because that was one roller coaster he wasn't willing to ride.

Quinn glared, hugging his wife close. It would have been the proper time to issue an apology. It would have made things better, for certain. But Gage didn't know how.

Instead he slipped his Beretta into his jacket and said, "Let me tell you what happened tonight."

When the story was finished, the circus began. Quinn called it in, and then followed Gage back to his place. There they were met by a dozen uniformed cops, the detectives Brisbane and Trenton, paramedics, and eventually the coroner, everybody marching all over his house as if he wasn't even there. He felt like a ghost at an estate sale following his own death. Carmen soon showed up too, pissed that she'd heard about it on the scanner rather than him calling her himself.

The bartender's name was Robert Pence. Bob to most. Divorced three times, convicted of assault and battery on numerous occasions over the years, two restraining orders, moved to Barnacle Bluffs three years earlier from Los Angeles. Brisbane was sent to notify next of kin and question everyone who worked at The Gold Cabaret. After the body was carted away, the bloodstains on his linoleum looked like an abstract painting by Jackson Pollock.

Forensics crawled all over his place, gathering clues. Gage himself was grilled for a couple hours by Quinn and Trenton. There really wasn't much more that he could tell them that Quinn didn't already know. They figured the bartender injected him with something, but Gage wasn't ready to narrow it down to the bartender just yet. There were other people at that poker game—Jaybee, Hamlin, Logan. There was Jimmy Lourdenback. And there were other people he'd interacted with during the day.

Eventually, exhaustion over came him. His thoughts were like a weak radio signal, everything coherent lost in the static. His eyeballs felt like scratchy marbles. Carmen noticed Gage's sluggish responses to Quinn's repeated questions—who else did he talk to, where else had he been?—and asked if maybe they could pick this up again later, if needed. When Quinn gave his approval, Carmen took Gage by the elbow. It wasn't until they'd passed through his front door that he resisted.

"Wait a minute," he said. "Where we going?"

The first glimmerings of day appeared as a gray smudge over the trees. Their breath fogged in the porch light. A garbage trunk somewhere down the highway was beeping.

"My place," she said.

He raised his eyebrows. She rolled her eyes, exasperated.

"Don't get any ideas," she said. "You just can't stay here."

"I can't?"

"Garrison, someone tried to kill you tonight!"

He shrugged as if to say so what, and she shook her head angrily.

"I can't believe you!"

"I just don't want the rats to think they can chase me out of my own hen house."

"Garrison, you *can't* stay here."

She was right, of course. Was he really so shallow that he needed to prove his manhood? Yes, he was that shallow. But it was more than that. He had some kind of death wish. He was just too cowardly to pop some pills and say good night. No, he was like some drunk matador doing his best to piss off the bull. There was a case to solve. There was no time for his own games.

"All right," he said, and when she started for her car he added, "But I'm going to a hotel."

"What?"

"Just following your own logic, Carmen. If somebody's following me, I'm not leading them to someone else's place."

"Ah." There was disappointment on his face. It was unmistakable. "Okay. Well, you want me to drive you?"

"Thanks, but no. I've got the van."

"Okay. You want me to come over for a while?"

He saw the imploring look in her eyes. The risk she was taking.

"Probably not a good idea," he said.

"All right."

"Who knows who's watching me. No need to put you at risk too."

"I see."

But she didn't. He could see that by the way her eyes turned inward. The way she was falling away from him while still standing still. She turned toward her Toyota.

"Okay, I'll see you in the morning at the station."

"Carmen."

She didn't answer. He followed her. When she opened her door, he touched her on the shoulder.

"Carmen, hey."

She looked at him.

"Thanks for coming over. I appreciate it."

Carmen climbed into her car. There was laughter from within the house. It was jarring, but he knew it was just another way of dealing with the gruesome nature of the crime. Cops needed to cope, just like everyone else. He started to say something else, but she closed the door—not quite a slam, but close. Not looking at him, she turned the key. He saw his own vague reflection in her window, a dark shape. The moisture on the glass looked like plastic wrap.

She put the car in gear, still looking forward, but then didn't go. She rolled down her window a few inches. When she spoke, she still didn't look at him.

"It's okay to need somebody, Gage. Really."

He was still searching for a response when she eased down the drive. He watched her tail lights disappear into the pre-dawn darkness, like embers in a dying fire. What she said stung, but not so much the meaning. It was her calling him Gage instead of Garrison.

It was like she was already pulling away.

Chapter 19

THURSDAY MORNING, after waking at the Motel 6 a half mile from his house, Gage called the police station from the phone in his room. The front desk had no news for him, and neither Quinn nor the detectives were in yet.

The sky looked like wrinkled metal, but at least it wasn't raining, though it must have come down like a monsoon during the night. There were enough puddles in the parking lot that he had to be careful where he put his cane. His body felt like it had been taken apart and put back together with some of the pieces missing; joints he didn't even know he had hurt like hell. He also had a pulsing headache—the aftereffects of whatever nasty drug had gotten into his system, most likely.

He read both the *Bugle* and the *Oregonian* in the hotel lobby while inhaling generous portions of what passed for a continental breakfast—cold eggs and some bagels as hard as bricks. There was nothing in either paper about his ordeal the previous night, which was no surprise considering how late it had happened. The *Bugle* did have a story on the case, under the headline, "Girl's Tragic Life and Death Raises Many Questions." It was all about her life, from the moment her parents died up until the moment she was found dead on the beach by "a local hermit." He laughed out loud at that one.

There was an accompanying article about the police investigation. It didn't say much except that the police were investigating all possible leads, but there was a hint of criticism in it, a few words here and there that implied negligence or downright incompetence. He knew Quinn was going to hit the roof.

After a quick shower and shave, he headed home to check his place, stopping at Mattie's. It was a few minutes after seven when he tapped on the front door, but he didn't want to wait any longer. He had this gnawing sense of dread that he couldn't shake.

Zoe answered, rubbing her eyes, wearing a long black t-shirt and apparently nothing else. One of the black cats meowed around her bare legs.

"Sorry," Gage said. "Didn't mean to wake you."

"S'okay," she said, yawning. "It's just sleep. Not like I need it or anything."

"She up?"

She shrugged and walked away. He stepped inside, closing the door behind him. The place smelled of burnt popcorn. The curtains were all pulled. He heard faint music coming from the down the hall and assumed it was Zoe, but when he got closer he could tell it was coming from Mattie's room. He knew the singer, too—Harry Chapin, who was singing "A Better Place to Be," a soulful tale about love and loneliness. Gage knew the song well. Janet had been a big Chapin fan. She'd often joked that if Chapin had been the sort of guy to have groupies, she probably would have been one of them.

He nudged open the door. Surprising him, he found the curtains open, the room filled with early morning light. She was sitting up in bed, propped up by pillows, wide awake. She petted the orange tabby in her lap and smiled at Gage.

"Hello, old friend," she said.

There was color in her cheeks and sparkle in her eyes. Her gray hair, freshly combed, lay on her white lace nightgown like silk. It was the best she'd looked in months. The room smelled strongly of pine, and he didn't know why until he spotted the green candle at her bedside table, a tiny trail of smoke rising from the flame.

"Well, hello," Gage said, speaking louder to be heard over the music. "You certainly look chipper today."

"I feel as chipper as a wood chipper," she said. "But what about you? You look like hell."

"Thanks."

"No, seriously now. What happened to you?"

"I fell in the tub."

"Uh huh. I think it has something to do with all those cop cars going up towards your place yesterday. I'm thinking you're getting mixed up with the wrong folks, that's what I think."

"Like you, you mean?"

She snorted. "Go ahead and make jokes. But I ain't no wilting flower, darling. I can take the gruesome stuff too."

"I don't doubt it."

"And I would have appreciated you letting me know you were okay."

"Next time I fall in the tub, I'll let you know."

"All right, all right, you don't want to talk about it, that's fine. Let's talk about something else. Go ahead and turn off the juke box, hon. It's right here on the end table. I'd do it myself, but I want to conserve my energy to talk to you."

"We can listen to the rest of it if you want."

"I've listened to it three times already, darling. Really, I don't even need it on anyway, because I can listen to it anytime in my head. Go ahead now."

He turned off the little boom box, then sat on the edge of her bed. She was so small and frail, hardly more than a skeleton, that it was hard to tell what was her and what was merely a wrinkle in the bedspread. Still, he was glad to see the life on her face.

"He's quite a singer," Mattie said. "He always makes me think about things."

"I like Chapin too."

"Do you? That's good. You know, one thing I always take away from that song, and everything I been going through lately only makes me believe it more. You get a chance for love, Gage, you jump at it. It might end quick or it might last forever, but it's always better to jump. You hear me?"

He thought about Carmen. He thought about all the years of loneliness that stretched out before him. It was funny. He hadn't thought of them as being lonely years until lately. Something had definitely changed.

"I hear you," he said.

"So I'm glad you stopped by," she said.

"Oh?"

"Yes. I've been thinking maybe it's about time we contacted hospice."

"I see."

She nodded. "I can tell this isn't really what you expected me to say, was it? You were waiting for me to say something about custody of Zoe. Well, that's coming too. But first things first. It's about time I got somebody in here to be my . . . how should I put it? My chauffeur on that last drive, I guess."

"Mattie, please."

"Well, it's true," she said. "And speaking of Zoe, I can't put her through this no more. I can't believe I did it this long. I'm going to kill her right along with me. So here's the problem. It's why I've been putting it off. I just flat can't afford it."

"I'll take care of it," Gage said.

"Yeah, I figured you would. I figured you'd offer just that fast, too. I'm not even going to pretend to be noble—telling you I'll make it up to you, pay you back, that sort of thing. Because we both know that ain't true. All I can say is I appreciate it. I do. It'll help Zoe, and that's the thing makes it easier to swallow. So thank you."

"You're welcome," he said.

She took his hand and placed it on top of her other hand, sandwiching it between the two. Her skin was surprisingly warm. "But it does make it harder to go ahead and ask you this other thing. I need to sign over Power of Attorney to you."

Gage started to pull away, not even realizing he was doing it until she held him firm. "Now?" he said.

"Yes, now."

"But—but you're looking better. We've got time—-"

"No, Garrison, I'm on borrowed time as it is. We both know it. Let's not play this little game. If you're going to do this thing, you've got to do it now."

"You've got the papers here?"

She looked at the end table. Next to the boom box, there was a white envelope partially sticking out of a black leather bible. He noticed the envelope, and then he also noticed the bible. He'd never seen a bible in her room before.

"That's it?" he said.

"Yep," she said. "Right there in the Book of James."

"But don't we need a—"

"—a notary?" she finished. "A friend of mine, a man I used to date, is a notary in town, and I already got him to sign it. I've put my name on it too. Now all you have to do is add your John Hancock."

"That's not exactly how it's supposed to work," Gage said.

"Well," she said, "my life wasn't supposed to work this way either. He'll say he was here, so it'll stand up in court. That's all that matters."

She let go of his hand and retrieved the envelope, then took the paper out, smoothed it on her lap, and handed it to him. He skimmed it. It did look like everything was there that needed to be there. She got a blue ballpoint pen out of the drawer, scribbled it on a white pad, and held it out to him.

"Moment of truth, pal," she said.

He didn't look at the pen. He looked at her eyes. He saw how much she wanted this, how desperate she was. If he said no, then nothing he'd ever done for her would matter. Those were just little things. Easy things. If it was easy for him, if it didn't take something from him, then it didn't matter. Not really. This mattered.

Everything inside him screamed not to do it, that it would bring nothing but trouble for both he and Zoe. And that may have been true—he had every reason to believe it would be true, knowing how their personalities mixed—but he also knew, deep down, it was just fear. He'd never been entrusted with that kind of responsibility. It had been enough being trusted to take care of his wife, to be there when it mattered, and just look how that turned out.

"Mattie—" he began.

"Garrison, for fuck's sake, just sign the damn paper! I *need* you!"

It stunned him—not just her voice, but the pink pinpricks flashing on her cheeks, the bulging veins on her neck and her hands, her pupils as big as saucers. She thrust the pen out like it was a dagger. It shocked him out of his hesitation. There were two choices. No delaying. He had to choose now.

He took the pen.

He signed his name.

He handed it back to her.

She didn't smile. She didn't frown or laugh or nod. She didn't do anything but lay her head against the pillow and close her eyes.

"Thank you," she said.

Just like that, she fell asleep. It was so swift that he watched with alarm, making sure he saw her chest rise and fall with each breath, however shallow those breaths were. She wasn't dying. This wasn't her swan song. Not yet.

He put envelope in the bible, the pen on the end table, and slipped out of the room. On his way out, he hesitated outside Zoe's room, then left without knocking on her door.

After checking on his house—there was yellow crime tape over door, but no cops yet on scene—he drove down to the gas station and tried ringing Quinn again. A nasty old pick-up was spitting out clouds of diesel in his direction. This time the Chief came on the line.

"Kill anyone else last night?" he said.

"Not to my knowledge," Gage said.

"Might be a good idea for you to lay low, pardner."

"Yeah, I was thinking the same thing."

"Liar," Quinn scoffed.

"Hey, there's just a difference between thinking and doing."

"Based on your behavior at my place last night, I think a bit more thinking and a bit less doing would be helpful."

"It sure would. But while I'm doing some thinking, it would be nice to have an update on whatever you've found out."

Quinn sighed. "Well, there isn't much so far. We searched Pence's apartment, and there's some kinky porn there, but nothing that would indicate he kept any girls on the premises. Brisbane and Trenton are talking to some of the folks this morning at The Gold Cabaret to see if they can dig up anything useful on him. The hotel room where we played poker was already cleaned by the maid service, so there's nothing for us to check as far as glasses. Kind of doubt it could have been done by any of those guys, though. I've known them for years. But I'm going to do some digging just to be sure."

Gage still hadn't fully ruled out Quinn, much less anyone else, but he could do some of his own checking. "What about John Larson? He's about the same build. Maybe a little shorter, but I didn't get that great a look at him."

"Yeah, I thought the same thing. He flew out yesterday and there's no record of him flying anywhere afterwards. All right, I gotta call on the other line. Check back in later and I'll tell you if I've got anything new."

"All right."

"And Gage?"

"Yeah?"

"Stay out of trouble."

Chapter 20

GAGE HAD NO INTENTION of staying out of trouble. He thought about calling Carmen and decided against it. Not yet. He wanted to head over to The Gold Cabaret and ask some questions of his own, but first he'd see Alex.

The shop was technically closed Thursdays, but of course Alex was still there, the neon sign glowing OPEN in its big green letters. Alex was at the computer behind the counter, a stack of jacketless hardbacks next to him. He glanced at Gage over the rims of his glasses. The bags under his eyes looked bigger than usual.

"Can I help you find a book, sir?" he said.

"Yeah," Gage said, "I need a how-to book on investigating a murder. Got any good ones?"

Alex leaned back in his swivel chair, folding his arms across his chest. His perpetual frown deepened. "I think we're clean out."

"Well, that's too bad. Here's what I don't get. If you're going to be open every damn Thursday anyway, why not change your sign? It's confusing people."

"Hmm, " Alex said. "You do have a point there. You're quite a smart fellow."

"It's just a suggestion, for God's sake. You don't have to get snarky about it."

Alex nodded. "You're right. I'm being entirely too snarky. And I think you need to get yourself a dog."

"What?"

"Well, if you want to come home and kick the dog, then I'm a poor substitute. This, my friend, is what we call in the parlance of pop psychology, anger transference. What happened last night that put you in this foul mood?"

With someone else, it would have been enough to get a rise out of Gage, but they'd known each other too long. There was a dry look, a snicker, then they both laughed. The tension gone, Gage filled Alex in on his brush with death the previous night, his encounter with Chief Quinn, and everything else he'd learned.

"Wow," Alex said. "I thought those bruises looked fresh."

"Nice of you to notice."

"Oh, I noticed. I just figured you'd get around to it eventually. Still, the case isn't what's bothering you."

"Huh?"

"Come on, spill the beans. What's troubling poor old Garrison Gage?"

"I was nearly killed and that's not enough?"

"Not for you. What do I have to do, beat it out of you with a stick?"

Of course he was right. It was about Mattie and Zoe. Or more specifically, about the document he'd just signed giving him power of attorney over Mattie's affairs. Or even more specifically, about what that would mean if Mattie passed and Zoe became his responsibility. He told Alex all about this, feeling a little like a guest on a talk show. Tune in tonight. A retired private investigator who mostly hates people grapples with the possibility of raising a teenager. Ratings gold.

When he was finished, Alex drummed his fingers on his stack of hardbacks. After a moment, he said, "So what do you think?"

"About what?"

"What do you mean, about what? I mean what about Mattie

dying and you taking responsibility for Zoe."

"I think it's a terrible idea," Gage said. "I think I should find someone else. Not just dump her in foster care, but someone I know and trust."

"Good."

"Good? What do you mean good?"

Alex shrugged. "I mean I agree with you. You'd be better off finding someone else."

"Really? You don't think after everything I've done in my life that I can't watch over one sixteen-year-old-girl?"

"As a man who once had a sixteen-year-old girl of his own," Alex said, "I'd answer that with an emphatic no."

"Jesus. Have a little faith in me."

"It's not about faith. It's about my firsthand experience with budding female hormones. In fact, I'm learned in all matters related to the fairer sex. You should listen to me."

"Uh huh. How many times you have been married again?"

"Don't change the subject. My point is some men are cut out to be fathers and others aren't. You fall into the latter category. It's not the worst thing in the world. It's better to accept it about yourself *before* you get in over your head."

"Mattie's not asking me to be her father," Gage said.

"Oh, she isn't? What role do you think she wants you to play, hall monitor?"

"Zoe's pretty mature. She's practically an adult."

"Right. Then why does Mattie need you at all? Why not just emancipate her?"

"I said she's *practically* an adult. What I mean is she probably won't need a whole lot of watching over."

Alex smirked. "Right."

"I'm serious. It's just to make sure she stays out of trouble. Help her out if she gets into a fix. That sort of thing."

"My friend, that sort of thing by itself keeps most grown men pacing the floor at nights."

Gage shrugged. "I'm up most nights anyway."

"Believe me, it's not the same thing. Anyway, you're not going to be taking custody of her, so it's a moot point."

"But what if I was?"

"Was what?"

"Taking custody of her," Gage said. "What if it wasn't such a hypothetical? Is it such a crazy idea? Maybe I wouldn't be so bad at it. I mean, I've never even tried, how would I know? I certainly couldn't be any worse than a lot of the sorry excuses for fathers out there. Who knows where she'd end up otherwise? It'd be on my conscience if I pass the buck on this one."

Gage realized he'd been going on quite a bit, so he looked over at Alex and found that the bastard was wearing self-satisfied grin; he practically exuded smugness. Gage scratched his chin.

"I feel like I've fallen into some sort of trap," he said.

Alex feigned innocence. "A trap? Whatever are you talking about?"

"I'm thinking you did this whole song and dance just to get me to admit that maybe this isn't such a terrible idea after all."

"Did I?"

"Christ, Alex, stop with the shtick. You made your point."

Alex leaned back in his chair, hands behind his head, looking like a bookie who'd just cleared a cool million. "I didn't make any point. You did."

"Uh huh. Then why do you look so damned happy?"

Alex smiled. "Because, my friend, I just got you to talk to the only person you ever really listen to—*you*."

At that moment, the door chimed and a bedraggled looking man wandered into the store. He smelled like cheap wine and looked like he'd spent the last decade of his life sleeping in a cardboard box. His long braided blonde hair and gaunt face made Gage think of Willie Nelson. He placed a moldy paper sack full of books on the counter. His green ski parka was taped at the elbows with duct tape.

Duct tape.

"Oh my god," he said.

"What?"

"I think I just figured out who put that message on my doorstep," he said. He shook his head. "Duct tape. Of course."

"Duct tape?"

"I'll talk to you later."

"Gage?" Alex said. "Gage, come on, don't leave me in susp—"

But Gage was already out the door, hobbling as fast as his bad knee would take him.

It was one of those fortuitous coincidences that seemed to happen in every case, a moment or event that sparked a memory or helped him put a couple pieces of the puzzle together.

When the homeless guy had wandered into Alex's store, Gage remembered a different homeless man who'd wandered into a different store a few days earlier—the bum who'd come into *TP Piercings and Body Art* while Gage was talking with the owner. At the time, it hadn't seemed to mean anything, but looking back it was pretty clear the homeless man could have heard their entire conversation. Plus he was just the sort of jittery fellow who might have seen something happen to the girl but was too nervous to approach the police about it.

More importantly, the duct tape the guy had used to repair his boots was the sort of thing that would have made that strange footprint found on Gage's driveway. It was a leap, of course, and it might have been nothing, but the only way to tell was to find the bum.

The sky was clear except for a blot of clouds blocking the sun like a dirty tissue on a yellow button. Gage spent the next two hours cruising Highway 101, from one end of the town to the other, searching for the Jerry Garcia lookalike on a bike with a wooden trailer. He drove in alleys and parking lots. He searched Big Dipper Park, the library, and even the city parking garage. No luck.

Where else would a homeless man frequent? He checked the two main beaches on the north side of town and talked to a couple homeless people who told him the guy was known as Dan the Can Man, but they didn't know much about him except that he was fanatical about all his junk, calling it "the treasures of his travels." Gage headed south to some of the beaches down there.

He'd just passed the road that lead to his house when he heard the siren. He glanced in his rearview mirror and saw the ambulance blazing up the highway, lights flashing. Edging to the right, he started for the shoulder, thinking it was probably some unlucky tourist at the Inn at Sapphire Head, and saw the ambulance turn.

Onto *his* road.

All at once, his veins turned to ice, his breath caught in his throat, and his vision tunneled to the flashing light in his rearview mirror. He told himself it couldn't be. He told himself there was still a chance it was for someone else. She had so many more good days ahead of her—not forever, and maybe not for long, but good days, enough of them that she could stop counting them for a while. Enough that he could stop counting them too.

And he knew it was all a lie.

Turning the wheel.

Driving fast, screaming up the drive.

Seeing the ambulance on the lawn, lights flashing.

The front door to the house wide open.

Ramming into the boxwood bushes, laying them flat.

In the house, down the hall.

Voices. Radio static. Crying.

A human tent folded over Mattie, checking pulse, checking eyes.

Zoe crying in the corner.

Silence.

A dreadful silence.

At some point, hours later, after the medics pronounced her dead, after consoling a sobbing Zoe in his arms, and after the ambulance pulled away, lights off, two sober-faced men in dark suits carried the body that was once Mattie Pelling to a black limo and finally down the road to some hot oven where that body could be turned to dust.

Gage didn't remember getting in his van. He didn't remember driving across town to the *Bugle's* office, and he didn't remember walking up those rickety steps. He didn't remember any of that. He remembered Zoe shouting something at him, though he couldn't remember what it was, and slamming the door so hard plaster rained from the ceiling. Then he remembered standing in front of Carmen's desk, her hugging him tightly, pressing her face against him as his body suffered through some strange seizure-like convulsion that didn't feel like grief. He still wasn't crying. He just wasn't himself and his body didn't know what to do about it, a body that had been transported from Mattie's house (*no longer Mattie's house, someone else's house, something would have to be done about that*) into that embrace in a single instant. Even later, when things seemed clearer and he looked back on it all with a more dispassionate view, that feeling of being transported never changed. A door slammed and he jumped through time and space.

"What am I doing here?"

"Shh. It's all right."

"Carmen?"

"Yes. Lay back down. It's okay."

"Are we . . . at your place?"

"Uh huh. Come on. Lay against me now. It's okay. Shh. There now."

"I was in your office. I was in your office and now I'm here. I . . . Is that the rain outside?"

"Yes, it's raining."

"I thought maybe it was someone whispering out there. I thought maybe it was someone talking. What time is it?"

"Shh. It doesn't matter."

"I like that. When you rub my hair. My mother used to do

that."

"I know. You told me that earlier."

"I did?"

"Yes."

"Carmen?"

"Yes, Garrison?"

"Did we . . . ?"

"No."

"Okay."

"I wouldn't do that unless you wanted to."

"Okay. Good . . . Carmen?"

"Yes, Garrison?"

"I want to."

Chapter 21

GAGE LISTENED to the ticking of the clock on the wall and the rain tapping on the shake roof. He was naked except for a pair of boxers. His back and neck felt slick with sweat; the leather couch stuck to his bare legs. He was listening to his breathing, wondering what was making it happen, wondering why he took the breaths he did.

There was a concrete reality to it all, a certainty of person and place that had been missing the past twelve hours. He had been vapor and now he was ice.

"You okay?" Carmen said.

He looked up and saw her standing in the hall, the green light from the oven's digital clock playing across her naked body, all the shapes and contours and curves of her. He could hardly see her at all, a few triangles of flesh, a few crescents of shadow, but he saw her with his hands. His hands saw the silky smoothness of her blond hair, so soft he'd had to touch it twice to make sure it was really there. His hands saw the soft underbelly of her breasts, the slope of her thighs, the firmness of her calves. His hands saw the hollow place on her long neck, the little pillow of her belly, the coarse little hairs between her legs. She stood in darkness, but he saw her as if she stood under the glare of the sun.

He did his best to smile and it felt like his face was a plaster mold. "I'm okay."

"You don't sound okay."

"I'm really okay."

She sat next to him, placing a hand on his bare knee. Her hand felt moist and hot. Was she really that warm or was his own body that cold? She was like a radiator, a fire of flesh and blood.

"Do you want to talk about it?" she asked.

"Not really," he said.

"That's fine. You don't have to."

"I loved her, though."

He didn't know where it had come from. He'd never once thought of the words *love* and *Mattie* in the same sentence, but of course saying it out loud he could see that it was true. It was not a sexual kind of love. It was nothing like his love for Janet. He didn't know why he'd felt the need to say it out loud. It wasn't something he'd said much in the past. It had been one of Janet's complaints. He couldn't even remember saying it at his mother's funeral.

"It's okay that you loved her, you know," Carmen said.

"I just . . . didn't think this would ever happen. I know that's ridiculous. I know, sitting here, that it was obviously inevitable. But I still didn't think it would happen."

"That's okay too."

A thought suddenly occurred to him. "I need to check on Zoe," he said, rising. "Jesus, I can't believe I just ran off without—"

"Garrison—"

"—taking care of her. I've got to—"

"Stop," Carmen said.

She took hold of his hand, but he was too full of dread to stop, and his momentum pulled her to her feet. He started for the door, but she put her arms around him in a big bear hug, holding him tight, pressing her breasts against his back. She was so hot it was like being held by a branding iron.

"Carmen—"

"It's okay, Garrison," she said.

"I've got to—"

"We dropped her off, don't you remember? We went back to the house and she said she wanted to go to her friend Angie's. That Angie would understand. Don't you remember? You told me later that you understood, that she needed somebody she trusted and it was obvious she didn't trust you yet. That's what you said. Don't you remember any of that?"

It sounded true. They stood like that, body to body, skin to skin, swaying a little in the dark room. She moved her hands across his chest, spreading her fingers wide, sliding them through the hair and over his nipples. He felt a stirring below.

"Garrison?" Her voice was breathy and full of need.

"Yes?"

"Come back to bed with me. I want to show you something."

He didn't know how many times they'd made love during the night, but looking back later, this one would be the first he'd vividly remember. It was a desperate and hungry kind of love-making, a groping and a scratching and a clawing, as if there was something there that would be lost if it wasn't snatched quickly. By the time they made it to the bedroom, he was kissing the back of her neck, and then he was kissing her lips, probing the tender flesh, biting down on her chin. She kissed back hungrily, not one long passionate kiss, but a series of hard thrusts, mouth groping and tongue probing, like she was trying to mark every inch of his face. It was like they were two separate people making love in parallel tracks, each taking what they needed.

They drifted to the bed, but then he was kissing downward, raking his lips over the soft pebbled flesh of her nipples, down lower, making her groan. His knee began to give out, but it didn't matter because she was on top of him, pushing him down.

Then, finally, there on the carpet next to the bed, with his shoulder pressed up against the wooden bed frame and the coiled springs beneath the mattress like landmines at the edge of his vision, they moved in concert. They rocked and grinded together,

her palms flat against his chest, her head thrown backwards and her back arched. They fell into a steady motion, two bodies moving as one, a quickening of the hearts, a rising of the blood. The sound of the rain fell away, and then all sounds fell away. There was just the moving. Moving with Carmen. Moving higher. Moving on and on and even in the hunger and the desperation wishing it never ended.

The buzzer on the bedside table snapped Gage wake. He groped for it, stretched, and fiddled with the buttons until the damn noise stopped. He lay there, half-covered by the bedspread, letting his pounding heart slow.

Daylight splintered the draped windows, a dagger of light slicing across his pillow and hitting him in the eye. He groaned and rolled onto his back, pushing off the bedspread. He rubbed his eyes, glancing at the other side of the bed expecting to see Carmen. The bed was empty. The cat clock on the wall above the dresser read ten after eight.

He couldn't remember the last time he'd slept past eight. In fact, it might have been the first.

He slipped out of bed, feeling exposed in his utter nakedness. He found his pants and slipped into them, then padded barefoot into the living room. The hall's hardwood floor, cool against his toes, creaked and groaned in protest. He smelled bacon and coffee. He heard her before he saw her, a pleasant humming from the kitchen.

He was feeling the slightest bit of regret about the previous night, but when he actually saw her, standing at the oven in a thin pink silk robe, golden hair cascading down her back, he felt a surge of happiness absent so long from his life he'd forgotten how it felt. Then, when she actually smiled at him, the way her whole face transformed, there was no room for even a sliver of regret. The previous night may not have gone according to any plan, but he wouldn't have changed a minute of it.

Something else was different: He realized that he also hadn't thought for a second about his bum knee.

"Hello, gorgeous," he said.

"Sleep well?" she said.

"Best in years," he said. And then it hit him, the guilt. He thought about Mattie alone in the dark on a cold gurney, only yesterday alive and smiling at him. Here he was staying the night with a woman he'd barely known a week. What did that say about him?

"Uh oh," Carmen said.

"What?"

"You've got that look on your face. The serious Mister Gage look. Maybe I need to take you back in the bedroom to make it go away." She smiled impishly.

"Tempting. But I think I need to make a phone call first."

"Aww. You're not going to call your real girlfriend, are you? Sorry, bad joke. I know you're going to check in on Zoe. The kitchen phone is right there. If you want something more private—"

"The kitchen phone will be just perfect, Carmen."

"Because my cell phone is in my purse in the bedroom—"

"Carmen."

"—and I'd be happy to get it for—"

He stopped her by touching his fingers to her lips. She blinked at him with big doe eyes, and he kissed her. She leaned into him, and it would have been easy to give in to it, but his anxiousness about Zoe was rising. He pulled away, both of them grinning like school kids, the bacon sizzling in the frying pan. He picked up the olive green phone on the wall. She smiled at him and leaned over to look at a piece of paper stuck to the refrigerator with a seashell magnet. She read him Zoe's cell number and he dialed it.

The phone rang three times and then Zoe answered, sounding groggy.

"Me here," she said.

"Hi," he said. "How are you doing?"

She snorted. "How do you *think* I'm going?"

"Okay. Stupid question. Did you manage to get some sleep?"

"No. Did you? Where are you, anyway? With that reporter chick?"

He decided to dodge the question, at least for now. "I just wanted to see if you needed anything."

"What would I need? Hugs and kisses?"

"I don't know. I just thought—well, if you needed anything, you know."

"I don't."

"Okay. Well. Are you going to be there all day?"

"I don't know."

"You're not going to school?"

She didn't even answer that one. He didn't blame her.

"I'd like to talk to you at some point," he said.

"Okay. I'm probably going to go out later."

"What time?"

She sighed. "I don't know. Look, I gotta go. I'll see you, okay?"

"Zoe—"

But she was already gone. He held the phone out from his ear, grimacing at it. He looked up to say something to Carmen, but she was gone, and then he turned and saw her coming down the hall. She was holding a cell phone to her ear. He was going to make a crack about women and phones, something about needing two lines when she'd been the only one living in the house, but then saw how ashen her face had become.

"What is it?" he asked.

She thanked the person on the other end, then clicked it closed. She lowered it to her waist.

"What?" he said.

"You know that guy?" she said. "Dan the Can Man?"

"Yes." Gage vaguely remembered telling Carmen about him the previous night, during one of the times they were resting in each other's arms.

"I just got a call from my contact at the police station, the secretary there. She said he was killed last night—witnesses said a truck hit him when he was riding alongside the highway. They pronounced him dead on the scene."

"What?"

"He's gone, Garrison. She said it doesn't look like foul play, but you never know."

Gage cursed. No way it was an accident. If only he'd gone looking for him last night instead of getting lost in an emotional fog. And it was a mistake that had probably cost Dan his life. "He's really dead?"

"They got a couple bags of his stuff down at the station."

"Like what?"

"I don't know. She didn't say. Just junk."

Gage shook his head. The pieces on the chess board were moving. There were just too many pieces moving to know what was happening. He felt like he *should* know, that it was right there in front of him.

He looked at Carmen. "You want to go treasure hunting?"

Chapter 22

THEY WERE DRESSED and at the police station by a quarter after nine in the morning. Even a hot shower had failed to wash all the cobwebs from behind Gage's eyes. The cloudy sky looked like a bowl of oatmeal and the moisture in the air felt just as thick. Quinn was waiting for them in the conference room with a couple cups of coffee in paper cups, a stern look on his face, and two big black garbage bags in the middle of the wide walnut table. His thin blue tie was slightly crooked. One of the fluorescent lights above them buzzed.

"This better be good, pal," Quinn said.

"This his stuff?" Gage said.

" Just liked you asked. I'd bring his bike in here too, but there's not much left of it but a few pieces of metal and rubber. Now you want to tell me why this old bum is suddenly so important?"

"You have anybody else go through this yet?" Gage asked.

"Why would I?"

"Just curious. Maybe Brisbane or Trenton got their mitts in here."

"My detectives have more important things to do than rifle through a bum's garbage. Speaking of which, I'm still curious how you knew about this stuff so fast."

Quinn shot Carmen a look, who shrugged and reached for one the coffees. Gage set his cane on the table and opened one of the bags. The stench of mold and rot and other foulness wafted out. Carmen kept her distance, cupping her coffee close to her face.

The contents of the first bag were a medley of the kinds of things Gage might find if he'd been combing the beach the past five years instead of filling out crossword puzzles: sea shells, agates, Bic lighters, some flip flops, a couple of plastic flashlights, several different single gloves, and tons and tons of paper ephemera. There were wrinkled magazines, garage sale flyers, business cards, maps, and two water-stained John D. MacDonald paperbacks. There were dank sweaters and torn shirts and badly stretched socks. A faded black *Kiss* shirt. A coupon for Jaybee's. A deflated red and white beach ball. There was a yellow plastic dump truck, three Matchbox cars, and a medley of plastic beach toys—a little red shovel, two tiny buckets, and some cookie-cutter tools for making shapes in the sand.

"Find your wallet?" Quinn said.

Gage moved to the second bag. It was more of the same—a motley collection of everything that represented life in Barnacle Bluffs: little gold tokens from the Casino, rusty keys, every size and shape of rubber band, empty envelopes, two aspirin bottles, a stick polished by its years in the ocean. He rifled through it, getting more frustrated, knowing there had to be something that could help him, some clue that could lead him in the right direction. He found a plastic spider ring. Two earrings, both cheap plastic. A half a dozen pencils, none of them sharp. A woman's make-up kit.

"It's just crap, Gage," Quinn said.

Gage kept looking. He dumped both bags on the table, which elicited shouts from both Quinn and Carmen. He didn't care. He spread all the things wide, searching in all that flotsam for the one piece of gold, that one diamond in the rough, hands rifling through it, now sticky with grime. The stuff spilled onto the chairs and the floor. There was nothing. Nothing but trivial garbage turned into a man's life, his reason for being, his treasure. Finally, Gage stopped, hands pressed against the table, surveying the piles all around him.

"Well, that was entertaining," Quinn said. "I hope you're going to help me clean up this mess."

"It has to be here."

"I'm still not exactly sure *what* it is you think has to be here. Seems like a waste of time to me. But then, I guess you do have plenty of time."

Quinn bent over and picked up something off the ground, something that had floated down from the table to his feet. Gage looked at him, ready to snap some sarcastic comeback, and saw Quinn pick up the candy wrapper from the floor. When he rose with it, Gage saw *exactly* what kind of wrapper it was—a Jolly Rancher wrapper.

It was like someone put a key in the lock in his mind. Everything came to him in a flash.

He remembered Winston Hamlin on the deck at the Inn, reaching down to pick up a wrapper just like it.

He remembered the son, how Hamlin said he was addicted to the things. What was his name? Nathan. The build and height matched his second attacker. The kid could have been the one to spike his drink.

And what else? Nathan was a spoiled kid who'd lost his mother young. He always got what he wanted. Even the location of the Inn made sense. That was a big property. Was there something in the woods around the Inn, some little tool shed or garden house where he had taken Abigail Heddle? It was all just supposition built upon supposition, but it felt right. His father was so oblivious, so ridden with guilt about his failings, that it could have all been happening right under his nose.

Maybe the son was into art. The mother had been into art. Why not the son? Maybe that was where he had met Abby, at the Northwest Artist Colony. Maybe he was the guy who came into the Cabaret that night, the one that made Abby freak out when she saw him.

"What?" Quinn said.

"Hmm?"

"That look on your face. It's like you just thought of something."

Gage still couldn't rule out Quinn as a possibility. The whole thing may have been a wild goose chase, but even if it wasn't, he wasn't quite ready to bring Quinn in on it yet. "Oh, just thinking. There's some other stuff I have to take care of today. A friend of mine died yesterday."

"I'm sorry to hear that."

"Yeah," Gage said. "It definitely seems to be going around right now."

When they were safely ensconced in Carmen's Toyota, alone with the pine air freshener hanging from the rearview mirror and the dozens of jazz CD cases piled at his feet, Gage told Carmen his theory. On the lake across the road, the motorboats pulling the early-morning water skiers buzzed and whined over the water as smooth as glass. A couple of uniformed cops walked past, eyeing them curiously.

"It's plausible," Carmen said. "I know a little about Winston Hamlin. I guess he was quite a drunk after that car accident. Sent his son to live with an aunt for a couple years until he finally got cleaned up. And Nathan . . ." She shook her head. "That kid was a hell raiser. Graffiti. Shoplifting. You name it. Any other kid would be in jail by now, but of course Winston Hamlin has got powerful friends."

Gage looked at the police station. "One of them's in there."

"Yep. No secret that Quinn is buddy buddy with some of the movers and shakers in town."

"Doesn't mean he's dirty. Maybe he just likes to keep his fingers on the pulse." If Gage was in Quinn's position, it was something he would have done. It was something he *had* done from time to time in his old life—position himself somewhere in the middle of the web so he could feel the vibrations when something stirred.

She shrugged. "Who knows. All I know is Quinn doesn't get out as much as he used to, now that his wife is sick a lot. So what are you going to do?"

Gage had told Carmen about his fight with Quinn, but not about the marijuana bit. He didn't know if she'd be able to resist the temptation of printing it in the paper, and after his transgressions, he felt he owed Quinn his silence on that point. Assuming Quinn wasn't involved in some fashion with Abby Heddle's death. "I'm going to find Nathan Hamlin," Gage said. "Then I'm going to follow him. If he really has other girls like Dan said, then he's got to be seeing them on a daily basis."

Carmen shuddered. "I really hope that's not true."

"Me too. I think the kid lives with his father. You know where that is?"

"Oh yeah. It's right next to the Inn, a big castle like thing up on a bluff, with turrets and black iron gates. Can't miss it. What, you going to stake them out?"

"If it's possible to do it without being seen."

"I think you really should bring the police in on this."

"I will. I just need harder proof. After what I put Quinn through, I'm lucky he didn't lock me up. "

"You want me to come?"

He thought about it. "No, why don't you find out everything you can about both of them. I've also got something else to do first."

"What's that?"

"Talk to Zoe."

Even thinking about what he had to do, Gage felt a sinking sensation. The thought of staking out a possible murderer hadn't fazed him the slightest, but thinking how to get through to a teenage girl brought up all kinds of dread.

Carmen dropped him off at Mattie's house, where he'd left the van. She kissed him on the cheek and made him promise not to do anything stupid, to come for the police if he found the real killer. He watched her drive away and wondered just where she'd come from, this person who'd changed his life in just a week. It amazed him to think that they'd both been living in town these past six months, two derelict ships sailing on parallel courses a few miles apart, never once crossing paths.

He got in his van and drove away, trying not to even look at Mattie's place. The sun was a softening in the gray fabric sky over a gray ocean, fog floating over the highway like a living thing. Carmen had given him the address of Zoe's friend. It was only a half mile north, into the hills, a ten-unit apartment complex surrounded by oaks and Douglas firs, most of its green paint faded or chipped away, the roof coated with pine needles.

The girl who answered the door looked nothing like Zoe. He expected nose rings, dark clothing, Goth attire. Instead Angie was a short round girl with blonde curls, thick glasses, and a prim purple sweater over a white shirt buttoned all the way to her chin. He couldn't imagine a girl like this hanging out behind the bleachers, smoking dope; she belonged behind a stack of books in the library. The smell of chicken and garlic drifted out to him. He heard the clink of silverware from the other room.

"Oh hi," she said. "You must be Mister Gage. Zoe said you might stop by."

"You're not in school today either, huh?"

"Oh, I'm homeschooled."

"Ah. Do you know where she is?

"No. I'm sorry. She was helping me with my algebra, and then said she had to leave. She said to tell you that she wanted to be alone. She wouldn't say why."

"Did she go back to Mattie's place?"

"I don't know. You might try bible study later at the First Lutheran. Sometimes she comes to that with me, but I don't know if she'll show up today."

"Bible study?"

She nodded. "Yeah. She's been coming for a while. Mister Gage? I'm worried about her. She didn't seem like herself at all."

"Did she tell you what happened yesterday?"

Angie looked perplexed. "Something happened?"

When Gage told her about Mattie dying, Angie covered her mouth with her hands, and then she started babbling that she didn't know, that she had no idea, that she wouldn't have let Zoe leave if she had the slightest inkling that something awful like that had happened. Of course, being someone himself who generally liked to deal with his grief in solitude, Gage knew that leaving was the point.

He gave her Carmen's cell number and told her to call if Zoe showed up again. Then he returned to Mattie's place, but he didn't find anything there but a lot of lonely cats in a quiet house that made his chest tighten just walking through it. Dust floated in the stale air. He checked to make sure the cats had food and water, but it was obvious that Zoe had already taken care of that; there were four bowls of cat food and three bowls of water in the kitchen.

Gage felt like a bastard. Not once had the cats occurred to him the previous day. If he couldn't even remember to feed a bunch of cats, how could he look after a kid?

He crossed the highway to see if she was down at the beach, but she wasn't. Winded, sweaty, and his knee aching, he returned to his own house to shower and change clothes. He thought about driving around town to look for her, but where would he go? That's when it occurred to him how little he knew Mattie's granddaughter. He never would have guessed in a million years that she had even glanced at a bible, or helped a girl like Angie with her algebra.

He didn't know her at all.

Chapter 23

GAGE HAD BEEN on hundreds of stakeouts in his life. When he was starting out with his uncle, that was practically *all* he'd done that first year. Waiting for the husband to meet up with the girlfriend. Waiting for the woman in the neck brace to show up for her tennis lessons. Waiting for the guy that was dipping into the company safe to show up at two in the morning. That was probably why he hated stakeouts so much now. They all had one thing in common. There was a lot of time spent doing absolutely nothing.

With a light drizzle streaking his kitchen window, and a cup of coffee steaming on the table next to him, he pulled out a map of Barnacle Bluffs and located exactly where Carmen had said the Hamlin estate was. He decided his best bet was to park at the public beach access a few blocks away, then set out into the woods that surrounded their estate and spilled into the Inn at Sapphire Head property. It was like the tip of the forest from the other side of the highway, the one near where Percy Quinn lived, formed a triangle whose top point was the Inn and the Hamlin estate.

There was so much on his mind that it was hard to concentrate. There was Zoe, missing. There was Mattie's impending cremation, and of course all the things that followed. There was the house and all those belongings. The cats. There was Carmen, lovely Carmen, and the emotional soup that just thinking about her stirred up inside him. He wanted to put Abby Heddle aside for a little while just to catch his breath, to get some of the pieces of his own life in order, but he didn't have that option. This whole line of thinking, with Nathan Hamlin being the killer, may have been totally wrong. A dead end.

But what if it wasn't?

What if he had other girls right now?

It was that thought that allowed him to push all of his other troubles out of his mind, to burrow into this one thing. He thought about that night two weeks ago when he found Abby Heddle on the beach, and it made him angry. It was a good anger, the kind he could use.

The drizzle turned into a downpour, but even that didn't deter him. In fact, he thought it was a good thing for a stakeout, that it might make it harder for Nathan to see him or hear him in the crackle of the rain and the dreary gray that thickened the air.

He put on a pair of boots. He put on his heavy leather jacket. He slipped his miniature binoculars into his side pocket. He loaded his Beretta and tucked it inside his jacket, the weight of it like a rock against his heart. He had a feeling it might come in handy. He hoped it wouldn't, but there were lots of times when that feeling had turned out correct.

The rain fell in torrents, a blustery wind shoving the van first one way then the other. It came down so fiercely that traffic slowed, the passing cars a blur of headlights, streaks of metal and black rubber. The windshield wipers screamed back and forth across the windshield and did little good; he might as well have been driving with them off. When he reached the public beach access, his was the only vehicle in the ten-space parking lot. Clouds of mist rolled over the embankment and swept over the asphalt.

He couldn't see the ocean. It was all one gray smear. The pines towered over the lot, and marked the beginnings of the forest that contained both the Inn and the Hamlin estate, bowed under the cascade of gusts that rose off the ocean. Climbing out of the car, he had to push hard against the door, and when he did his cane slipped out and skittered across the parking lot.

He lumbered after it, gimpy on one leg, feeling like a fool for chasing this stupid little stick that meant so much to him. He hated that damn stick.

Finally, he got hold of it. Already he was winded, pant legs soaked from the onslaught, sweaty under the brim of his fedora. Looking up the sandy embankment that led into the Douglas firs and the live oaks, holding his hat on his head to keep it from sailing away, he wondered just why, exactly, he was here. He'd come to Oregon to get away from all of this. He hadn't wanted to find that damn girl on the beach. He wanted to be back home, in his easy chair with his leg up on the ottoman, a crossword in his lap, no troubles. He looked up at that embankment, turning his face into the rain and then wind, then gritted his teeth and started up.

The trouble with having no troubles, he'd learned, was that if you didn't have them you didn't have anything.

No troubles, no life.

It took excruciating effort to get into the trees, his boots finding no purchase in the damp sand, his cane a useless extremity he was forced to carry. He used the ivy at the top like a rope, finally getting under the lower leafy branches of the pines so that he was at least partially out of the storm. A bit more effort and then he was in the woods, where the dark canopy shielded him from most of the rain and the wind.

Water ran down his face in rivulets. His fedora was a soaked sponge, letting the rain straight through. His hands felt cold and numb. The bed of twigs and leaves felt as soft as a plush mattress. After studying the map, he had a good sense of where both the Inn and the Hamlin estate were, but once in the half-light of the trees, fully surrounded by forest, it was disorienting. Only the ocean and its ever present rumble, off to his right, helped keep him moving in the right direction.

The place smelled alive, with rich, wet earth, fresh pine, and thick ferns. It was only a few minutes before he came to a break in the trees, and then he saw it there through the gaps in the branches, a long winding road that lead up to a castle overlooking the ocean, the road bordered on both sides by this private little forest.

A castle was the only way to describe it, a sprawling stone castle as big as some of the hotels, with three turrets, a five-bay garage, and a gated circular drive that was bigger than some of the cul-de-sacs not far from where Gage lived. There was no reason to go up that road except to the castle, so he was glad he'd parked where he had. His only hope was at least partially preserving the element of surprise.

He found a place to hide behind a stump overwhelmed with ivy, where the hedge of ferns and the overhang of the fir trees would make it difficult to see him from the castle. He knelt in the damp earth, wincing at the sharp stab in his knee. The mud seeped through his clothes, cold against his flesh. It didn't matter. He was so wet now, even under all his layers, that getting a little wetter wouldn't make a difference.

The little binoculars steamed up as soon as he took them out of his coat, so he used his finger to wipe the lenses. All of the windows of the castle were dark. He swept the binoculars across them several times, hoping to see some activity, but there was nothing.

Maybe this was all a waste of time. Maybe the kid was just at the movies, the dad was at work, and Gage was watching an empty house for no reason at all. Getting wet. Getting cold. Feeling more miserable by the second. This was the real life of the private investigator, lots of hunches that led no where, lots of misery that you brought onto yourself. And for what? To help someone you didn't even know. In this case, it was even worse. He was trying to help someone who was dead. Even now, he wasn't doing this for Becky Larson. He was doing this for Abigail Heddle.

Or maybe not.

Maybe he was just doing this for himself, to see what it felt like to be somewhat human again.

Time passed. How much time he didn't know and he didn't

care. He could have looked at his watch, but what difference would it make? He would wait there until something happened or until dusk, when he'd have to start back for his car or risk being forced to walk along the road. At some point, as strange as it was out in the middle of a fierce storm, the wind pushing against him, big raindrops spitting against the brim of his hat and the arms of his jacket, he started to feel tired. Exhausted. He listened to the wind moaning through the trees, the rhythm of the falling rain, one curtain of water dropping after another. Telling himself he was going to just rest for a moment, he closed his eyes. He closed his eyes and let himself drift away.

"*He has other girls.*"

His eyes snapped open, his heart pounding. It was Janet's voice, a whisper mixed in with the wind and the rain. He'd been sure of it. Even stranger, what he'd thought was only a few seconds must have been much longer, because the daylight had waned. It was not quite dusk, but the shadows around him were deeper, the sky grayer. The twin street lamps standing sentry at the gate had flicked on, glowing yellow bubbles in the mist.

The house was still dark. The rain still fell.

He looked about him, peering into the trees. Was someone there? It was all darkness and shadows, slants of limbs and broken shapes. The mind saw what the mind wanted to see. A bulging stump could have been a hunching person. A leafless branch was an outstretched hand. Everything looked like a person and nothing looked like a person. But somebody was whispering. Somebody was whispering his name, over and over, a sound just barely above the kiss of the wind.

"Janet?" he said.

There was no reply. After a while, he didn't hear his name any more. He shivered. He was struck with a morbid thought, one that hadn't occurred to him in years but used to come to him all the time. He thought about Janet, down in her casket, under all that wood and dirt and grass. He thought about her pounding on the roof of the coffin, wanting to get out. She was still alive down there. She needed him.

Back then, he'd often found himself halfway to the graveyard, a shovel in his truck, before he realized what he was doing.

It was approaching the time when he'd have to head back through the forest. He felt depressed at the way things had panned out. Somehow, magically, he thought this was it, that this was the moment when the case would crack open and all the answers would be revealed. Murderer confesses. Innocents are spared. Garrison Gage saves the day. He should have known it wouldn't be that easy, that more misery awaited him.

Then he heard the groan of an engine coming up the road.

He heard the swish of tires on the pavement. He climbed to his feet and eased himself back into the deeper shadows just as he saw the flash of headlights on the trees. A black Honda SUV rolled past, stopped at the gates until they opened, then drove into one of the garages.

Gage trained his binoculars on the garage. He got a glimpse of Nathan Hamlin's jeans and boot, stepping out of the Honda, before the door came down.

Bingo.

The adrenaline had Gage fully awake now, his pulse racing, all his senses engaged. He watched the windows, waiting for the lights. First one downstairs lights came on, then another. Then those went off and for a long time the whole castle was dark again. Had the kid already gone to bed at four-thirty in the afternoon? He'd no sooner thought this than one of the lights came on in the turrets, illuminating the narrow rectangular windows that surrounded the turrets, one after another a foot apart.

As soon as Gage pointed his binoculars at the windows, he saw Nathan's face, looking right at him.

It was so unexpected that he actually jerked back in surprise. He dropped the binoculars, and then of course he saw the face in the window as only a pink smudge inside the glass, and realized how unlikely it would be for the kid to see Gage out here, tucked into the forest, with the light failing. Impossible. He raised the binoculars and looked again, but by then the kid had disappeared.

Scanning the other windows, Gage saw him, sitting in the

middle of the room. He sat in profile, looking at something, and Gage couldn't figure out what he was doing until a hand came up, armed with a paintbrush. Of course. His hunch had been proven right.

Still, was he just sitting here watching some kid paint?

Where was *that* going to lead him?

The turret went dark, not a light on anywhere in the house. Maybe the kid was going out, another movie, another night on the town. The seconds ticked by and nothing happened. Off to bed then? Gage wondered. Then he saw something, a flicker of movement on the side of the house, down beneath the turret where the kid had been painting a few minutes earlier. It was a black shape moving from the turret into the cover of the trees.

He only saw it for a second, but it was unmistakably a human shape. If he hadn't been watching attentively, he would have missed it.

He picked up his binoculars and pointed it there, just catching the kid walking south before he vanished into the shadows. Dressed in dark sweatpants, a hooded black pull-over, and black boots, he was practically invisible.

Now the hard part—following. Gage surged to his feet, but he did so too fast and his knee buckled, sending him back down, landing hard on his palms. He rose again, hands coated with cold mud, and started around the perimeter, toward the castle and the turret. It was too risky to go across the road, too easy to be seen by someone watching from the forest.

Ferns whipped at his pant legs. With the light fading, he had a hard time seeing the roots buried in the leaves, and they grabbed at his boots. He had to move fast. From where they'd started this race, the kid had a good five minute lead on him. Hurry now, hurry. Get that old body moving, Gage. In the darkest shadows, he used his cane like a blind man's walking stick, trying to ward off low-lying adversaries.

When he reached the castle, there was a supporting stone wall that held back the hill. The wall wrapped around the ocean side, and Gage followed next to it, sliding his hands along the rough surface, boots slipping in the sand. Exposed as he was, the rain and the wind whipped at his face. The ocean, muted behind that wall, now roared in his ears. He squinted into the haze and saw the ocean swells a dozen yards away, gray and flat under a low sky, dark coils bunched tightly together, pressing down on the ocean. The embankment dropped a few feet to his right, down to the boulders and the driftwood where the night surf sometimes reached.

It took an eternity to round the castle to the other side, where the forest started up again. Precious minutes lost. He really had to hustle now. Under the cover of the trees, the light seeped away again; it seemed darker than before. His heart thundered in his chest, his pulse loud in his ears. Under his jacket, his shirt felt like wet tissue stuck to his body.

He had to be careful not to be too loud, though it was almost impossible as he stumbled and flailed his way over the vines and fallen tree limbs. He was grateful for the storm. If not for that, the kid surely would have heard him.

Using the tree trunks as cover, he moved from one to the other as fast he could. After a few minutes, he finally saw the kid ahead, a dark loping shape. The kid was barely distinguishable from the tree trunks. He wasn't moving too fast, thankfully, though Gage still had to push himself. His knee felt like a glass vase which had shattered and then was stuck back together with gum; the pain seared up his leg and into his spine.

Darkness was closing around him like a fist, squeezing the last bits of daylight out of the forest. Where was this kid going? It wouldn't be long before they reached the golf courses that bordered the Inn at Sapphire Head.

That's when the kid veered to the left. At first Gage didn't notice, and he continued forward, momentarily losing sight of his target. Then he saw the dark shape float to the left, a column moving among columns. Gage's trajectory had moved him temporarily closer, more in the kid's line of sight, so Gage ducked behind the thickest tree trunk near him.

He waited a beat, then peered around the trunk. The kid's

shape was still moving.

Off in pursuit again, he followed in the kid's wake. They were getting farther from the ocean, the moaning wind drowning out the ocean waves. He passed under an opening in the trees and the rain crackled on the ferns and beat against his fedora. They walked for several minutes, two shadows in a world of shadows, going deeper into the forest.

Then a light flashed up ahead, a starburst that quickly went dark. Gage fell to a crouch.

A flashlight. It had to be. He started edging forward, using his cane as little as possible, relying on brute strength to keep his knee from letting go on him. He lurched from one trunk to another.

A jangle of keys made him seize up again, waiting. He heard a door creak open, slam shut. Moving again, Gage saw what was emerging from the gloom—a concrete structure, a garden house or a power shed of some kind, fully tucked under the protective embrace of the forest.

Gage hesitated, deciding what to do. He could go back and get help, bring the police in on this, but he'd have egg on his face if he was wrong. No, he needed at least a little more proof that his hunch was right. If he got closer, maybe he could see or hear something that would give him that little extra bit of evidence.

He crept forward. The structure took on more definition. He saw a green metal roof, mossy stone walls, a rusty iron door. He heard the crackle of the rain on the roof, like marbles on glass. The structure was bigger than he'd thought at first, a cottage in the woods with a half a dozen barred windows. He heard something else, too—the murmur of a voice. Or was it voices? He moved closer.

The ground beneath him changed, became hard and smooth. He looked down and saw concrete partially buried in the dirt— an old path. Following it, he saw it wind into the trees, toward where the golf course must have been. He heard the voice again. He unzipped his jacket, reaching for his Beretta. He wanted to know that it was close, that it was ready.

There was a metallic click off to his right, then a sharp prick in his neck.

Then darkness.

Chapter 24

GAGE WAS DROWNING. Water pounded him from all sides, so much water, wave after wave crashing over him, tossing him about like a rag doll. The cold—it hardened his muscles, turned them to ice, made it hard to move. Salt water burned in his eyes and choked in his throat. He thrashed and kicked and flailed, trying to find the surface, trying to find air. It was a colorless world, a patchwork of gray fabric, some dark, some light, tightening around him, pressing against him like a shroud. He was driftwood. He was garbage, tossed aside. No one wanted him. Someone had dumped him here.

Finally, he burst into open air, gasping. The ocean was the color of oil, and he struggled to keep his head above the surface, riding the ocean swells up and down like the sea foam sprinkling the surface. Black clouds hovered over him, close enough to touch.

He heard someone else break the surface, and spinning around, saw him—a man, gagging, spitting out water, the back of his head as shiny as a seal's. He went under again, popped up, went under. He was going to drown unless Gage did something. Gage paddled toward him —first up, like climbing a mountain, then sliding downward as the ocean sank. He grabbed the man's jacket, dug his fingers into the leather, spun him around.

The man had no face.

"Wake up, good fellow."

A voice in the darkness. He'd heard the voice before—a refined voice, a gentleman's voice.

"Come on now, Garrison. Time really is of the essence."

His head throbbed, a pulsing from within, a thousand tiny fists punching the inside of his skull. His eyes felt like they'd turned to wax. His mouth felt like steel wool. He became conscious of something cold, damp, and hard pressing against his left cheek—a grittiness to it, pebbles against his skin, dirt on his lips. He smelled piss and mold. Heard the ticking of water. Something else. Something shuffled not far from him. Something moved.

He groaned.

"Easy now," the man said. "It does take a while for the tranquilizer to wear off."

He opened his eyes. Concrete. A sheen of muck. Streaks of moss. He swept his arm underneath him and propped himself up, bones cracking. He blinked away the fog in his eyes, focusing on the shape standing across the room. Someone was in a doorway, behind bars, someone so short Gage at first thought it was a child. When his vision cleared, he saw that it wasn't a child at all.

It was a man in a wheelchair.

"Surprised to see me, Mister Gage?" he said.

The shrunken figure of Winston Hamlin stared at him from his place on the other side of an iron gate, the bars orange with rust. His tan trench coat draped his spindly body like a flag on a flagpole, hiding all but the wheels of his wheelchair, making it appear as if he was crouching like an old tiger. Droplets of water sprinkled his green wool hat and his long pointed beard, but his thick glasses were clear and his eyes were bright. He rested his gloved left hand on the long, thin barrel of the tranquilizer gun in his lap. His right hand pointed Gage's Berretta through a gap in the bars.

"It's a nice piece," Hamlin said. "I imagine it's seen a fair amount of action back in New York. You've kept it in excellent condition, despite its disuse these past few years."

Gage brought his knees up, got them under him, managed to rise. A million needles pierced his knee. It was all he could do to keep from screaming. The bones there felt like a bag of gravel. Where was his cane? He didn't see it.

"Oh, yes, the cane," Hamlin said, as if reading his mind. "It's so hard to be dependent on something like that, isn't it? Believe me, I know. But unlike you, I don't let it limit me. I'm quite resourceful, you know. It may never have occurred to you that a man in a wheelchair could be hiding in the trees, but then, I took the dirt path down from the Inn —a fair bit easier than the way you came, though the path *is* barricaded to detour nosy guests. Of course, since I'd been expecting you, I made sure to bring this tranquilizer gun. One must be prepared. And my son was quite helpful moving you in here—he's much stronger than he looks. That's another lesson for you, Gage. It's never good to go it alone. Look at you now. All alone and with no options."

"Where—where is he?" Gage said, his voice groggy.

"Nathan? Oh, we'll get to that in a moment."

A light bulb hung from a chain next to Winston, the shadows from the bars striping the slick floor. The room made him think of a World War Two army barracks he'd visited as a child on the Washington coast, a cave of concrete hardly wider than the span of his arms. He teetered on his feet, head woozy, trying to focus. There was a shuffling from behind him again, like a scurrying rat. He craned his head to see what it was.

He almost didn't see them. He saw a gray wall, the pale yellow light speckling its beveled, slick surface. He saw a barred window with cracked glass, the bars no more than four inches apart, the shapes of trees outside like cloaked monks, the sky between them purple-black as the daylight gave its last gasp. It was only when one of them moved that he saw them, two girls crouched in the corner, spindly arms and legs tangled and pressed so tightly together that his mind saw one person at first, a deformed monster of white flesh and cavernous eyes. They melded into the corner like moths.

"I see you've met the other guests?" Hamlin said behind him. "Girls, this is Garrison Gage. He's a detective of sorts. Kind of like Sherlock Holmes, but obviously not as talented."

One was utterly naked, her knees tucked up against her tiny breasts, her ribs like a crude accordion fashioned from flesh and bones. She looked at him through a greasy tangle of blond hair, the place where her eyes should have been as dark as the hollows of a skull. The other girl wore red lace panties, the brightest color in the room, like a splash of blood on a monochrome print, and a sports bra that may have once been white but now was smeared with mud. Her short black hair stuck to her head in chunks, like wet leaves. Bruises and needle marks marred their arms. They could have been fifteen or twenty-five or anywhere in between.

The naked one, the blonde, held a long serrated knife, the hilt pressed against her hollowed belly, the point aimed directly at Gage.

"How long . . . have I been sleeping?" Gage asked, without turning to look at Hamlin.

"Oh, what does it matter?" Hamlin said. "Look at me now. We have something important to do and little time to do it."

The world was tilting on its axis. He remembered an old client of his, a physicist by trade, once telling him that if it weren't for gravity, we'd all be flung out into space at a thousand miles per hour—a billion human rockets blasting for the stars. And nobody really knew why gravity existed. They knew what it did and how it did it, but not the why. It just existed. He felt like that, like at any moment he was going to be hurled into space. He managed to get himself around, gravity still holding him.

Hamlin was smiling. It was a cold and toothless smile. With his clay fingers, he readjusted his grip on the Beretta. The end of the barrel looked huge to Gage, like an open mouth.

"I want you to listen very carefully," Hamlin said. "You're going to do something for me, and you're going to do it in the next . . ." He looked at the gold-plated watch on his right hand.

"In the next four minutes and nineteen seconds. If you don't do it, then someone precious to you is going to die. If you do it, then this person lives. It's quite simple. Do you understand?"

Gage felt like he did the few times in his life when he'd allowed himself to have one too many beers, his head shrouded in fog, his thoughts like sparrows darting through his mind. He had to think. He had to get a grip on himself. He bore down, using the full weight of his will, forcing his mind to clear.

"Who is it?"

"I think you know."

"Another girl?"

"Yes. But more than that to you."

Then Gage knew, and the full terror of it descended on him like a winter storm, chilling his heart and clearing the mist in his mind all at once. It was Zoe. It had to be Zoe. There was a reason she had been missing, and it had nothing to do with her state of mind.

"You're lying," he said, even as he knew that Hamlin wasn't.

"She was quite an easy catch," Hamlin said. "My son found her wandering the beach alone, obviously crying. It was such an easy thing to take her. She didn't even know. A rag soaked with chloroform was all it took."

"I don't believe it."

Hamlin sighed, then looked at his watch again. "Three minutes twenty-nine seconds. We can fritter away the last moments of her life, or you can listen to what I want you to do. What will it be?"

"Where is she?"

"Not far, not far."

"Let her go," Gage said. "She doesn't have any part in this."

"Ah, but the same can be said for you, my dear Garrison. The same can be said for you. You had no part in this either, but that didn't stop you from thrusting yourself into the middle of things. If you'd just kept to yourself, none of this would have happened. That girl, when she got out, it was a careless mistake. My son, he can sometimes be careless. But no one would have thought of some girl washing up on the beach, some girl that no one cared about, unless you started asking questions. I knew right away that eventually I'd have to clean up after Nathan again, as I often do." He glanced at his watch. "Two minutes, forty-six seconds. Ready to listen now?"

"What do you want?"

"Oh, it's quite simple really. I want you to wrestle away the knife from that girl. Then I want you to kill them both."

He said it the way a man might tell a dim-witted underling to restock the supply cabinet. Put the reams of paper there, by the manila folders, and make sure you lock up when finished. It made the threat all the more believable. Hamlin was not a man who was used to having people disobey him. One of the girls behind him whined like a wounded cat.

"You're crazy," Gage said.

"If you *don't*," Hamlin said, "then the consequences will be quite severe, I assure you. You see, my son is expecting a call in the next . . . two minutes and twenty-one seconds. If he doesn't get that call from me, then he will do as I have instructed him to do, and sadly, a few days from now another poor girl will wash up on the beach. People will just assume she committed suicide, of course, so distraught she was about her grandmother's death."

"Why are you doing this?"

"Why? What a foolish question, Garrison. There are things we do for our loved ones that we would never do for others. My son—he is all that matters to me."

"You have a funny way of showing your love."

Hamlin sneered. "Spare me your judgment. One minute, fifty-eight seconds."

"You blame yourself," Gage said. "I know. I've been there."

"My dear Garrison, do you think I have a choice? Once I discovered my son's unfortunate addiction, I could have either turned him in or . . . enabled him. I know what I am. I'm not proud of it. But I have my son. That's more than you can say for your wife . . . one minute, thirty-six seconds."

"What about Bob Pence? You enabled him too?"

"That was my son's doing. They had a . . . special relationship. One minute, thirty seconds."

"Hamlin. Don't do this."

"I have no choice. "

"We always have a choice."

"You seem to be under the mistaken impression that I don't mean what I say. He *will* carry out my instructions. He is a very good boy, despite his problem."

"And what if I don't? You shoot me?"

"Of course. I shoot all three of you. But I'd prefer to frame you for all the murders first in a way that's quite convincing. You will not survive, Garrison. But Zoe can."

"You'll kill her anyway."

Hamlin shook his head. "No. I am a man of my word. You may find me despicable—frankly, *I* find myself despicable—but I have never been a liar . . . exactly one minute left now. I hope you've said your goodbyes. She was such a talented girl."

There was no point in arguing with him. He was a madman, and he was the father of another madman. Gage's mind raced, trying to think of a way out of this. Zoe was obviously up on some bluff nearby, ready to be pushed into the ocean just as Abby had been. Hamlin had a cell phone on him, and Gage had to get to it. But how? If he even took a step in that direction, Hamlin would shoot him dead.

"Forty-six seconds," Hamlin warned.

He turned toward the girls. They jerked backwards, melding even more into the stone, moaning pitifully. The knife trembled in the girl's hand. A plan sprang up in Gage's mind, one that would give him a chance, a tiny sliver of a chance, and it depended on everything going just right.

He advanced a step. One of the girls screamed. Hamlin chuckled. Gage focused on the knife. It all depended on that knife, on getting it out of the girl's hands as swiftly as possible, on doing what needed to be done without hesitation.

Gage lunged. Both girls screamed. There was a flailing of arms, a swinging of elbows; he took it in the jaw, eyes blurring, but then he had her by the wrist. He pried the knife loose with the other hand. Both girls were shrieking, the noise deafening in the enclosed space, and he'd counted on that. Noise could cover lots of things. His back was to Hamlin. There was no hesitating—he sliced the knife across flesh.

His own.

His palm opened up, a pulsing slash of red. The girls jerked and spasmed like they'd been struck by lightning. He pressed his palm against the girl's chest, right between her breasts. Their eyes met, and he hoped she'd understand, that there was still enough of her in there to figure it out. It was a play, darling. Play your part. She stopped spasming, going still, her eyes vacant. Was it shock or was she really in control?

The other girl screamed, obviously not comprehending what was happening. Gage moved slightly, as if he was going for the other girl, making sure to give Hamlin a clear view of the girl's blood-stained chest.

Hamlin applauded.

It was the moment Gage had been waiting for, some sign, however small, that Hamlin was not pointing the Beretta at him. If he was applauding, he'd put the gun down, and that was the one thing Gage needed to have a chance. Now it all depended on his body cooperating.

Gage's wounded hand throbbed. His heart roared in his ears. He turned, one swift movement toward the door.

Hamlin's eyes widened, his clapping hands freezing. The Beretta lay in his lap, just as Gage had hoped.

Gage propelled himself forward, pushing through the agony, ignoring the white hot pain flaring up from his knee.

Hamlin went for the Beretta.

Gage closed the distance. He managed one running step and it took a lifetime. People lived and died in the time it took him to take a step. Hamlin fumbled the weapon, not much, just a slight bobble, but it allowed Gage to take another step.

Now Hamlin was bringing the Beretta up. Gage wasn't going to make it. It wasn't even going to be close. In the span of a second, Hamlin would have the gun up and discharging a bullet streaking through the air, long before Gage could take another step. He had to throw the knife. He knew that. He'd known that all along, which was why he'd been retracting his throwing arm in the same movement. It was all about getting close enough. Another step. Increasing his chances of getting it through the bars. Of striking Hamlin in the throat. Of bringing his captor down before the gun could fire.

His arm was moving.

He was leaning.

The Berretta aimed at him.

Gage threw the knife.

Chapter 25

THERE WERE THINGS in Gage's life that he would always remember with absolute clarity. He would always remember the look on his mother's face the day he told her he was dropping out of the FBI, the way the wrinkles around her eyes revealed her disappointment. He would always remember the sound of his father's voice when he called to tell Gage the news, the hitch between the words "Mom" and "cancer." He would always remember, like a photograph seared into his mind, Janet's limp hand draped over the side of the bathtub, a puddle on the white tiled floor beneath her fingers. Most memories receded into the gray mists of his past, indistinguishable from another. But not these. These could have happened ten years earlier or ten seconds, it made no difference.

The knife sailing through the air was like that, instantly imprinted on his consciousness for the rest of his days. Later, he would not be able to say a lot about much of what happened in that room, but he would never forget the knife. Amber light glinted on the metal blade. The hilt propelled away like a receding torpedo, the bottom as black as coal.

He could not have aimed any better; it streaked right between the bars like a football through the middle of the goalposts, a perfect shot.

A shot discharged, a deafening boom in the coffin of a room, followed immediately by shattering glass. One of the bars had deflected the bullet. The knife found its mark. Hamlin dropped the gun and grabbed his neck as if he was choking himself, blood streaming around his fingers. He toppled forward, his head slamming into the bars and ringing them like a bell.

Gage was still moving, lunging for the bars. Time was short. Had he lost his chance already? Had the kid already dropped Zoe into that deep dark sea? His only hope was that Hamlin had padded the deadline. Either that, or it was all a lie, a ploy to get Gage to do what he wanted.

Crunched against the bars, Hamlin spasmed and convulsed, even his useless legs twitching. He coughed and spat up blood; there was blood everywhere, on his trench coat, his arms, the concrete floor. Gage, on his knees, fumbled inside Hamlin's trench coat for the keys. He had to get the keys. That was the first thing, the keys.

But they weren't there. Precious seconds ticked away. He searched the trench coat pockets, his own hand leaving smears of blood. He searched the pockets of the man's trousers and he found the cell phone, which he grabbed, but no keys. Hamlin's body stilled, the dying body coming to rest. Gage searched the pockets of Hamlin's dress shirt. Nothing. Zoe was going to die if he didn't find them.

A skeletal hand reached past his face, into the blood-drenched collar of Hamlin's shirt, and pulled out a chain containing a single key.

Gage turned and there was the girl, the one who'd played dead when he'd streaked her chest with his blood. Out of the shadows and up close, he saw her eyes and they weren't skeletal at all. They were deep and dark but full of hope.

With no time to even thank her, he grabbed the keys and fumbled with the lock. They slipped out of his fingers and he cursed. He tried again and this time he managed to unlock the gate. He pulled himself up, arms burning, legs shuddering in protest, and swung the gate inward. Hamlin stared up at them with vacant eyes.

Gage pried the Beretta out of Hamlin's death grip. Ignoring the pain flaring out of his body, he limped out the door. He flipped open the cell phone, tried to get a dial tone, but there was no signal inside the concrete bunker.

Down the hall. Pushing open the big metal door, creaking. Night wind cooling his sweat, darkness painting the forest black. He was going to fall. He was going to go down. Limping over uneven ground, muck sticking to his boots. Clutching the handle of the gun tightly, hoping the pressure slowed his bleeding palm. It was not raining, but the air was so thick that his face was instantly damp, his eyes blurring. Where was his damn cane? A thousand straight shadows criss-crossed his path like Tiddlywinks. His cane could have been any one of them. The one time he really needed the damn thing, he couldn't find it. Of course it would be like that.

Staggering into the swaying Douglas firs. The ocean was up ahead somewhere. He checked the phone again and this time he got a bar, a single bar, and he hit the redial button. Praying it worked.

One ring. Two rings. Three rings.

It was too late. She was dead. Gone.

Four rings. A click, and then a voice: "Dad?"

Gage said nothing. He held the microphone away from his mouth, not wanting the kid to hear him gasping for breath, but keeping the speaker close to his ear. He pushed his damn crippled body forward as fast as it would go, hoping the kid was up there somewhere close, hoping it wasn't already too late.

"Dad?" he heard Nathan say. "Dad, you want me to do it?"

Relief flooded through him like ice water. The temptation was to answer, to scream no, but Gage knew that would only produce the opposite. His only hope was that the confusion would lead to delay, and that the delay would give him the few moments he needed to reach her.

"Dad?"

Tripping over the exposed root of an oak. Slipping on a pile of pine needles, catching himself. Kicking at a tangle of ivy. Sweat pouring off his face. The pounding in his ears. The throbbing on his palm.

He heard it—the ocean, a murmur above the wind.

He was climbing, staggering onto a bluff. Out of the jumble of shapes ahead, he saw a bit of solid gray in the gaps between the trunks—not quite black, but close, a matte of ocean and sky. He worried that he hadn't heard Nathan's voice in a while (was she dead? was she gone?), and then he saw him—a man in silhouette, on a sandy bluff where what little moonlight squeezed through the clouds painted his outline a milky white. Scrub grass rippled around his legs like thousands of slender fingers groping his pant legs. The kid was holding a phone to his ear.

He was alone.

The dread that stabbed Gage's heart was almost enough to freeze him on the spot, but he kept going, putting one foot in front of the other, bringing the Beretta to bear on his target. But Nathan must have spotted him at the same time, because he ducked behind a wall of thick ferns.

Gage cast the cell phone aside and limped into the clearing. Exposed, no longer protected by the trees, waves of mist buffeted against him. The bluff ended a dozen yards ahead, the ivy and the scrub grass curling over the edge, into an unseen abyss. The ocean stretched out dark and flat, blending into the sky.

The kid emerged from behind the ferns, this time with the limp body of a girl propped under his arms. Gage blinked away the moisture in his eyes, struggling to see if the girl was who he thought she was, but it was too dark now. He couldn't tell.

"Where's my dad?" Nathan yelled.

"He's fine," Gage said. "He's safe."

"Liar!"

Gage took another few steps. Nathan was so close to the edge, just inches from where the sand sloped into the darkness. One wrong move and they would both go down. They were becoming clearer to him, the kid's dark clothes more distinguishable against the night. He saw the kid's black sweatpants rippling. He saw the glint of the girl's nose ring—it had to be Zoe, it just had to be. Her arms were milky white; she wore a t-shirt and underwear and nothing else.

"Stay back!" Nathan cried.

"I'm not going to hurt you," Gage said.

"I'll throw her over, I swear!"

They were separated by less than twenty feet, a silver of sand and grass, with all that endless black ocean all around them. Gage stopped, still pointing the Berretta at them, knowing they were too close together to get off a clear shot.

"Put the gun down!" Nathan cried.

Gage knew that the Beretta was his one advantage, that if he had to fire to stop the kid from throwing Zoe over the edge, he would do it. The chances of her surviving the fall were slim to none. He could hit her, it was true, but at least she would have a chance.

"You don't have to do this, Nathan," he said, edging a little closer. "It's not too late for you. You—"

"Stay back!"

"You can put her down. You don't want to hurt her. Look at her, Nathan. Do you know her name? Her name's Zoe."

"I'm warning you!"

"Zoe didn't do anything to you. She's a good kid. She's sixteen years old. She listens to heavy metal bands on her iPod and she's good at algebra and—"

"Stop!" He made a motion toward the edge, as if she was a sand bag and he was preparing to throw her onto the dike. "You don't know! You don't know anything!"

His voice sounded frantic. He looked at Gage and back at the edge, jerkily, with lots of false starts and wasted movement, like a drug addict in the first stages of withdrawal. Gage tightened his grip on the walnut handle of his Beretta, psyching himself up, reminding himself what this kid had done to Abigail Heddle and the girls back at the concrete bunker. And who knew how many others? Gage was no natural born killer, but this kid was a disease. It would be no waste to kill him. But if he hit Zoe . . .

Then it occurred to him that there was one last tactic to try. "Zoe's a lot like you, you know. She lost her mother too."

"Shut up!"

"In fact, Zoe lost both her parents. Can you imagine what that's like, Nathan? She's all alone in this world. Zoe is alone. She always feels alone."

"I know what you're doing!" he cried. "I know what you're doing and it's not going to work! Put the gun down!"

"Zoe even lost her grandmother yesterday. That was why she was crying on the beach. She lost the one person she really loved. You don't want to kill her, Nathan. You don't want to kill someone who's suffered like that. Put her down. It's okay. Just put Zoe down and we can walk out of here. All of us."

The kid's jerky movements, all the twitching and trembling, stopped. He stood tall and silent, a dark outline against a dark sky, his sweatpants and his jacket wrinkling in the wind. The air had turned cool, heavy with the smell of salt and the pungent odors of seaweed and kelp. Nathan held the limp body of Zoe as if he was making an offering, and he looked down at her, gazing into her face. It caught what little light there was just right, and Gage was close enough now that he could really see her, those pale white cheeks, those dark full lips. Still as she was, her face not contorting with sarcasm or disdain, she seemed much younger to him, a child. She wasn't grown up yet. Not yet.

"You know I loved her," Nathan said. "I loved all of them."

It was in that moment, when Nathan seemed the most distracted, that Gage lunged. The kid realized at the last second what was happening, but by then Gage had clamped down on Zoe's bare arm.

A fierce tug-of-war ensued; they grappled and pushed and shoved, the boy cursing, Gage staying focused on keeping his grip. Zoe moaned.

Hamlin had been right. The kid was stronger than he looked—no way Gage could win this fight, especially in his present condition. They teetered close the edge, the grass rippling over the abyss. Then Gage swung the Beretta. His positioning was awkward, so he only managed a glancing blow on Nathan's chin.

It was enough. The kid, stunned, relaxed his grip and Gage managed to tug Zoe free.

For a moment, Nathan teetered on the edge of the cliff, eyes bone-white. He flailed his arms frantically like some kind of crazy bird. For one brief moment, Gage actually thought the kid was going to fly. He would fly up into the darkness, carried away by the ocean winds, disappearing forever.

But of course he didn't. He fell. He fell like everyone who's haunted by such demons must fall, a black stone plummeting past the sand and the crabgrass, out of sight, to the boulders hiding under the shallow waters. He fell out of Gage's life and out of everyone's, to the death that awaited him below and beyond, falling farther, still falling, to some private hell that only the most miserable on Earth could ever understand.

Chapter 26

AFTER THE POLICE and the medics arrived, after Gage had been assured that Zoe was going to be okay, and after he'd answered all of Quinn's questions, Gage asked Carmen to stop at The Gold Cabaret on the way to the hospital. She wanted him to get stitches pronto, but he told her it would only take five minutes. When he told her to wait in the car, she protested, but she quieted down when he said he'd answer all her questions when he returned.

The rain soaked his hair, stung in the cuts on his face. A dozen waterfalls poured from the overhang, aglow in the neon orange LIVE NUDE GIRLS sign. The bouncer raised his eyebrows at the bloodied bandages on Gage's hand, but Gage offered no comment. The music pulsed in his ears. A pasty-faced girl was giving a lap dance to a fat guy sitting at one of the tables. There was a new bartender behind the counter, a Hispanic man with glassy eyes and tattoos all over his neck. He didn't stop Gage from heading to the back office.

When he stepped inside, Pam looked up from behind her desk, pausing in the middle of counting a stack of twenties. She wore a white bookie cap, her orange hair flowing out the top. Instead of a Betty Boop t-shirt, she wore a Minnie Mouse one;

her big breasts made Minnie's ears look massive.

"A knock would have been nice," she said, and then, noticing his appearance: "Jesus, what happened?"

Gage shut the door. His knee was killing him, so he settled into the folding chair across from her even though he didn't plan on staying long. He could still feel the pulse of the music through the thin walls.

She must have seen the seriousness in his yes, because she swallowed. "What is it?"

"I've been doing some thinking," he said.

"Oh?"

"Yeah. You see, I know you told the police you had no idea what was going on with your bartender. I just don't think it's true."

She stared. He noticed that her gaze flitted briefly toward the gun cabinet before returning to him.

"What are you talking about?

"I don't have any proof yet, but I think that will turn up soon enough."

"You're insane!"

There was some rainwater dribbling into Gage's eyes and he wiped it away. "You won't get much argument from me on that one. I'm pretty sure I am insane. But that doesn't change anything. You see, I got to thinking about this place, about what you told me. How you've had to struggle to keep from going under. I got to thinking about it and I wondered. I wondered if maybe you knew a bit more about what was going on with your bartender and one of your former dancers than you were willing to let on."

"That's nonsense! Why would I do that? I—I don't want to hurt anyone."

"Maybe not. But staring a pile of bills in the face can make people do funny things. I got to thinking, you know, what would have happened if Sue went to Hamlin and demanded some money to keep quiet. That sure would have made it easier to keep her doors open when it was obvious to the world she didn't have the business to justify it. I figure once the cops start digging through Hamlin's financial records, they'll find some strange checks from his Inn to your bar. Because, you know, Hamlin was kind of a stickler about pretending all the stuff was above board. I played poker with him once and found that out first hand."

The color drained from her face.

"Oh yes," Gage said, "I know all about Hamlin. Just came from talking to him. Though he won't be talking much any more. Neither will his son. What a pair those two made, though it sounds like your bartender and Nathan were more than just friends. Who would have thought it, huh? Though I bet you knew about that too."

"I—I don't know—I mean—" she stuttered.

"Time will sort this out, but I figure Nathan met her over at the Northwest Artist Colony. She managed to get away from him that time, but then she came to work here. Nathan came in one time and recognized her, and the next day she was missing. Good old Bartender Bob probably knew who Nathan was—unlike your bouncer—and he put two and two together. Only instead of turning him in, he wanted a piece of the action."

"I don't know what you're talking about."

"You probably didn't. At first. I'm giving you the benefit of the doubt, of course. I'm assuming you weren't in on the actual raping and imprisonment."

"Get out!" she cried.

"Maybe you told yourself Abby was already dead," he said. "Or maybe you told yourself that if she wasn't dead, there wasn't much you could do. I don't know. Honestly, I don't care. I figure most of the blame is on Nathan Hamlin and Robert Pence, but you know, they were rotten to the core. It's when people who know better convince themselves to stand on the sidelines when something awful's happening that really gets to me. Personally, I'd like nothing better than to haul you down to the police station."

She didn't move.

"But you're old," Gage continued. "You're banged up and

decrepit, kind of like me. I don't know how you'd fare in prison. I'm thinking not well."

"You're telling—you're telling me to run?"

"Oh no. You wouldn't get far. I'll be calling this in as soon as I get to my car. I just wanted you to have this information so you could . . . ponder it a bit."

Just as he expected, her gaze drifted to her gun cabinet. Gage waited to see what she would do, and when she didn't do anything, he rose.

"I could be wrong, of course," he said. "Maybe there's no paper trail leading from Hamlin to you. Maybe I just came in here and upset you for nothing. If that's the case, well, pretend I was never here. It should be easy for you. You were pretty good at pretending Abby Heddle was never here—at least not in any way that mattered. Even if nothing else I said is true, you're going to have to live with that. And if what I said *was* true, well . . . I don't know how *anybody* with a conscience can live with doing something so callous."

She had the kind of numb expression of someone who'd just survived a terrible traffic accident. He left without another word, hobbling back through the strobing lights and thumping bass. He stopped and briefly watched the gyrations of the young girl on stage, this pencil stick kid with the plastic purple hair and dirty snow eyes, wondering who she was, wondering where she'd came from and whether she was running or hiding—and then with slumped shoulders headed outside. He might be able to find somebody's killer, but he was no good helping someone who was alive. That was something *he* was going to live with.

When he was standing on the stoop, he heard the roar of the shotgun deep within the bar.

Chapter 27

TWO WEEKS LATER, at the agreed upon time, the three of them climbed the trail under a tinfoil sky. It was a bright and colorless gray, the sun invisible but still somewhere present, burning off the last of the mist that clung to the ferns and the blackberry bushes. They had not seen the sun in days. At the peak, almost to the bluff, the ivy rippled in an unseasonably warm breeze, and fine particles of sand pebbled their faces and made them squint.

A month earlier, Gage would have been annoyed at the sand in his eyes, but now he didn't care. It made him feel alive.

The previous two weeks had been an exhausting whirlwind, but it was finally beginning to calm down. Besides food and rest, the two girls who'd been held captive mostly needed counseling. Lots of counseling. The cut on Gage's hand turned out to be the most serious medical condition among them, requiring seven stitches. He'd had worse.

Hamlin was pronounced dead at the scene. His son's body washed up on the beach three days later.

The press, both local and national, descended like vultures. Gage refused all interviews, hoping it might preserve what little anonymity still remained for him in Barnacle Bluffs, but his name and face were all over the news anyway. The two girls in the bunker were both runaways, one missing for four months, the other nearly a year. The police found three more girls buried near the bunker, and there was speculation there might be more. One of the girls, an autopsy determined, had been dead for five years.

Forensics matched the pants Dan the Can Man was wearing at the time of his death with the fibers found on the bumper of Winston Hamlin's white Cadillac. Beyond that, most of the major press ignored Dan, but Carmen ran a nice article about him, doing a fair amount of research to dig up his past—a schizophrenic who'd lived with his aging mother until she'd passed away five years earlier, then ended up on the streets. Carmen turned it into something of an expose on the growing homeless population on the Oregon coast. The writing was good enough he figured she'd win a Peabody.

The financial records confirmed what he'd suspected about the owner of The Gold Cabaret. The place closed down to clean up the mess in her office and still hadn't reopened. He wasn't betting it ever would.

Climbing the bluff under a gray sky, Gage was the first to the top. He rammed his cane into the sand like a mountain climber planting a flag, his bandaged hand throbbing, then turned to help Carmen. She gladly took his hand, smiling up at him, blond hair billowing around her red windbreaker. He'd been looking at that blond hair a lot lately. He'd been looking at those blue eyes too. He'd been getting used to them, starting to count on them.

Zoe came next, holding the silver urn tight against her black sweatshirt. She gazed up at him, and though her face still looked hollowed and pale, though she still wouldn't talk about losing Mattie or any of the other awful things that had happened, there was more hope on her face than had been there lately. She didn't smile, but she did take his hand and allow him to help her onto the bluff.

The wind was stronger, whipping at their clothes. The surf crashed on the rocks and the driftwood below. They gazed out at the vast ocean under a vast sky. High above, a few seagulls riding the thermals cawed a few times, but otherwise they were alone. And yet, for the first time in a long time, with Zoe on one side and Carmen on the other, Gage did not feel alone. He did not know what the future would bring, and it scared the hell out of him, but he was not alone.

Zoe waited until the wind waned, then stepped to the edge of the bluff, bracing herself with one foot on a battered stump. They'd talked about saying a few words, a poem or a prayer, but Zoe insisted Mattie wouldn't want it that way. She pressed the silver metal to her lips, a long and tender kiss, then opened the lid and let the ashes spill onto the breeze. The ashes plumed in the air, up to the seagulls and the gray sky, already indistinguishable from everything else.

Then they watched. They watched and said nothing, three souls alone with their thoughts but not alone. They watched the ocean swells. They watched the seagulls on the breeze. They watched the shifting layers of the sky, the different shades of gray all moving in concert.

"I think I see the sun," Carmen said.

They all looked. There it was, a brightening in the west, a place where the gray was not quite so gray. It may have been the sun or it may have been a trick of the eye. It all depended on how the clouds changed. It all depended on what happened next.

"I see it too," Zoe said.

17309244R00162